THE SENATOR AND THE SIN EATER

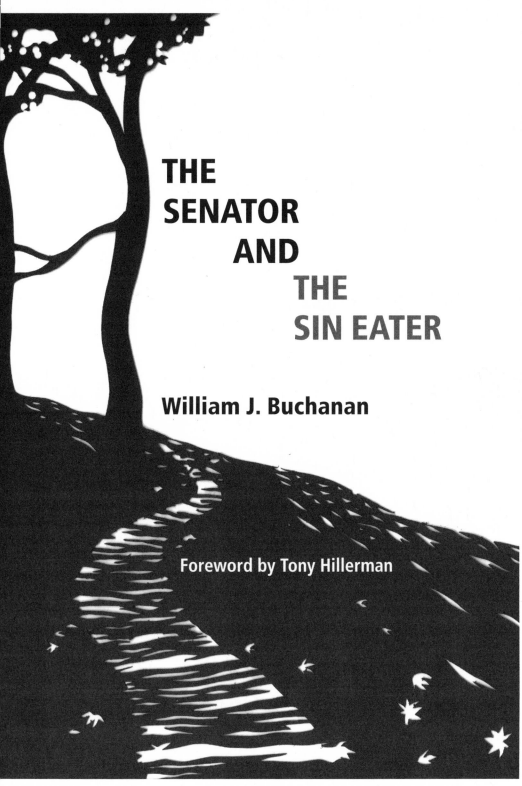

THE
SENATOR
AND
THE
SIN EATER

William J. Buchanan

Foreword by Tony Hillerman

UNIVERSITY OF NEW MEXICO PRESS | ALBUQUERQUE

© 2007 by the University of New Mexico Press
All rights reserved. Published 2007
Printed in the United States of America

12 11 10 09 08 07   1 2 3 4 5 6 7

LIBRARY OF CONGRESS CATALOGING-IN-PUBLICATION DATA
Buchanan, William J., 1926–2005.
  The senator and the sin eater /
William J. Buchanan ; foreword by Tony Hillerman.
    p. cm.
  ISBN 978-0-8263-3894-5 (ALK. PAPER)
  1. Racially mixed people—Fiction.
2. Authors—Fiction. 3. Mountain life—Fiction.
4. West Virginia—Fiction. 5. Murder—Fiction.
6. Political fiction. I. Title.
  PS3552.U332S46 2007
  813'.54—dc22
                    2007009885

Book and jacket design and typography by Kathleen Sparkes
Jacket art by Mary Sundstrom
This book was typeset using
Trump Mediaeval LT Std and Frutiger LT Std

Foreword

Any time you pick up a book with Bill Buchanan's name on the cover, there is one thing of which you can be certain: Colonel Buchanan always deals with his characters kindly and gently. *The Senator and the Sin Eater*, his last book before his death, provides a perfect example of this in its opening pages. There you meet a Seneca Falls postman and a few of his patrons— all nice folks. By the end of that brief opening chapter, the postman is doing his job beyond the call of duty, but without violating post-office ethics. He notices an odd glitch in the usual conduct of mailbox owners, acts on it out of that sense of human and community responsibility for which Buchanan's characters are noted, and consequently discovers a murder.

As you read on you will find this murder is indeed mysterious, but *The Senator and the Sin Eater* is much more than a murder mystery. It is an examination of what sometimes goes wrong in a small, friendly town that is Southern enough and old enough so that when one refers to the war, the hearers presume you are discussing the War between the States. The community is also old enough so that the usual patterns in American society have developed, stratified, and hardened. In providing the solution to the murder of the wealthy and powerful man found dead because of Buchanan's conscientious postman, the author takes you through a beautifully done examination of a small town in a part of America that fought on both sides of the Civil War.

Like the murder victim's brother—who returns to Seneca Falls for the victim's funeral, and who subsequently becomes the central figure in the intriguing tale—Buchanan knows the place and the people involved. He spent much of his boyhood in the shadow of the Kentucky State Penitentiary, where his father was warden. The penitentiary had been noted for the number of its executions, but when the elder Buchanan retired, he spent years campaigning against capital punishment. Perhaps that is part of the explanation for the author's kind heart.

Buchanan's kindness might also be explained by his military career, which spanned World War II, the Korean War, and the cold war. Buchanan's job was in military intelligence, where he specialized in radar and other electrical systems that had proliferated. During his career, he controlled, from Quemoy Island, spy systems in Communist China; worked with the DEW Line in Alaska; and, from a base in Iceland, tapped into Soviet radio signals.

I first encountered the colonel's prose in a *Reader's Digest* article back about 1960. Today I can't remember the name of the article, but I do recall it concerned dogs, horses, and good people, and it left me smiling. Later I met him in person in Albuquerque when we both happened to have articles published in *True*. We were at the magazine rack in the late Norman Zollinger's Little Professor Bookstore, admiring our work. I told Buchanan I admired his story. He said he liked mine. Norman joined the conversation. Bill and I both complimented Zollinger on his novel *Riders to Cibola*. We continued a three-way book talk over coffee and cookies, and became lifelong friends.

But enough of this. Read *The Senator and the Sin Eater*. It's much more interesting.

Tony Hillerman

THE SENATOR AND THE SIN EATER

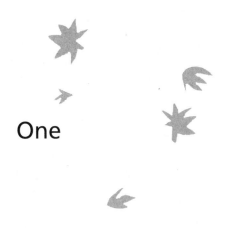

One

To anyone else in the small town of Seneca Falls, West Virginia, that sweltering July morning, nothing would have appeared out of order at the white brick mansion on the high knoll overlooking Fourth and Mountain View streets. The stately elms that lined the winding driveway were beginning to fill in nicely following an early cropping that spring. The two giant oaks standing sentinel near the east wing shaded the columned portico as they had each morning since two decades before the Civil War. Just below the west courtyard, a gardener maneuvered a ride-on mower between blooming dogwoods, white-laced spiraea, mountain ash, golden forsythia, and other flora that decorated the two-acre estate. Nothing at Twin Oaks seemed amiss.

Nonetheless, Charley Hodges was concerned.

Charley had delivered the mail in Seneca Falls ever since he mustered out of the army following the Korean War, over forty years before. For the first twenty years he served his customers on foot. When the town population reached three thousand, the postmaster assigned him a Jeep and doubled his route. Charley didn't mind. He knew everyone in town and where they lived. He knew whether they got any mail, and if they did, from where and from whom. Charley made it a point to chat for a spell with folks regardless of whether or not they got mail. The Jeep made it possible to talk to more people.

On this Monday morning when he pulled up at the Dunning family estate, Charley noticed that the mail he had put in the curbside box Saturday was still there. That was unusual. When the senator was away, he arranged for his housekeeper or his secretary at his office in town to pick up the mail that was delivered to the house. When he was in residence, the senator usually walked down the hill to retrieve the mail himself, often timing the walk to intercept Charley for a neighborly chat. Like any astute politician, Stewart Dunning kept his hand on the pulse of his community, and there was no better sounding board in Seneca Falls than Charley Hodges.

In the distance beyond Twin Oaks, a darkening weather front rose high above the Alleghenies, giving promise of afternoon relief from the scorching heat. Charley mopped his brow with a handkerchief, eyed the sky hopefully for a moment, and then returned his thoughts to the senator's mail. It was out of order. Charley didn't like things out of order. He liked things neat, in place, on schedule, routine. But things seldom were. Concluding that there had probably been a screw-up in communication between the senator and his aides, he pushed the Saturday mail aside, deposited the morning's delivery in the box with it, and continued on his route.

Shortly after two o'clock Charley turned onto a rutted dirt road leading to the Bottoms. In this section of Seneca Falls, a development of low-income tract houses—surrounded by weedy yards and sagging fences—sprawled along the lowlands of the Potomac River. It was the far extension of Charley's route. Midway through the neighborhood, he pulled to a stop in front of an aging stucco house where neatly trimmed privet hedges and a well-cared-for lawn made it stand out from the rest. He was thumbing through the mail when he spotted Viola Brown weeding a row of bush peas in the vegetable garden in her side yard. He was surprised. Viola was Senator Dunning's cook and housekeeper. Her job almost always kept her at Twin Oaks until seven o'clock, or later, every evening on weekdays.

"Afternoon, Viola," Charley called. He separated the top two pieces of mail from the others in his hand.

A hefty black woman of sixty, Viola straightened up slowly

and kneaded the small of her back with both hands. "Afternoon, Charley." She gave the rear of her jeans a tug to make walking more comfortable and came to the curb. "Anything but bills, hear? Don't hand me more bills today."

Charley laughed. "No bills. Bulletin from your church. Congregational picnic's gonna be up at Spring Run this year. And here's a postcard from Sonny. Says he's getting along just fine in his new job at the refinery down in Bluefield. Says he might get up to see you soon. I figure he's getting hungry for some of your home cooking." Sonny was Viola's nephew.

Viola chuckled. You never had to read the postcards Charley delivered. He always did that for you.

"That boy," she exclaimed. "Four months, four different jobs."

"Needs a good woman to settle him down's what he needs," Charley suggested. He paused. "I saw Dub up at the manor mowing the senator's grounds."

Viola nodded. "Needed doing for days. I called him down at the paper office Friday and told him to get up there and get it done. He said he was having trouble with the mower. I reckon he got it fixed."

"He didn't pick up the mail I put in the box Saturday."

"Dub Oliver?" Viola gave a scornful laugh. "He knows better than to put a hand in that mailbox. No one picks up the mail at Twin Oaks but me and the senator. Or someone from his office when he ain't home." She gave a frown. "Which he ain't. You say there's mail in the box?"

"From Saturday and today."

Viola thought a moment. "Well, all I know is he gave me the week off starting Friday and told me Carolyn would have somebody from the office take care of ever'thing—includin' the mail." She gave a sigh. "Guess I better get up there and get it."

"No . . . no," Charley countered. "Enjoy your time off, Viola. I'll take care of it. I can hold everything at the post office. You get on back to weeding those peas. I'll expect a jar when you get 'em put up, hear?"

"You'll get 'em," she promised. "Thanks, Charley."

"Don't mention it. See you tomorrow." He climbed back into the Jeep and drove off.

Tuesday morning when Charley pulled up at Twin Oaks the

mail was still in the box. Just as he'd put it: Saturday's delivery in the back, and Monday's in front. Exasperated, he took it all out and put it in the pick-up box in the back of the Jeep.

That afternoon after deliveries, he went to the carriers' desk in the back of the post office and dialed the senator's office in the Seneca County Bank.

"Senator Dunning's office."

"Carolyn . . . Charley Hodges. The senator's mail's been piling up in his box. I don't wanta leave it overnight . . . *again*." He was being accusatory, but this was the United States mail, for God's sake. "I got it here at my desk when you get ready to pick it up."

"His mail?"

"You're supposed to pick it up, ain'tcha?"

Carolyn paused before responding.

"No, Charley Hodges, I am *not* supposed to pick it up. And I don't like your tone of voice, either. Viola Brown is supposed to pick up the house mail all this week since Friday. Stewart told me so just before he left for Charleston. Said I wasn't to worry about it. Damn! That woman!"

Charley's thoughts spun rapidly. He knew Carolyn Wright well. She was a pretty, well-liked brunette who nonetheless could be meaner than a rain-soaked wildcat when riled. And she was genuinely riled. "Okay, Sooky. Okay," he said, attempting to mollify her with her popular high school nickname. "Simmer down. Has Stewart called you?"

"No."

"No? Well . . . look, I'll take care of it, hear? I'll hold everything here at the post office. Just you be sure and let me know when he gets back in town. That suit you?"

"Sure. All right, Charley." Her voice was less strident. "When he calls I'll find out what's going on."

Charley put the phone back in the cradle. What the hell *was* going on? Senator Dunning had told his housekeeper that his secretary would pick up the house mail. Then he told his secretary that the housekeeper would do it. As it turned out, no one was doing it. Dunning was not that absentminded. And he hadn't called his office since leaving for Charleston Friday. Unlike him. Strange. Not orderly.

Charley picked up the phone and dialed two numbers. Hesitant, he replaced it in the cradle and stared at it, wondering if making the call was the right thing to do. After a while he uttered, "What the hell," and picked up the phone again. This time he completed the dial.

"Sheriff's office."

"Bob . . . Charley Hodges. Is Russ there?"

Moments later a gruff voice came on the line. "Sheriff Hess."

"Russ . . . Charley Hodges. I think you better take a look-see up around Twin Oaks." He explained what he knew, including the conflicting directions the senator had given his housekeeper and secretary.

"Pretty slim evidence to go poking around somebody's private property, Charley," Sheriff Russell Hess responded. "You got some other reason you don't care to mention?"

"C'mon, Russ . . . you know me better'n that. I been deliverin' mail to Twin Oaks longer'n you and Stewart are old. You develop a second sense about folks on your route in that time. Call it a hunch, toss me in the clink if I'm wrong, but I say there's something fishy up there."

After a short silence, Hess said, "All right, Charley. I'll send Bob up to look around. But, hunch or no hunch, we're not breaking in. And if Dunning comes down on me about this I just *might* toss your ass in the clink."

Fifteen minutes later Deputy Sheriff Bob Mares was walking around the outside of Twin Oaks, tugging at locked doors and rising on tiptoe from time to time to peer through one of the first-floor windows. He had just decided to call it a boondoggle when he spotted Charley Hodge's red, white, and blue postal service Jeep speeding up the driveway toward the house. Charley pulled to a stop and dangled something from his hand.

Spotting the key, Mares exclaimed, "You outta your damned skull, Hodges?"

"Viola lent it to me." He held the key out to Mares. "Now you don't have to break in. Besides, you got just cause. It's legal entry."

Charley knew his man. Hess or no Hess, there was no way Bob Mares was going to pass up an opportunity to see for himself what the inside of Twin Oaks looked like. It was surely the only chance he would ever get.

Mares took the key. "Okay . . . official business. But only me, got it? You wait here."

"Sure, Bob . . . whatever you say."

Mares climbed the steps of the columned porch, turned the key in the massive oak door, and entered. Charley Hodges leaned back against the Jeep hood to wait.

Thirty seconds later Mares stumbled back out onto the porch and slammed the door shut. For a long moment he leaned against the doorframe, ashen. Then, barely making it to the railing, he leaned forward and vomited into a bush of blooming azaleas.

Charley rushed up the steps. "Bob . . . what's wrong?"

Mares focused watery eyes on the mailman. "Charley! My God!" Fighting for composure, he lost, turned back to the azaleas, and upchucked again. Between heaves he grabbed Hodges by the arm and pushed him back down the steps.

"Go get Hess, Charley. Go get Hess. Now!"

Two

Joshua Chacón adjusted the lamp on his helmet, knelt, and ran his finger along the serpentine pattern etched several inches along the alabaster wall. The man standing above him shined his flashlight on the pattern for better illumination.

"It's a breccia pipe," the man said. "Secondary."

"Sorry, Mel," Chacón responded. "I'm not that much into geology. Speak English."

"A conduit carved by water," Mel Simmons explained. "That one's eons old, formed when the pre-Cambrian sea that covered this desert was subsiding."

"And you say that means trouble now, a million years later?"

"With a capital *T*," Simmons replied. "I've taken core samples for three miles in all directions. That pipe's no orphan."

Josh Chacón stood, dusted his hands on his trousers, and beamed his handheld light around the cavern. At this level, they were two hundred feet beneath the surface of the Querecho Plains, an expanse of alkali desert northeast of Carlsbad, New Mexico. In the panned light, the crystalline salt-encrusted walls reflected eerie patterns on the cavern floor. Josh gave an involuntary shiver. He didn't like caves, didn't like being underground. "Well," he observed, "it's drier down here now than high noon in the Mojave."

"And it could stay that way for another hundred years . . . or a week. A breccia pipe, even a secondary one, means aquifer. Water has been here; water can be here again. Lots of it. Josh, in just a few weeks the DOE is going to start storing transuranic . . . uh, nuclear waste."

"I know that one, Mel."

"Okay. Transuranic waste will be stored at WIPP, barely fifty miles west of here on a down-plane level. WIPP is carved out of pure bed salt. If these pipes mean what I believe they mean, that storage site—and the metal drums that will contain the waste— could eventually be exposed to water seepage. Water plus salt equals brine; brine means corrosion and a possible build-up of explosive gases; and that spells a potential disaster for us or future generations on a scale we can barely imagine."

Josh collected his thoughts. He had known Mel Simmons for only a week. Yet, in that time, he had sized up the University of New Mexico geology professor and found him to be a level-headed professional, far from the wild-eyed alarmist the publicists for the Department of Energy made him out to be. Still, despite the political skulduggery that tainted the site-selection process, it would be foolish for an objective observer to assume that the Department of Energy geologists who developed the Waste Isolation Pilot Plant were all imbeciles. And Josh Chacón prided himself on being an objective observer.

Simmons sensed his skepticism. "Josh, I didn't pick your name out of the Yellow Pages, you know. I checked around, talked to people, read your books."

"Then you must know that this isn't exactly my kind of story."

"You write about people; you write about injustice," Mel said. "Well, WIPP may very well be the greatest injustice of all time to the people of this country—certainly this state." He paused, as if choosing his next words carefully. "I also know that you've been . . . well, looking for a suitable story for some time now."

Diplomatically put, Josh thought.

"This is a suitable story, Josh," Mel continued. "My colleagues and I have every confidence in you."

Josh gave an appreciative nod. "I'll have to think on it, Mel."

"Understandable. Just don't leave us hanging. If you decide to do it, you'll get first-rate technical support. And with your name on the story, it's sure to get wide coverage."

All the more reason to be careful, Josh thought. He said, "Give me a week."

"Fair enough."

"Now," Josh said with a shudder, "lead me out of this damned hole in the ground."

At 3:15 that afternoon, Josh turned off Highway 380 onto Interstate 25 and set the cruise control on his Honda Accord LXi for sixty-five miles per hour. Ninety miles to the north, resplendent against the background of an azure sky, rugged Sandia Peak towered like a regal sentinel above other giants in the southernmost Rocky Mountain chain. He studied the scene for a moment, and then returned to his thoughts.

He had left his apartment on Canyon Road in Santa Fe yesterday for the drive to the Querecho Plains and his meeting today with Mel Simmons. Now, on the return trip, he had already driven three hours since leaving Simmons in Artesia, and he faced another three before he would get back to Santa Fe. He didn't mind. He liked driving. Liked the privacy it afforded him to think. He had even turned off his car phone, and left it off, to assure that privacy. At the moment, the only sound competing for his attention was the soft strain of the "Theme from Ruby Gentry," but he didn't consider that a distraction. As always when driving in the high country, he had the Dolby-enhanced radio tuned to KIVA, the Albuquerque easy-listening station. Despite being born into the rock 'n' roll era, he rarely listened to any music written after the fifties, a penchant that frustrated his closest friends and provoked others to derision.

After listening to the melodic theme a while, he turned his thoughts to the WIPP exposé that Mel had proposed. Despite vigorous statewide opposition, the Feds had already scheduled the first twenty-five thousand drums of nuclear waste to be shipped to the southern New Mexico desert for burial, with nearly a million more to come.

Fait accompli.

But federal bureaucratic bullying alone didn't justify the time and effort a book project would require. Nothing new there. No, what had piqued his interest enough to lure him to the Querechos

Plains was Mel Simmons's theory that WIPP was a world-magnitude disaster in the making—a man-made nuclear-poison pit that some-day would erupt to wreak havoc on generations yet unborn. *That* was worth serious consideration.

A glint of burnished gold distracted him. He glanced across the highway, surprised to see a familiar scene of piñon rooted sparingly among crimson and annatto rocks. He was climbing La Bajada, the final steep ascension from the lower Rio Grande valley to the Santa Fe plateau, once the route of conquistadors. He had been so engrossed in thought, that he had lost track of time and place.

As he did often on La Bajada, he pulled to a stop on the side of the road, got out of his car, and walked to the edge of the west embankment. With heavy heart, he surveyed the rugged terrain below. By the time he became old enough to ask questions, no one could pinpoint for him exactly where it had happened; where, on that ice-bound December night, his parents' pickup truck went out of control, plunged into a deep ravine, and burned—but not before the impact had expelled him, an infant at the time, into the cushioned safety of a nearby snowbank. For years now, since that day he had returned as a stranger to this strange but fascinating land of his birth, he had come to La Bajada often.

Seeking what? Communion?

That's what Annie Zah said. Like her Navajo ancestors, Annie believed that an earthbound spirit of the dead dwelled forever at the place of death. Well, her explanation was as good as any. Yes, he came to this rugged ravine for communion. A yearned-for closeness with whatever spirits might remain here of the parents he never knew. A consuming need to gain some insight into a past that haunted him and eluded understanding. Other days—always on the anniversary of the accident—he would visit their common grave in the pine grove near the Dedication Centrum in the National Cemetery in Santa Fe. There, near the base of a shel-tering ponderosa, a plain granite marker bore the inscription:

ESTÉVAN CHACÓN
1932–1960
SERGEANT
USMCR

On the back of the marker was inscribed:

JENNIFER COLLIER CHACÓN
1932–1960
HIS WIFE

Dead at twenty-eight. When he had reached and passed that age himself, the dates on that stone moved him deeply. To be older than his parents. To view their grave, and contemplate what little he knew of their lives and his from the vantage of an age they had never attained. It was as if the child and parent roles had somehow reversed.

The piercing blast of an air horn jolted him. He turned to see an eighteen-wheeler aggressively riding the tail of a Chevrolet in the southbound lane. The car eased toward the shoulder. He watched the truck pull around and away from the cowed Chevy, wondering if the commercial markings on the trailer were authentic, or a cover for a DOE shipment headed for WIPP. Mel said transuranic wastes were often transported like that. Incognito. Made the natives less restless.

He returned to his car and glanced at the dashboard chronometer: 5:02 p.m. He had been away from his apartment for thirty-six hours. He wondered if Annie had any messages for him.

God bless Annie. He had written a dozen books over the years, with little recognition and even less financial reward. Then, following a tip from a well-placed source, he wrote *Evil Witness*, an account of how the federal government's witness-protection program damaged innocent people while shielding some of the nation's vilest felons. The book was so unnervingly accurate that the United States attorney general denounced Chacón publicly and threatened to subpoena the author to reveal his sources. The resulting publicity caused sales of a lackluster midlist book to skyrocket overnight, and the book subsequently enjoyed sixty-four weeks on the *New York Times* best-seller list.

Chacón followed that with a yearlong probe of sweatshops in California, Texas, and Arizona. The result was *Cargo of Shame*, an exposé of brokers on both sides of the border who smuggle children and teenagers from South and Central America into the United States to become cheap laborers. The book brought him a

Pulitzer, and his phone began to ring every five minutes, making work impossible. It was then that he had signed with Annie, and he never regretted it. Wheelchair-bound Annie Zah operated her answering service from her home and treated her clients more like family than employers. She knew which messages were important, which could wait, and, in most cases, which could be ignored.

They still came, the calls and messages and invitations, despite the fact that he was now in the third year of a barren hiatus in output. Following the Pulitzer, things began to go sour. Words wouldn't come. Ideas that once would have galvanized him no longer turned him on. For a while he wasn't concerned. He had banked and invested more royalties than he would ever need. Fame and recognition, the book tours, and the talk circuit had been ego fulfilling. Then, as time passed, he became obsessed with a notion that haunted his brain like an unshakable tune: *Is this all there is?*

In the past he had attacked his demons at his word processor. It had worked, and maybe could again. When the unexpected invitation to go caving with Mel Simmons had come, he accepted. Perhaps beneath the rugged Querecho Plains he would find the inspiration he needed to work again.

He had seven days to make that decision.

He switched on his cellular phone and pressed the precoded key for his own number. Annie answered on the second ring, "Chacón residence."

"Hi, Annie."

"Well, about time. How was spelunking?"

"Not for me. Anything important?"

"Call from your agent. Same old thing. She wants to know if you've started anything new."

A persistent query these days. "I'll call her tomorrow. Anything else?"

"Five requests for speaking engagements. Three want you gratis; I tossed 'em out. Two for fee: one an insult; one for good money, a library association in Phoenix. You might be interested."

"I'll look it over," he replied.

"Glenn Barrett called from Taos," she continued. "They're auctioning the Martinez collection at La Fonda this weekend. He says there are a couple of Remingtons in the lot. He wondered if he should bid for you, if you can't attend."

Josh's collection of western art was famous among Santa Fe dealers. Barrett had acquired most of the paintings for him.

"I'll call him."

"Okay. Oh, Vicki Armijo called to remind you that she's grilling T-bones for the two of you at her place tonight. I like this one, Josh. How about you? Is it serious?"

"You're a nosey Navajo, Annie."

"That's better than a stupid gringo."

"Half gringo," he replied.

"Yeah. And Pancho Villa was Irish."

He laughed, but there was little mirth in it. There was no bullshitting Annie Zah. She had sensed his dilemma long ago.

She said, "All I know is it's time for you to stop dicking around—time to make a real commitment before you wake up old someday and find out just how lonesome that king-size bed of yours can be. Anyway, Vicki wants you to bring the libations."

"I'll pick up a six-pack of Coors."

"Uh-uh. Zinfandel. Sandia Shadows, last year's vintage."

"New Mexico wine?"

"Don't be a snob. It beats most of the swill they import here at five times the price."

"How come you know so much about booze, Annie?"

"It gets me through the night. Don't knock it."

He let it go at that.

Annie continued, "There was a weird call early this morning. You know a guy named Hess?"

"Hess? No. Wait . . . Russell Hess? From West Virginia?"

"That's the one."

"Yeah, I know him. But I've got no desire to see him. What's he doing out here?"

"He's not out here. He called from . . . just a minute, it's on my notes . . . here it is—Seneca Falls. Wanted to talk to you. Asked a lot of prying questions when I told him you'd been out of town a couple of days. Then said something crazy. Said your brother's dead. I told him he had the wrong person. You don't have a brother."

Josh was silent.

"Josh?"

He didn't answer.

"Josh . . . you there?"

"I'm here." There was a strange tone to his voice.

"Josh, you *don't* have a brother, do you?"

"Yeah . . . I have a brother."

"Madre de Dios . . . I didn't know, I swear it."

"It's okay, Annie. Did Hess say what happened?"

"Josh, I'm so sorry. He said he was . . . murdered."

Murdered?

Josh's mind raced. Who would want to kill . . . ?

He paused in midthought. It was a witless question; there were plenty of people who would be delighted that Stewart Dunning was dead. His thoughts turned to Aunt Martha. Would she need him now?

"Josh . . . you all right?"

Annie's voice was faint. He saw that he had put the phone down on the passenger seat. He didn't remember doing that. He picked it up again. "Annie, I need your help. Call Vicki. Tell her I can't make it tonight, and that I'll make it up to her later."

"That it?" Annie said.

"No. Call Barrett. Tell him to use his best judgment on the Remingtons. Then call my agent. Explain that I'll be out of touch for a couple of days and will call her as soon as I can. Then book me on the first flight out of Albuquerque to Dulles"—he looked at his watch—"anytime after 7:30 tonight. And have an Avis rental car on hold for me at Dulles. Can you do all that?"

"No problem. Anything else?"

"That's everything. I'll call you from Seneca Falls. And Annie, thanks."

"Don't mention it. Josh . . . I *am* sorry."

He put the phone down, started the engine, and pulled back onto the highway. He tried to imagine Stewart dead. Egotistic, ambitious, damn-whose-toes-get-stepped-on Stewart Dunning.

Annie, who didn't even know Stewart existed, had said she was sorry.

Am *I?* Josh wondered. He didn't know.

She was waiting for him at his apartment, seated on the couch where they often sat while watching late-night movies. "I let myself in. Is that all right?"

"Sure. That's why I gave you the key."

He went to the bedroom, picked out his lightweight gray suit from others in the closet, and hung it on a hook on the door. She followed and sat on the edge of the bed and studied the floor. He was sorting through his ties when he caught her melancholy reflection in the mirror. She was wearing tan slacks and a short-sleeve saffron blouse with a wide collar. A thin gold necklace bearing a tiny cross adorned her throat. Her raven hair was short and brushed back at the sides, boyish style. But no one would ever mistake Vicki Armijo for a boy. On other occasions, in this very bed, he had held her close throughout the night while trying to divine his true feelings for her.

He turned. "Look, Vicki, about tonight. Did Annie explain?"

"Yes. I'm sorry about your brother. How long will you be gone?"

He took a small suitcase from the closet and set it on the bed. "Three days at most. Will the steaks keep?"

"I'll stick them in the freezer. I didn't even know you had a brother, Josh."

"Few people do. I don't talk about it."

She shook her head. "I can't understand that at all. Family is everything. How could you be so distant?"

"It's an Anglo affliction."

"You're not Anglo."

"Annie would argue with you about that."

He grabbed a pair of Jockey shorts from his dresser drawer and started for the bathroom. "How about throwing a couple of shirts and stuff in that bag for me while I shower. I'll only be a few minutes."

She had the bag packed when he came out of the bathroom. "Don't forget your razor," she reminded him.

"Oh, yeah." He retrieved his Norelco and other items from the bathroom. Vicki got a Ziploc freezer bag from the kitchen, sealed the toiletries in it, and packed it with the other stuff. Then she sat back on the bed and watched him dress. After a while she said, "Andrew called me this morning. The network was impressed with the series

I did about women and AIDS. He said the co-anchor job in Wichita is mine . . . if I want it."

"Oh?" It took him by surprise, and his face showed it. "I thought you liked your job in Albuquerque."

"I do. But I won't get a chance to anchor there for another two years at best. Andy says I can have a few days to think about it. That's what I wanted us to talk about tonight. That and . . . well, you know . . . everything."

He finished dressing and stepped over to the bed and put a hand on her shoulder. "I'll be back in a couple of days. Can it wait?"

"I guess so." She stood and pressed her body to his and kissed him with ardor. "I love you, you know."

He returned her kiss with equal warmth. But he said nothing.

Three

The old statue was just as he remembered it, tarnished bronze and caked with bird dung. A replica of a World War I doughboy—eyes alert, rifle at ready—perpetually guarding the entrance to the ivy-encased, red brick Seneca County Courthouse. Elsewhere on the columned portico, other markers honored Seneca Countians who had served in World War II, Korea, and Vietnam. A more recent plaque commemorated the county's sole casualty in Desert Storm. But it was the doughboy that had stuck in Josh's memory over the years, as it had in the memory of every Seneca Falls High School senior since 1921 whose class had commemorated graduation by decorating the silent sentinel with a mortarboard and cape of purple and gold—fighting colors of the good old Seneca Falls Vikings.

He had driven to the courthouse after seeing Stewart interred in the spacious Dunning family plot in Elm Hill Memorial Gardens, alongside eight generations of Dunnings reaching back to the mid-eighteenth century. Those generations certified Stewart's status as an entitled member of this tight little community in the Potomac Highlands of West Virginia, where anyone with fewer than two generations entombed at Elm Hill was regarded as an outsider.

The funeral had been the largest in the town's history, with mourners overflowing Main Street Presbyterian Church far beyond its four-hundred-seat capacity. Latecomers crowded the sanctuary walls and the narthex outside, where hastily rigged audio speakers brought them the words from the pulpit. From a rear pew, where he sat with his aunt Martha, Joshua Chacón studied the somber faces in the crowded sanctuary. Governor Kane was there, having flown in from Charleston to pay final homage to the man who most likely would have succeeded him in office. Kane's attendance was also a wise political move, Josh mused. The ambitious politician was running for the United States Senate and would make capital out of his close association, if not actual friendship, with Stewart Dunning. Seated next to the governor was Stewart's father, Harold Dunning Jr., in from his summer home in Bar Harbor, Maine. No point in offering condolences to him, Josh thought, recalling past humiliations. The pews behind Dunning and the governor were filled with every Republican member of the West Virginia State Senate, plus a sprinkling of mossback Democrats. There wasn't a liberal politician in sight.

Josh switched his attention to other, more meaningful faces from the past. There was Carl Travis, editor of the *Seneca Falls Ledger*, who had given him his first job as a reporter. Josh made a mental note to drop by to see Carl before departing Seneca Falls tomorrow. In the front pew across the aisle from the Dunnings was Angus Munroe, patriarch of the Munroe clan, ever imperious, as great wealth sometimes causes a man to be. Standing against the wall near Munroe, with his eyes dutifully turned toward the audience rather than the pulpit, a tall, neatly dressed man with crew-cut blonde hair bore all the markings of a bodyguard. A sign of the times, thought Josh. Next to Angus was his daughter-in-law, Constance, still breathtakingly beautiful. Her husband, David—the old man's son—was nowhere in sight. Seated beside Constance was her daughter, Beth Munroe Dunning, now Stewart's widow. If she was feeling any emotion for this somber affair, she was holding it well in check. Josh studied her more closely. Though he had steeled himself for the moment when he would see her again, he felt a rekindling of old hurts long suppressed. If Beth knew he was there, she gave no sign of it.

Two pews behind Beth, resplendent in his best tan and brown uniform, was Sheriff Russell Hess. Throughout the service, while others paid respectful attention to the speakers who eulogized the deceased from the pulpit behind the elegant bronze casket, Hess's gaze had remained fixed on Beth. How appropriate, Josh thought. So close, yet still so far.

Now, after the graveside service, it was Sheriff Hess who Josh had come to the courthouse to see.

Tossing the doughboy a hasty salute, Josh peeled off his suit coat, threw it in the car, and mopped his brow with his handkerchief. He'd forgotten how oppressively humid the East could be. Inside the old courthouse, a musty-scented wood corridor extended the entire length of the building. The first door on the right had a frosted glass pane that read:

SENECA COUNTY SHERIFF'S OFFICE
Russell Hess, Sheriff
Robert Mares, Chief Deputy Sheriff

Josh smiled at the second name. He didn't know Mares, but he knew he was the only other officer on the county payroll. He guessed that Mares had been awarded the title "Chief Deputy" to mollify him for the lack of a decent wage. The door was slightly ajar. Josh rapped twice and entered.

Still in dress uniform, Hess was seated at his desk talking to a comely redheaded woman holding a steno pad on her lap. The sheriff looked up at Josh, then back to the woman. "Just finish it up in your own words, Agnes. I'll sign it after lunch."

"Yes sir."

The woman rose, gave Josh a cursory smile, and left, closing the door behind her.

In a glance, Josh saw that nothing much had changed. Two plain wooden desks in an equally plain office; timeworn oak floor; green plaster walls, sorely in need of repainting; nail-mounted clipboards bordering an oversize map of Seneca County; five army-surplus four-drawer file cabinets, secured by combination locks; a small pine conference table with four straight-back chairs. The odor of stale coffee permeated the room. Mares was not there.

Hess leaned back in his chair and eyed Josh critically. "See you're wearing shit-stompers these days, Chacón."

Without invitation, Josh sat down in the chair the redheaded woman had vacated and crossed one leg over his knee, offering the sheriff a better view of his custom hand-stitched Lucchese cowboy boots. "Seemed appropriate, Russ."

The two men locked eyes for several seconds. Hess broke the silence first. "Surprised you'd show up around here again, big shot you are nowadays. When *did* you get back, by the way?"

Josh chuckled. "You got me on your suspect list, Russ?"

"Just answer the question."

Josh shrugged. "Twenty-four hours ago I was crawling around inside a cave in New Mexico. Yesterday afternoon the lady who manages my answering service told me you had called to check if I was in town, and then passed on the news about Stewart. At 8:50 last night I caught a red-eye out of Albuquerque to Dulles International. There's a red Corvette parked out front that I rented at the Avis counter at Dulles this morning. I drove straight here and got a couple hours sleep before the funeral. Any more questions?"

"What flight?"

"American 245."

Hess made a note on the tablet. "You staying at Martha Collier's?"

"Where else?"

Hess stood and went to a hot plate on a table near the window and lifted the coffeepot. He took his time filling his cup, not offering any to his visitor. He was a strapping man, two inches over six feet, with a ruddy complexion and close-cropped brown hair. He was still as erect and muscular at thirty-eight as he'd been at eighteen, Josh noted. And still as brusque.

Hess brought the cup back to his desk and sat down. "So, why did you come? And don't give me no crap about brotherly love. I know there was no love lost between you and Stewart."

"We had the same mother," Josh replied. He felt no need to explain further. "I'm not planning to stick around, if that's worrying you."

"You don't worry me one bit, Chacón."

Hess took a swig of coffee and cradled the cup between his hands. "I take it this isn't a social call. What's on your mind?"

"I want to know what happened to Stewart . . . and why."

"Just like that?"

Josh didn't reply.

"Maybe you're asking the wrong person," Hess said. "Governor Kane's thinking of putting Colonel Gregory in charge of the investigation. That'd put it outside my jurisdiction."

"Bullshit, Russ. Nothing in Seneca County is ever outside your jurisdiction. If you let the state police go on the hook for this one, it's because you want it that way."

Hess acknowledged the backhanded compliment with a smirk.

"Russ," Josh continued, "just this once, put the past aside and tell me what you know about Stewart's death."

Hess sat for a long moment without comment. Then he put down the cup and swiveled in his chair to reach a field safe beside the desk. He took out a large manila envelope and handed it to Josh. "What you see doesn't leave this office. Got it?"

"Got it," Josh agreed.

He loosened the clasp on the envelope and pulled out an assortment of eight-by-ten photographs. At the sight of the first one he looked away, swallowing hard. "Oh God!"

"Doc said he'd been dead for four days," Hess said. "It was pretty hot over that weekend."

Josh looked at the photo again. Captured in sickening full color, Stewart Dunning's blackened and bloated body lay atop a long harvest table in the middle of the large kitchen of Twin Oaks. The body was covered below the waist with what appeared to be a green shroud. The arms, protruding from a midsleeve Oriental robe, were arranged so that one hand lay atop the other, like those of a corpse laid out in a casket. The head was resting on a brocaded cushion. Two burned-down candles sat waxed to the table on either side of the cushion.

"That's a drapery covering him," Hess said. "Torn from one of the dining room windows. The pillow's from a chair in the living room."

Josh was stupefied. "For God's sake, Russ, this has the earmarks of a demonic sacrifice!"

"Uh-huh, except he wasn't offed there; that took place in his office in the manor. Shot in the face, close up. We dug the slug out of the seat of the couch. Twenty-two caliber. No trace of the weapon."

The next photo was a close-up of the right side of Stewart's face, or what remained of it.

"It was a dumdum," Hess explained.

Josh took a deep breath. "Any fingerprints?" he managed to ask.

"A few. The FBI lab in D.C. is working them up now."

Josh held one of the photos up to the light. "Who took these?"

"I did."

"You develop them?"

"Yeah. Why?"

"Just wondering," Josh said. He began to look through the other photos. "Why did it take so long to find him?"

"No one knew he was in town that weekend. He took pains to make people think otherwise. Probably was meeting someone he didn't want to be seen with, or vice versa."

"A woman?"

Hess shook his head. "Stewart didn't give a damn who knew about his women."

"Not even Beth?"

Hess snorted. "That fire went out long ago. She hasn't lived in the manor for years."

"Oh?" Josh pondered this news with interest. After a moment he asked, "What about robbery?"

"He had a three-thousand-dollar Rolex on his wrist. There was fifteen-hundred bucks in his money clip upstairs, and another twelve grand in the office wall safe. Televisions, DVD players, four stereos—all in place. Silver, crystal, artworks—none of it missing. The computer on his desk was still turned on. Way I figure it, Stew had been working late, stretched out on the couch to rest, and whoever offed him took him by surprise."

"Working? With only a robe on?"

"Viola said he often worked that way."

Josh pondered that. "Okay. How about the killers? Why did they—?"

"*Killers?*" Hess eyed Josh askance.

"Stewart was a big man, Russ. Why did they carry him to the kitchen and lay him out like that? Is that somebody's idea of a sick joke?"

Hess reached across the desk. "Through with those?"

"Huh? Oh." Josh gave the photos another quick look, then shoved them back into the envelope and handed them to Hess. "You didn't answer my question."

Hess locked the photos in the safe and then turned back to face Josh. "It's sick, but it's no joke."

"That's no answer."

"It's all you get."

Josh pressed it. "Russ, Stewart wasn't just another rich kid whose daddy bought him a seat in the Senate. He was a power in his own right, high profile. He could get an invitation to the Oval Office any day of the week with a simple phone call. He was a shoo-in to be the next governor. Now, who would be so brazen as to walk into the home of a man like that, blow his brains out, and then lay him out like a sacrificial offering in a Druid ceremony?"

"Whoever got his pockets lined to do it," Hess replied.

"A hit?" Josh exclaimed. "C'mon, Russ, get real. This is West Virginia for God's sake."

Hess wasn't swayed. "Don't you have newspapers out there in Arizona, Chacón?"

"New Mexico."

"Wherever."

Hess leaned across the desk and lowered his voice. "Now, I'll say this once, then this conversation's ended. If you don't know who's behind Stewart Dunning's death, you're the only damned person around here who doesn't. But nobody'll ever be able to prove it. Not me, not the state police, nobody."

He splayed a hamlike hand on the desk and pushed back in the chair. "You want more, talk to your old buddy Carl Travis."

"Carl?"

"I don't think that needs explaining."

Josh agreed. It didn't. He rose. "I know your heart wasn't in it, Russ. But thanks, anyway."

He left.

Hess turned toward the window and watched Josh walk down Virginia Avenue toward Second Street. He was still watching when Deputy Mares entered the office.

Mares set a Dairy Queen sack on his desk. He hung his hat on a rack, dropped into his chair with a weary sigh, and took out a burger and shake. "I never seen so damned many cars. Bumper to bumper all the way up Cemetery Hill. Half those plates were outta county—lots outta state."

Hess didn't respond.

Mares stretched toward the window to see what was distracting the sheriff. "That Chacón?"

"Yeah," Hess replied. "That's Chacón."

"Never did understand that relationship." Mares was from Greenbriar County and knew little about Seneca County other than what he'd picked up since becoming the deputy four years before.

"He and Stewart had the same mother," Hess said.

"I know . . . Jenny Collier, Martha Collier's kid sister. What I don't know is why Jenny'd leave someone as loaded as Stewart's dad was, to run off with some damned greaser." Mares took a bite out of the burger.

"The world's full of stupid broads, my friend."

Hess tore off the top sheet of his tablet, rose, and grabbed his hat. "I'm going home to feed Pop." He laid the sheet on Mares's desk and tapped the flight number and date he'd written down there. "Call American Airlines at Dulles. Find out if Joshua Chacón was on this flight."

Mares glanced at the note Hess had made.

Hess continued, "Then I want you to cover the office. I'll take patrol. I'm going to keep an eye on Chacón until he leaves town."

Mares looked up from the paper. "You don't like him much, do you, Boss?"

"I don't like him at all," Hess replied.

Four

Constance Munroe dried herself vigorously with a towel, then slipped into her white velour robe, and stepped from the steamy bathroom into her bedroom. The spacious four-room suite she occupied was one of four on the second floor of Greenleaf, the stately home that was the centerpiece of the vast Munroe estate atop Mount Canaan, thirty miles from Seneca Falls. She pushed the kitchen call button on her phone; ordered a small plate of cottage cheese, a glass of carrot juice, and six wheat wafers be sent to her room; and then went to her dressing table. The funeral that day had kept her from her customary morning ride through the deep Mount Canaan forests on Thunder, her favorite quarter horse gelding. During the lunch hour she had compensated for the missed canter by swimming a dozen brisk laps in Greenleaf's Olympic-size indoor pool. This daily regime of strenuous exercise combined with a carefully regulated diet had paid striking dividends for the one-time Miss America runner-up. Stunningly beautiful, she possessed a body that was the envy of women half her age.

She looked among the items on the vanity, found the eyebrow pencil she wanted, and began her makeup. She had almost finished when her husband entered the room. David Munroe was a slender, graying man who regarded the world through chronically dilated eyes. He was working on his fourth luncheon martini of the day.

"I do wish you would knock, David," Constance complained, observing him in her mirror.

"Sorry."

He slumped into a chaise lounge by the window. "I hear that writer fellow was at the funeral—the one Beth used to fool around with in high school."

"There was more to it than fooling around," she said, continuing with her makeup.

"Did Beth notice him?"

"She has eyes."

"She say anything?"

"Not to me."

"Wonder if he's the reason she left town right after the funeral. She didn't even stop by Greenleaf, you know. I'd liked to have seen her."

"You could have, if you'd gone to the funeral. Anyway, it's a bit late for you to start feeling paternal, don't you think?"

He started to reply, decided against it, and turned to the window. Far below, in the wide expanse of the Canaan Valley, a man and a woman were launching a canoe laden with camping gear into the river. David watched until they shoved off, paddling upstream. Heading for the Canaan wilderness, he thought wistfully. Far removed from everything.

He said, "I understand that Father did quite well at the funeral this morning, considering."

"Considering what?" Constance replied.

"Considering that most people in this state, from Governor Kane on down, believe it was Angus Munroe who sent Stewart Dunning to his grave."

"Do you?" She set her lip gloss aside and picked up a hairbrush.

"Do I what?"

"Believe your father sent Stewart to his grave."

He swirled his martini, took a sip, and replied, "No, I don't believe it. Angus likes nothing better than a fight. And Stewart was his only worthy adversary still living. Angus would never have forfeited the opportunity to destroy him—by other means."

She made a final sweep through her sable hair. "Where is Angus, by the way?"

"Where else?" he sniffed. "At the river. Hunting for his precious flints."

"It gives him pleasure," she said.

"Oh, sure . . . whatever gives dear Father pleasure, right?"

He fixed his gaze on the canoe as it rounded the far bend in the river. "We used to do that, you know—Mother and I. We used to spend days on end backpacking in the Canaan wilderness, just the two of us, fishing, hiking, scrounging the stream banks for artifacts. Father would join us on occasion. But after Mother died, something happened to him. There was no room for me in his grief. He never considered that I may have been grieving too." He paused. "Of course, you wouldn't understand."

She had heard the chronic lament dozens of times over the years, and she knew the doleful expression on his face without having to look. "Your mother was very much alive when we got married, David. I understood your relationship with her quite well. She made certain of that. And I've watched you wallow in self-pity ever since she died."

There was a momentary silence. Then, turning from the window, David said, "Huh? What did you say?"

"Nothing important," she replied.

There was a rap at the door.

"Come in, Clara," she called.

A young woman, dressed in the crisp gray uniform of a maid, entered bearing a tray. She placed on a table near the vanity the meager lunch Constance had ordered. "Will there be anything else, Miss Connie?"

"No. Thank you, Clara."

When the maid left, David erupted: "*Miss Connie . . . Miss Connie!* I despise that! You're my wife, damn it! *Mrs. Munroe.* Why don't you just instruct her call you 'Miss Scarlet' and be done with it."

She ignored his diatribe, as she always did, and sipped the carrot juice.

After a moment David said, "Marshe called again, while you were at the funeral."

"Who?"

"Professor Marshe, from the university."

Her face clouded. "You didn't talk to him, I hope?"

"No. Mary took the call. He was trying to get through to Father again. Bad business, Connie. Bad business."

"I'm Angus's business manager, David, not you," she said, bringing her ire under control. "I'll decide what's good or not good for business."

She finished her lunch, stood, and stepped out of her robe. She draped it across the vanity chair and went to the bed where Clara had laid out her clothing for the afternoon. Sitting on the edge of the bed, she kicked off her mules and reached for her panties. At the sight of her nude body, David sucked in his breath. He put down his drink and went to her and cupped one of her still-firm breasts in his hand. "Connie . . . can't we . . . ?"

Her anthracite eyes fixed him with an icy stare.

After a moment he removed his hand. "I see," he said. He retrieved his drink, downed it in one gulp, and left.

A half hour later Constance Munroe was driving her robin-egg-blue Rolls Royce convertible north on Pike Road. Her mind was still on David. Recalling the touch of his hand on her body, she gave an involuntary shudder. He was becoming more disgusting every day. Of course, he had not been much to begin with. Still, her mother had summed it up neatly soon after that night in Richmond years before, when Constance walked away with the Miss Virginia crown, and her entourage of lusting suitors multiplied prodigiously. On learning the identity of one of the pack, a foppish playboy from West Virginia then in his junior year at Yale, Mama said, "Well, sweetie, whatever else he may be, he *is* Angus Munroe's sole heir."

That had been enough, in the beginning. There had even been a few good times following the birth of their daughter, Beth. But it wasn't enough. Notwithstanding, she had endured. And she *would* endure. For David Munroe was her legitimate claim to Greenleaf and all it stood for. And she *would* have Greenleaf.

Just ahead, a signpost read Davistown—1 Mile.

She reduced speed and pushed thoughts of her husband aside. There were more serious matters to tend to at the moment. She rounded the final curve into the picturesque ski-resort village on the north slope of Mount Canaan and pulled to a stop at the only full-service gas station in town.

The manager greeted her with the obeisant salute he reserved for his best customers. "Afternoon, Mrs. Munroe. Scorcher today, huh? Fill 'er up?"

"Afternoon, Martin. Yes. And whatever else needs doing. I forgot something; have to call home."

"Use my desk phone if you wanta."

She made a face at his grimy hands and they both smiled. "I'll just use the booth," she said.

She stepped across the paved apron to the phone booth, closed the door, and dialed long distance. An operator intoned, "Please deposit seventy-five cents for the first three minutes."

She dropped three quarters into the slot. On the third ring, a brusque voice answered, "Hullo."

"Manny?"

"Who wants to know?"

"Miss Mollie."

Pause. "That spelled with a *y*?"

"No . . . *i-e*"

"Hold on."

Moments later a more familiar voice said, "Yeah?"

"Marshe called Greenleaf again today. This is the third time."

There was a long pause before the response. "Anyone talk to him?"

"No."

"I'll handle it." Click!

Five

Carl Travis—owner, publisher, and editor
of the *Seneca Falls Ledger*—spotted his one-time protégé crossing
Virginia Avenue and heading for the Ledger Building. He rushed to
the door to meet him. "Joshua." Carl grasped the younger man's
hand warmly. "Come in, come in. I was afraid you might have left
already. Couldn't get to you at the funeral. What a mob. Marvelous
tribute to Stewart . . . marvelous. We're making that the lead story
in this week's edition. Come . . . my office . . . there's so much to
talk about."

It would be like that for a while, Josh knew. Small talk.
Chitchat. One could seldom initiate a serious discussion with Carl
until Carl was ready. Josh followed the graying rail-thin editor
into the unpretentious office he had occupied for forty years.

Carl sat down at his rolltop desk, swiveled around in his
chair, and motioned for Josh to sit on one of the nearby chairs.
"What're you working on these days? Tell me everything. You
married yet?"

"No. You?" Josh asked, still standing.

"Ha! Who'd have an old turkey buzzard like me?"

A framed cover from *Newsweek* adorned the office wall. Josh
recognized the montage of his own likeness superimposed on the
book jacket from *Cargo of Shame*. The legend read: "The flesh

traders—a flourishing atrocity." It had been the cover story the week Josh won the Pulitzer.

Carl lowered his chin to better see through the upper lens of his trifocals and saw that Josh was studying the cover. "I keep it there to remind me of what I spawned," he bragged.

"Amen," Josh agreed.

Next to the magazine cover was a series of black-and-white photographs, pictures of every Seneca High School graduating class since 1955. Josh sought out the photo of a much later class and studied the familiar faces of his classmates. There were twenty-two of them—ten boys and twelve girls—all so very young, so full of hope, their plastic smiles frozen in time.

Josh studied one pert brunette. "Frances Baccus. Whatever happened to her?"

"The noblest profession," Carl replied. "A journalist. Owns her own newspaper in Kentucky."

"I'll have to go see her someday." He scanned another face. "Lois Arquette?"

"The *oldest* profession," said Carl. "Manages a place called the Bunny Ranch out in Nevada."

Josh laughed. "Well, I just might go see her, too."

His merriment faded when his eyes fell upon the face of a stunning blonde girl standing at his side in the top row. Though it didn't show in the picture, they had been holding hands while they faced the camera that day. For a protracted moment he gazed at her likeness in silence.

"She's still lovely as ever," Carl said.

Josh started to say that he knew, that he'd seen her in church at the funeral.

"I thought once that you two might hitch up someday," Carl added.

"She had other ideas," Josh replied. He didn't expand.

Carl was perturbed. From the beginning, his relationship with Joshua Collier, as Josh had been known in Seneca Falls, had been deeper than friendship, closer to paternal. No one in the town, not even Josh's Aunt Martha Collier, had been more torn up when Josh, like his mother had done years before, left family and home to find a new life in New Mexico. No one was prouder when Joshua Chacón—the name he reverted to in the land of his father—began to receive critical acclaim for his work. But now there was a moodiness about the young man that didn't befit one who continued to win accolades from both the public and his professional colleagues alike.

"Josh, forgive me if I'm off base here, but did you find what you were looking for out there?"

"Does anyone ever?" Josh replied.

It spoke volumes, but Carl decided not to press it.

Josh sat down on the brown Naugahyde couch across from the desk. "Carl, Russ Hess says you know things about Stewart's death that haven't been told."

Carl frowned. He picked an apple from a bowl on the desk and started peeling it, using the time to weigh his answer. Josh noted the bowl of Winesaps and remembered that fruit was the only food his old mentor ate for breakfast and lunch.

Carl dropped a long spiraling peel into the wastebasket. "Russ shoots his mouth off too much."

"Uh-uh. I haven't been around here for a while, but I'm no stranger. Russ doesn't make careless statements. Carl, if you know something, tell me. I think I deserve that much before I leave."

"When is that?"

"Tomorrow."

Carl offered Josh a slice of apple. "What'd Russ say, exactly?"

Josh declined the apple. "He implied it's an open secret around here who killed Stewart. But that no one would ever be able to prove it. Did you see the photos of the body?"

"I was there when Russ took them."

"Then explain the bizarre way Stewart was found. Hess couldn't . . . or wouldn't. What the hell's going on, Carl? Is there a satanic cult in these hills that no one wants to talk about?"

Carl shifted in the chair, uncomfortable about this turn in the conversation. Josh knew his old mentor well enough to guess the problem. On the day he founded the *Seneca Falls Ledger*, Carl instituted four policies that the paper adhered to for four decades: (1) print every subscriber's name in the paper at least twice a year; (2) devote an entire page of each issue to recipes and women's issues; (3) print nothing that might upset an advertiser; (4) avoid controversy. It was an axiom among Seneca County residents that if murder were committed on the very steps of the Ledger Building, subscribers would not read about it unless it was picked up first by one of the major dailies that covered the area—the *Washington Post* or the *Cumberland News*. With any contentious story involving Seneca County, it was Carl's practice to wait until it had been run in one of those giants. Then he would rehash it for the *Ledger*, taking care to sanitize it for his readers. Whatever the merits of his policies, they worked. The *Ledger* was successful, and Carl Travis was one of the best-liked and most-respected people in the state. And it was universally held that he knew far more about everything and everybody in Seneca County than any other person.

Sidestepping Josh's question, Carl pushed a button on his intercom. "Miss Angie . . . have Dub bring me the wire folder for the last couple of months, please."

Minutes later a tall heavyset man wearing ink-stained overalls entered, carrying a file folder. When he spotted Josh, the man's countenance brightened. "Hullo, Mr. Collier!" He spoke in the deliberate drawl of one who must weigh every word to get it right. "Ya gonna be workin' here again?"

Josh rose and shook Dub Oliver's hand.

"Good to see you again, Dub. No, just visiting."

He started to explain that he no longer went by the name "Collier," but decided that would be too confusing. Now in his midfifties, Dub Oliver had been retarded since birth. Had it not been for Carl Travis making a job for him at the *Ledger*, Dub would have become a ward of the state years ago. The childlike man handed the file to Carl and sauntered off on feet heavy with shoddy brogues.

Carl thumbed through the folder, pulled out a number of clippings, and handed them to Josh. They were releases from the Associated Press, Los Angeles Times, Chicago Tribune, and other wire-service associations. Josh concentrated on the first, datelined Charleston, West Virginia:

DUNNING STRIP-PIT BILL ANGERS MINERS
Enraged miners from a tristate area of Appalachia
descended on the state capitol here today to protest a bill,

introduced Wednesday by State Senator Stewart Dunning, to close existing strip pits and ban future strip mining in Seneca County, West Virginia.

Although the bill would affect only Seneca County, a spokesman for the mining industry claimed that an anti-strip-mining movement anywhere threatened strip mining everywhere. "We're talking thousands of jobs here. Not just miners, but truckers, sorters, equipment operators, mechanics—working-class Americans trying to make a decent living. We're not about to let our livelihood be flushed down the drain by some over-privileged blue blood who never did a day of real labor in his life."

Succeeding paragraphs included a short history of past anti-strip-mining movements throughout Appalachia, as well as background on Senator Dunning's growing involvement with the issue.

The other press releases heralded a similar message.

Josh looked up over the clippings. "So, what's new? There've been anti-strip-mining bills introduced in every legislature since stripping began."

"What's new is that Stewart was going to win."

"Oh, bullshit, Carl. West Virginia will never outlaw stripping."

"You've been away too long, Josh. It's a new ball game. You don't know what's been happening up on Mount Hazard once the coal's taken out. We've become the dumping ground for the eastern seaboard. New York, Pennsylvania, New Jersey—all have contracts to ship their trash in here to be buried in those played-out pits. Trainload after trainload, around the clock."

"Contracts with whom?"

Carl shot Josh a pointed look.

Josh got the message. *That* had not changed. There was only one person among the mining moguls who had the power to negotiate a deal like that. "Angus Munroe," he said, brow furrowed. "Stewart locked horns with *him*?"

"None other. Russ and I both tried to warn him. But Stewart was never one to back off from a fight with anyone, particularly Angus Munroe. And a lot of folks around here were pulling for Stewart. You just can't imagine some of the stuff that leaches out of those garbage pits into the streambeds. Remember the trout fishermen who used to vacation here every summer? Take a drive up the fork and look around. You'll see a lot of vacant cabins along the river today. Even over the Fourth it was like a ghost camp. Ecologists from the university predict that if the dumping continues, our drinking water'll become so contaminated in the next ten years that we may never be able to clean it up. Bottled water was unheard of around here before. But stop by the A and P and watch how many jugs they ring up now. People are scared . . . and damned mad."

"What about the Feds—the EPA? What're they doing about it?"

Carl scoffed. "The whole state'll be poisoned before they get their act together. Anyway, Stewart always kept his finger to the political winds. He saw all this coming. He started hitting Munroe Mining Corporation hard in the legislature. Even made it a campaign issue. The voters were beginning to swing over to him. And where the voters go, the politicians follow."

Josh thought about it. Of course, none of what Carl had said had ever appeared in the *Seneca Falls Ledger*, which Josh continued to subscribe to, although with each issue he wondered why. "And you're telling me, in your roundabout way, that you and Hess believe Angus Munroe killed Stewart."

Carl shook his head. "Angus doesn't have to do his own dirty work. But it gets done, just the same. Of course, saying it is one thing; proving it is another. Even if anyone was stupid enough to try."

It was the echo of Hess's appraisal.

"All right," Josh said, still skeptical, "explain the way Stewart was found—the sacrificial altar. How does that fit into your theory?"

"I can't answer that, Josh. No one can; it has everybody stymied. That isn't common knowledge, by the way."

"So Russ implied."

Josh looked again at the photo of his high school class. "Russ tells me Beth and Stewart split."

"Some years back. She's got a town house in Georgetown. Much esteemed as a hostess. Her name's been linked with a couple of White House power brokers. Anyway, she doesn't get back here often."

"Divorced?"

"Not that I know of. She still goes by the Dunning name."

"Then she's Stewart's heir."

"Most likely. But if you're looking for a motive there, you're barking up the wrong tree. Beth Munroe's worth more in her own right than Stewart ever hoped to be."

Josh tossed the press releases onto the coffee table. "So, we're back to Angus Munroe. And if what you're suggesting is true, he'll get away with murder, right?"

Carl was surprised by the agitation in the younger man's voice. "Josh, something puzzles me."

It was an invitation to pose a question. Josh made a go-ahead gesture.

Carl said, "I remember what it was like for you growing up around here, after you found out who you were. And I know who was behind it. Stewart Dunning was just as much a pompous ass when he was three, or thirteen, as he was the day he died. And like all the Dunnings, he was an insufferable bigot. He loathed the fact that anyone with less than certified WASP genes could be related to him. He treated you like so much dung, and he made sure that a lot of others did too."

He let the recollection register. Then he continued, "Now, what I'd like to know is, why do you give a damn what happened to a horse's ass like him?"

Six

Martha Collier entered her small office in the rear of the Collier Hardware Store and tossed her hat and purse on the desk. She glanced at the catalog near the calendar. She had left it open to an advertisement for one of those newfangled electronic cash registers that keeps a running tally of sales, computes the change due a customer, and even prepares an updated inventory of stock at the end of each workday. At least once a week the old-fashioned push-button register she inherited from her father would jam, and she would vow to replace it. But once she got it working again, the urge passed. After all, it had been Papa's.

Stewart's funeral that morning, and the memories it invoked, had left her with a headache. She stepped into the bathroom just off the office, pulled a paper cup out of the dispenser near the sink, and filled it with water. She took a bottle of aspirin from the medicine cabinet, shook two tablets into her palm, then—remembering that each was only 325 milligrams—shook out another. She gulped down all three with the water. She detested taking pills; they usually made her gag. This time they went down easy.

She tossed the cup into the wastebasket, returned to the office, and dropped into the deep leather chair across from the desk. Resting her head against its high back, she began to massage her temples.

She had considered reopening the store after the funeral, but now decided to keep it closed for the remainder of the day.

The aspirin began to take effect. With a twinge of nostalgia, she ran her hand across the old chair's rich leather arm. This is where Jenny used to sit. She'd thought a lot about her sister since Stewart's death. Dear, headstrong, ever-restless Jenny, the prettiest girl at Seneca High; the shopkeeper's daughter who astonished everyone by snaring the county's most eligible, and richest, bachelor—Harold Dunning. To Martha's question about why she would marry a man she considered an insufferable snob, Jenny replied, "He got me pregnant." It was the only explanation anyone ever got.

Five months after Hal Dunning and Jenny Collier were married, their son Stewart was born in their private suite on the second floor of Twin Oaks, the palatial Dunning family mansion in Seneca Falls. Immediately, the baby was placed in the care of a live-in nanny chosen by the elder Dunnings.

Within a year, the marriage, like all other ventures in her young life, began to pall on Jenny Collier-Dunning. One day when she came to visit Martha at the store, she found the doorway blocked by a tall, raven-haired man with tawny features. With a flourish, the man removed his dove-gray western Stetson and held the door open. "Señora," he said, bidding her to enter. For a prolonged moment they held each other's gaze. Then, with a slight bow, he left. Jenny watched until he disappeared around the corner, and then went to the counter where Martha had taken it all in with amusement.

"Who is that *adorable* man?" Jenny gushed.

"That *adorable* man is Mr. Estévan Chacón, from New Mexico. He's a new engineer for Munroe Mining." Martha waved an order form. "And he just put in a substantial order."

"An order? You mean you got his phone number?" Jenny snatched the form from Martha's hand. After a moment she flashed a wicked smile and handed the form back to her sister.

Four nights later the phone beside Martha's bed roused her from a deep sleep. She glanced at the clock—2:12 a.m. Who could be calling at this hour? She picked up the phone. "Hello?"

"Martha,"—It was Jenny's voice, throaty and excited— "Hemingway was right . . . the earth *does* move!"

Jenny's affair with Estévan Chacón alarmed Martha. "You've played fast and loose before," she admonished her sister, "but this time you're close to the fire. Nothing goes unnoticed here. Nothing."

One month later, in a world that no longer held surprises, Jenny announced to Martha that she was leaving Harold Dunning and moving to New Mexico.

It needed no explanation. "And your son?"

Jenny frowned. "Hal insists on keeping him."

The following December, Martha received a card from Santa Fe announcing the arrival of Joshua Chacón. "Estévan chose the name," Jenny wrote, "from one of his biblical heroes. He's so happy. He never had a family, you know. I call the baby 'Josh.' You *must* come to see him."

On the day of Josh's first birthday, Martha called Jenny. "If you still want a visitor, I'll be there to spend Christmas with you."

"I'll believe it when I see it," Jenny retorted.

"The twenty-second," Martha said. "American Flight 185 via Dallas, arriving in Albuquerque at 11:45 that night. Can you meet me?"

"With bells on," Jenny exclaimed. "Oh, Martha . . . it's been so long. It's going to be so good to see you . . . so very good."

American Flight 185 from Washington International to Albuquerque arrived that December 22 on a clear star-bright night. The inclement weather predicted for New Mexico had confined itself to the higher elevations around Santa Fe. There was no one at the airport to meet Martha. She waited a half hour, then called Jenny's number. No one answered. Thirty minutes later there was still no answer. She considered taking a cab. But what if they passed each other on the road? She had no way of getting into Jenny's apartment. At 1:20 a.m. she dialed Jenny's number again. This time a strange voice answered. Puzzled, Martha asked, "Is Jenny there?"

"Who's calling, please?" The speaker used an officious tone.

"Martha . . . Martha Collier. I'm Jenny's sister. I'm calling from Albuquerque. She was supposed to meet me at the airport."

After a pause, the strange voice said in softer tones, "Miss Collier, this is Sergeant Chavez, New Mexico State Police. There's been an accident . . ."

Later she was able to recall only a few of the words that followed: "icy road . . . La Bajada . . . fire . . . one survivor. A child . . . not a scratch . . ."

A nightmare! Too young . . . too young, she thought.

"Hello. Miss, are you all right? Hello."

She forced herself to speak. "Where . . . where is the baby?"

"Here, asleep. Look, Miss. There's a traveler's aid office in the airport. Wait there. I'll have a patrolman pick you up and bring you to Santa Fe."

On Christmas Eve, Martha sat in a metal folding chair beneath a temporary awning near the Memorial Centrum in Santa Fe National Cemetery and watched as two coffins were lowered into a common grave—Estévan's first, and then Jenny's. The dark-complexioned baby Martha cuddled in her lap slept peacefully through it all. That afternoon she hired a local probate lawyer to place all funds from the estate into a trust for Joshua. Then she packed what she could carry of his things into a separate bag and arranged for everything else to go to the orphanage where Estévan was raised. That evening in Albuquerque, with Josh in her arms, she boarded a return flight to Washington. On the ticket, as she would on all records thereafter, she registered the boy's name as Joshua Collier.

He became a blessing. After her fiancé, Boyd, had been killed in Vietnam, she resigned herself to a life of lonely spinsterhood. Instead, Martha Collier became a mother.

And I did a damned fine job of it, she complimented herself, thinking of the handsome man who sat beside her that morning at his half brother's funeral.

A blinking light on the desk signaled an incoming call. She stood and picked up the phone. "Collier Hardware."

"I was lonesome last night."

"Me too."

"I guess tonight's out of the question."

"It won't be much longer. He's leaving tomorrow."

"Sounds like that makes you sad."

"It does."

"But it's all so silly. Why don't you tell him about us. I'm not ashamed."

"Oh, no . . . it's not that. It's just . . . well, he's had this terrible conflict about his mother and me."

"You should have told him about that years earlier than you did."

"I know. But what's done's done. I don't want to make it worse. Not at this late date, anyway."

"Martha, he's a grown man."

"Please . . . let's not argue about this."

After a long silence he responded, "All right. I guess I understand. Soon?"

"Yes, soon," she said, and returned the phone gently to the cradle.

Seven

Sometime after midnight, sleep eluding him, Josh got up and switched on the light in the upstairs bedroom that had been his while he was growing up. Soon after she had revealed his true identity, Aunt Martha told him it had been his mother's room, and it helped appease the hurt. Later, when he left Seneca Falls and she was convinced that he would not return, Aunt Martha had converted it to a reading room. On the wall across from the sleeper couch where he had tossed fitfully before rising, six shelves of well-thumbed books attested to Aunt Martha's enduring passion for reading. His own works, he noted with amusement, were bracketed between the collected works of Shakespeare. He grinned at the arrangement. He had never shared Aunt Martha's passion for the bard's torturous syntax and often remarked that he would just as soon read the latest issue of the telephone book, at which times she would cluck her tongue and allow as how no aspiring writer who disparaged Shakespeare would ever amount to much. Now, he sat on the edge of the sleeper couch thinking about Aunt Martha's reaction to his meetings yesterday with Hess and Travis. She had scoffed at their suspicions about Angus Munroe. "Angus has done more good for Seneca County than Russell Hess or Carl Travis could do in a hundred lifetimes," she rebutted, as if that dismissed the matter once and for all.

He slipped on his shorts and stepped out onto the screened balcony just off the bedroom. Often during the muggy summers of his youth, he would forsake his bed for a pallet on this balcony, even after Aunt Martha installed air conditioning. This airy porch, sheltered by the ageless black gum tree in which he had once built a private hideaway, was his favorite place in the old apartment above the Collier Hardware Store.

On this bright night he could see the North Fork of the Potomac flowing quietly in the distance. A white moon hung low above the Alleghenies, casting a burnished reflection upon the water. He pulled a high-back wicker chair to the railing, settled into its plump cushion, and let his gaze follow that shimmering pathway across the shoals to the far bank. There, visible against the backdrop of a starlit sky, a precipitous bluff overlooked the river.

Make Out Point, he mused.

He wondered how many impassioned couples were parked along that wooded ridge this night, as so many others had done on other feverish nights. He felt an urgent rekindling of an old ardor and wondered if he should permit that long-repressed memory to take root. It was part of his past—perhaps the best part. But it was the past that had robbed him of sleep and tormented him since that moment in New Mexico when Annie Zah told him about Stewart. That was less than thirty-six hours ago. It seemed like weeks.

Stewart. "Why do you give a damn what happened to a horse's ass like him?" Carl Travis had asked. It was a question Josh had asked himself long before Carl voiced it. Years before, when Aunt Martha dropped the bombshell that his name was not really Collier, he was hurt and angry. Throughout that long night they sat at the kitchen table while she told him about his mother and father, his mother's previous marriage to Harold Dunning, and his half brother, Stewart Dunning. One day soon after that all-night session, he approached Stewart at school and suggested that brothers should be friends.

Stewart had bridled. "Chacón," he declared, loud enough for everyone in study hall to hear, "*never* call me your brother again!"

The rebuke left a scar that would not diminish with time.

He turned his gaze back to Make Out Point. One night during spring break from college, he and Beth Munroe parked there in her new canary-yellow Thunderbird. "Grandfather Angus buys me a new one every year," she said. She played with the radio until she hit upon the silky voice of Andy Williams singing "Moon River."

She sat back and took off her blouse. "I just love the golden oldies," she said. "Don't you?"

"Yeah," he agreed, although he hadn't given it much thought before then.

She turned her back to him. "Unhook me."

He removed her brassiere and kissed her bare shoulder. "Do you think Stewart knows about us? Everyone knows you're engaged."

She gave a mirthless laugh. "I don't know. I don't think I care." She turned to him. "Anyway, that should make this all the sweeter for you."

It did.

"Russell Hess cares," he said. "He's been nuts about you since grade school."

"That loon," she exclaimed. "I wouldn't come within a mile of him if he were the last man on earth."

"He threatened me once. Said he'd cut off my balls if he caught me with you."

She laughed and gave him a lingering kiss. "Come on . . . let's christen the backseat."

Now, years later, he pushed back the wicker chair and stood, trying to erase the bittersweet memories from his mind—memories of a distant past so much closer now that he was back in the little town where it had all happened. He stretched wearily and turned to go back into the bedroom. Just then something caught his eye. Dimly visible through the branches of the gum tree that overlooked the balcony, a small light glowed in the distance. It was coming from the knoll up around Fourth and Mountain View streets. Too faint for a car. The beam faded, then reappeared moments later, as if passing from window to window.

Twin Oaks!

Someone was inside the Dunning mansion. He went to the bedroom and looked at the clock: 3:30 a.m. The estate had been sealed off since the murder. Who in hell would be fooling around up there at this time of night? Hess? Mares? They didn't patrol at night unless called out, and that would likely be due to an accident on one of the mountain roads out of town. It would be most unusual for anyone else in this sleepy little village to be up and about at this hour.

He wondered if he should call Hess, but decided against it. The sheriff was antagonistic toward him as it was, and a false alarm would only make things worse. He returned to the bedroom and pulled on his pants, shoes without socks, and shirt. Then, stepping quietly, so not to awaken Aunt Martha, he slipped down the back steps to his Corvette.

At the corner of Mountain View and Virginia he switched off the lights and parked a full block from Twin Oaks. He took a flashlight from the glove compartment, thought better of it, and put it back. Then, keeping to the layered shadows, he walked in a crouch the remaining distance to the estate. Chirping crickets grew silent as he carefully worked his way up the long sloping lawn to the front of the house. Backlighted by the moon, the sprawling mansion loomed like some imposing setting for a gothic movie. He took shelter behind one of the large azalea bushes bordering the porch and waited a full ten minutes, watching for the light to reappear. It did not.

He eased around to the west wing, pausing from time to time to watch the windows on both floors. Nothing. It was the same at the rear and at the east wing. No cars. No movement. No sign that there was anyone else anywhere on this darkened estate other than him. Back at the front, he climbed the steps to the broad porch and was confronted by the yellow tape Hess had strung across the entry: CRIME SCENE—DO NOT CROSS. The solid oak door was locked; so were the windows. He descended the steps and circled the house again, checking the remaining doors and windows. They were all locked tight.

At the west wing he leaned against one of the massive oaks, waited, and watched. Fifteen minutes later he began to wonder if he had been mistaken. No, he decided. He knew what he had seen. There *had* been a light in these windows. Someone had been here tonight. And antagonistic or not, Hess was going to hear about it just as soon as the sheriff got to his office this morning. The inside of the mansion should be searched as soon as possible.

He started walking down the elm-lined driveway toward the street, wondering if he should go back to bed or just forfeit sleep for the rest of this unsettling night.

Suddenly the unmistakable sound of tires scorching gravel shattered the silence, followed by the roar of an engine closing fast behind him. He whirled, and his blood turned to ice water. Less than thirty feet away, a vehicle with its lights off was bearing down on him. He dived toward the side of the driveway and landed hard on the exposed root of one of the guardian elms. The vehicle sped past, turned west at the intersection, and raced off into the night. But not before Josh got a glimpse of its box-shape body in the moonlight.

He sat for a moment, fighting for breath. He thought about running to the Corvette and giving chase, but he knew he couldn't get to the car in time. When he got to his feet, a sharp pain in his left knee caused him to wince. He rested a moment against the elm, wondering if he had sprained the knee when he jumped out of harm's way. And he *had* been in harm's way. Whoever was driving that . . . van? truck? carryall? . . . had intended to run him down. Had his reflexes been a fraction of a second slower, he would now be a shattered corpse on his murdered half brother's front lawn.

Where in hell had it come from? He limped downhill to the Corvette, started it, and drove back up the winding driveway to the mansion. Thirty yards behind the house, the double doors to the garden barn stood open. He was certain they had already been closed when he circled the mansion. He maneuvered the Corvette so that the lights fell on the front of the barn. That's where he waited, Josh thought. Parked alongside the ride-on mower now visible in the headlights. Watching me all the time. The thought sent a shiver through his body as he drove away.

Back at the hardware store, he had to grasp the railing in order to climb the steps. In his bedroom, he switched on the light and sat on the edge of the bed to study his knee. He was surprised to see that his trousers were torn. Beneath the tear, an inch-long bloody cut in the side of his leg had congealed over. He probed the cut, wincing now that the sight of it brought more pain. No way did I sustain this from an elm root, he thought. The vehicle had struck him!

He removed his pants and went to the hallway bathroom. There was a bottle of hydrogen peroxide and a box of cotton balls in the medicine chest. He used them to cleanse the wound, and then taped an oversize Band-Aid over the cut. He went to his room and lay down on top of the bedcover.

A ringing phone awakened him at dawn. He heard Aunt Martha answer. Moments later she knocked on his door.

He sat up on the side of the bed. "I'm awake, Aunt Martha."

She pushed the door open. "That was—Josh, what's wrong with your leg?"

He didn't feel like explaining it now. "I hit it on the bed frame. No big deal." He noticed the anxiety in her face. "What's wrong, Aunt Martha?"

"Carl Travis just called." Her voice was as somber as her countenance. "He wants you to come to his office right away. Sheriff Hess is on his way to arrest Stewart's killer."

Eight

The drive up Mount Canaan was perilous. Now and then the twisting blacktop wound past phantom farms where deserted houses, long since peeled paintless by the elements, sat in fallow fields overgrown with weeds and scrub brush, testimony to hardscrabble life in Appalachia. On one switchback curve Carl Travis braked late, causing the Buick station wagon to skid within inches of a sharp drop-off.

White-knuckled, Josh gripped the shoulder strap tighter. "Damn it, Carl, slow down or let me drive!"

"Sorry. Forgot you're not used to West Virginia roads anymore."

"Oh sure," Josh retorted.

Carl eased back on the accelerator. "I want to get there as soon as possible in case there's any problem. I know Dub better than Russ does."

Josh shook his head. "I just don't get it. How did Russ come up with this pea-brained idea?"

"Colonel Gregory called from Charleston early this morning. The FBI lab in Washington identified Dub's fingerprints at the murder scene."

"Well that's just brilliant," Josh said. "Dub Oliver's done odd jobs for the Dunning family since before Stewart was born. He's been in and out of Twin Oaks for over forty years. What the hell does a fingerprint prove?"

"These were in blood, Josh. Stewart's blood. Two prints on a cabinet door in the kitchen, one on the couch in Stewart's office. Russ says there's no question they're Dub's."

Just ahead, a red fox was tearing at the innards of a white-tailed doe that lay bloated at the side of the highway. Josh watched the scavenger scurry into the woods as they drove by. "Carl—your honest-to-God, gut feeling—do you really believe Dub killed Stewart?"

Carl let the question hang for a moment. Choosing his words carefully, he replied, "I don't know. I do know Dub . . . well, he could be provoked . . ." He let the sentence drop.

Josh shifted in the seat and fixed his eyes on his old mentor. "Carl, I've got to catch a flight out of Dulles tonight. Whatever it is you know, don't make me wait to read about it in the *Washington Post*. Just spit it out, okay?"

Carl shot his passenger a wry smile, and then looked back to the road. "You ever hear of Matthew Dawes?"

"Matthew Dawes?" Josh filtered the familiar-sounding name through his memory file. "Wait a minute. *Televangelist* Matthew Dawes? Temple of the Divine Shepherd in Richmond?"

"That's the fellow."

"What's that fruitcake got to do with anything?"

"He operated in Seneca County for a while, you know."

"Here? No, I didn't know."

Carl slowed and turned off the paved highway onto a rutted dirt lane, one of many unimproved access roads that were bulldozed into Seneca County's trackless forests during the heyday of the logging boom, over a half century ago. Alongside the road, pools of stagnant water gave evidence of the recent rains that had drenched the mountain.

"You'd already moved away," Carl continued. "Dawes came here from Ohio. Powerful-built man, shock of long, yellow hair, voice like a Mount Hazard thunderstorm. Set up shop over near Grove Center— giant tent, folding chairs, sawdust floor—regular Elmer Gantry. Pulled big crowds, too. Every night and three times on Sunday, he fulminated against cussing, boozing, and fornicating. All were transgressions, by the way, that the good preacher indulged in copiously.

"Couple of months after Dawes opened for business, Agnes Poole brought her seven-year-old grandson Robbie to my office. Poor kid's back and buttocks were black and blue. Agnes told me that the reverend was an advocate of what he called 'God's cleansing discipline.' One of his favorite sermons was from Proverbs 13:24. Recall that one, Josh?"

"Afraid not."

Carl quoted: "'He that spareth the rod hateth his son; but he that loveth him chasteneth him often.'"

"Sometimes when the congregation got filled with the spirit, Dawes would call a parent with a youngster in tow up to the altar. He'd strip the boy—always a boy, mind you—then hand the parent the briar cane he always carried and command the parent to 'thrash the Devil from out' the kid's body. Agnes's daughter—Robbie's mother—was one who got called up."

"Oh for God's sake!" Josh exclaimed, heatedly. "Don't tell me people like that still exist."

"You're not that naïve, my friend. Of course people like that still exist. And not just east of the Mississippi," he added pointedly, "if that thought's crossed your mind."

Josh accepted the admonition without comment.

Carl resumed his account. "I took Polaroid shots of the boy's back. Then I called Dawes. Told him that this was one story that wasn't going to come out in the *Cumberland News* first, and that I was going to put those photos on the front page of my next edition."

Josh was growing impatient. "Carl, what's this got to do with Dub Oliver?"

"Hold your horses. After supper that night I went back to my office to work on the story. Around 9:30 Ruby called me—Ruby Warfield, my housekeeper. She was mighty upset. Said that Dawes had just been to the house looking for me. Said he was drunk, and madder'n a wet hornet.

"Well, I figured if the preacher wanted a confrontation, I'd give him one. Then Ruby said something that made me change my mind awful fast. She'd spotted a pistol stuffed under Dawes's belt."

"Pistol-packing preacher," Josh quipped, with a laugh.

"May sound funny now," Carl said, "but it sure as hell wasn't then. I hung up and ran to lock the front door. Too late. Just as I got there, Dawes came storming through. He was in a world-class rage, eyes ablaze, stinking of bourbon. His breath would have felled an elephant at ten yards. He called me an 'abomination unto the Lord.' Then he raised that briar cane and said he was there to cleanse me from Satan's clutch. I'm no coward, but I'm no match for a man like that. He shoved me back into my office and pushed me facedown over the desk. I tried to yell, but he had me so tight I couldn't breathe.

"All of a sudden, Dawes screamed and let go of me. When I got up, I saw that Dub had the preacher pinned to the wall—by one hand at his neck, mind you. Dawes's eyes were bulging and his face was turning purple. His feet were barely touching the floor. He was just hanging there, kicking and squirming. There was a thud, and I saw that the preacher's pistol had dropped all the way through his pants leg onto the floor. It was a pearl-handled .22. Dub picked it up and stuck the barrel in Dawes's face. I grabbed Dub's arm and pleaded with him for the gun. I don't know who was sweating most, Dawes or I. Dub finally let me have the gun. Then he dropped Dawes. The preacher hit the floor and lay there moaning. When he caught his breath, I told him to get out of there before Dub changed his mind. I didn't have to tell him twice. Couple of days later, the good reverend packed his tent and departed West Virginia for healthier climes."

Carl shifted down to ascend a steep hill. "Funny thing was, I didn't even know Dub was there that night. Sometimes he sleeps on a pallet back in the equipment room. Fortunately for me, he decided to do it that night. Josh, I know as sure as I'm sitting here that if I hadn't intervened, Dub would have blown Dawes's brains out."

The implication was clear.

"But he was protecting you," Josh protested. "Seems to me that's a hell of a lot different from what happened at Twin Oaks."

"Maybe. All I'm saying is, I've seen what can happen when someone riles Dub bad enough."

Josh pondered the point. "So, if the FBI is right, the question is, what did Stewart Dunning do to rile Dub Oliver enough to lead to violence?"

"Yes," Carl agreed. "That would seem to be the question."

Where they were driving now, an almost impenetrable barrier of oak, black gum, and maple trees crowded the road, forming a broad canopy that blocked the morning sunlight. It gave Josh a sense of déjà vu. He wondered why.

A mile and a half into the forest, they entered a narrow glen fed by a shallow creek that was muddy with runoff from the rains. A ramshackle log cabin sat facing the creek, its front door less than two yards from the water's edge. Sheriff Hess's patrol car was parked near the rear of the cabin. Carl pulled to a stop next to the sheriff's car.

"How does Dub get back and forth from here?" Josh asked.

"Hitchhikes. Everybody around here knows him. He walks in from the main road. Sometimes I bring him," Carl said.

The area around the cabin was piled high with old orange crates and rusting oil drums filled with hubcaps, bottles of all sorts and sizes, engine parts, frayed sheets and blankets, old magazines and newspapers, cracked dishes and pottery, skillets and pans, and broken tools. Near the doorway, a dilapidated foot-powered sewing machine sat alongside the remnants of a cast-iron coal range. Other bits and pieces of junk, most of them unidentifiable, were strewn along the stream bank next to the cabin.

"Dub likes to collect things," Carl explained.

"So I see."

"Mostly it's harmless. Sometimes though, he'll pick up a trinket in the Five and Dime or one of the other stores in town. They're aware of his problem, and they simply send me a bill. It never amounts to much."

Despite the early hour, exiting the air-conditioned station wagon into the sweltering July heat was like stepping into a sauna. Josh wiped his brow with his hand. "What does he do with all this junk?"

"Saves it," Carl replied.

"For what?"

Carl shrugged.

Hess was nowhere in sight. The cabin door was closed. Carl knocked. No response. A small window beside the door was partially open. Josh tried to look inside, but the view was blocked by a raveled curtain.

Carl yelled, "Russ!"

Silence.

"Dub!"

Still no answer.

"What the hell's going on?" Carl asked.

Flies swarming around a garbage barrel set up a drone that muffled the sounds of the creek. Shooing the insects away, Josh walked around to the side of the cabin. There were a shovel and a pickaxe hanging on pegs nailed to the wall. Standard equipment at cabins in Appalachia, Josh knew, where many families dug their own fuel from countless hand-excavated shafts tunneled into these ancient hills.

"Josh . . . JOSH!"

Josh raced back around the cabin and through the open door. A foul odor assaulted his nostrils. "What?"

Just inside the cabin, Carl stood staring at a frayed overstuffed chair that sat in the middle of the room facing the door. The high back and one side of the seat cushion were covered with blood. A blood-splattered copy of *Life* magazine lay open on the floor nearby.

Carl dropped to one knee and ran a finger across the chair seat. The blood was not yet dry. He looked up at Josh, bewildered, just as Russell Hess entered the cabin, his .45 automatic drawn, cocked, and ready for use. The sheriff's uniform was soaked through with sweat. His boots and pants cuffs were caked with mud.

Hess looked at the kneeling editor, then at Josh. "What the hell are you doing here, Chacón?"

Carl stood. "He's here because I asked him. What happened here, Russ? Where's Dub?"

Hess continued to stare at Josh for a few seconds; then he released the hammer on his gun and holstered it. "You tell me. I've circled this cabin twice, close in and far out. Checked the woods on both sides of the valley. Nothing."

"Footprints?" Carl asked.

Hess shook his head. "Just Dub's, leading in from the main road. No other footprints, no motorcycles, no tote goats, no off-road vehicles of any kind. There hasn't been a car in here for weeks."

"Is that . . . Dub's blood?"

"Who else's?" Hess replied.

While the others talked, Josh looked around the one-room shack. The cabin had been ransacked. Clothing, magazines, pots, pans, and canned goods pulled from now-barren shelves strewn about the floor. An army cot near one wall was overturned, a soiled army-surplus blanket beside it. At the foot of the cot, a shabby chest of drawers lay on its side, emptied of its contents. The charred wick of an oil lamp on the table was still in the extended position. Josh noted that the chimney was blackened with soot, an indication that the lamp had not been turned off, but had flickered out from fuel starvation. In the rear of the shack, a propane hot plate sat atop an unpainted pine table. There was no sink, only buckets for hauling water—from the creek, Josh assumed, since he had seen no well. Several empty food cans, some encrusted with mold, lay beside the hot plate. One, labeled "Campbell's Pork and Beans," had a spoon resting in it. Josh ran his finger around the inside of the can. The bean sauce had not yet dried. This had been Dub's supper.

Josh wiped his finger on a handkerchief and turned his attention to the wall above the overturned cot. Every square inch was pasted or stapled with pages torn from magazines and books. Josh stepped closer and saw that the flimsy sheets had been torn from the King James Version of the Bible. Some verses had been underscored in ink. Other walls, too, were adorned with religious objects—posters, likenesses of Jesus cut from magazines, and hand-carved wooden crosses of various sizes.

In one corner, a potbellied Franklin stove rested on a fieldstone base that was heavy with coal dust. One side of the stove was indented with a fresh groove that exposed bare metal. Josh knelt for a closer look.

"Don't touch that!" Hess yelled.

Carl looked around to see what had caused the outcry.

Josh was sighting along the groove to a telltale hole in the cabin wall.

"The bullet ricocheted off the stove," Hess said. "We still may be able to read it."

Carl looked from the bullet hole to the bloody chair. "This isn't making sense, Russ. What did Dub have here that anyone would possibly want?"

"Good question," Hess replied. "And the answer is *nothing.* This has nothing to do with robbery. Whoever did this didn't want Dub Oliver doing any talking. Any thoughts on that, Chacón?"

"Not at the moment, Russ. I'll let you know if anything comes to mind."

"Yeah. You do that." He turned to Carl. "There's something else."

Just outside the cabin, beside the door, a small mound of brush was piled against the wall. Some of the twigs were charred. "He tried to torch the place. Not a boy scout for sure. These branches are green—and wet from the rain."

"Why burn the cabin?" Carl asked.

"To make it look like Dub died in a fire."

Hess nodded toward the cars. "Mares is on his way up with the lab kit. We're gonna dust the cabin, dig out that slug, and make a more thorough search of these hills. You two'll have to leave. We don't need you tracking up the place any more than you already have."

Carl took another long look around the cabin. "Let me know if you find . . . anything."

"Sure," Hess said.

Carl fished his car keys from his pocket. "You'll have to drive, Josh. I'm afraid I'm not up to it."

They drove along the old logging road in silence. Carl sat with his face turned to the window, eyes on the forest, unseeing. At the turnoff to the main highway, Josh asked, "You okay?"

Without turning from the window, Carl replied, "There hasn't been a murder in Seneca County for over forty years, Josh. Now this. What's happening to our tight little community?"

Josh wondered whether to tell Carl about the near-miss hit-and-run attempt on his life last night at the manor, but decided to play that card close to his chest for a while longer. He asked, "Did you notice the blood?"

"Who could miss it? Why?"

"Dub, or whoever was in that chair, bled a hell of a lot before he moved."

"Or was moved," Carl said.

Josh shook his head. "I don't think so. He wasn't dragged, or there'd have been a bloody trail. If he was lifted up, where did they put him? No sign of a car or footprints around the cabin, remember?"

"Then where the hell is he?"

"Good question," Josh agreed. After a moment he asked, "Carl, could Dub read?"

"No. I tried to teach him. He just couldn't grasp it."

"There were a lot of magazines in the cabin."

"Oh. I gave those to him. He liked to look at the pictures."

"What about the wall decorations?"

"Dub was a Pentecostal, deeply religious. He carved all those crosses himself. That was his perennial Christmas present to everyone he knew . . . and liked."

"Some of those Bible verses were underlined."

"Really? Well, Dub didn't do it."

Josh looked at his watch: 8:30 a.m. His return flight to Albuquerque was scheduled to leave Dulles at 6:00 p.m. Still six hours or so before he had to start the long drive to Washington. "Who is Dub's best friend, Carl? Besides you, I mean. Is there anyone else close to him?"

"Most everybody in town likes Dub. But the person who knows him best . . . that'd have to be Viola Brown."

"Stewart's housekeeper?"

"She is mighty nice to Dub. He boards with her winters."

Josh geared down for the final descent into town. Far below, sheltered between the foothills of the Blue Ridge and Allegheny mountains, Seneca Falls lay nestled alongside the Potomac like an Alpine scene from a postcard. He picked out a small cluster of houses next to the river. "She still live in the Bottoms?"

"Same house. Looks like it always did."

"Think she'd remember me?"

"Ha! Everyone in the county remembers you. Or claims to. Not many from here have made the name for themselves that you have. Why do you ask?"

"I've got a few hours before I have to leave. Soon as we get back, I think I'll go pay my respects to Viola."

"Mind if I ask what you're looking for?"

"I don't really know. Reporter's instinct, I guess."

It was an answer Carl could appreciate.

In town, Josh pulled up beside his Corvette at the hardware store and got out of Carl's car. Carl slid across to the driver's seat. "I'll be at my office. Don't leave town without coming to see me. I'll want to hear about your visit to Viola."

"Deal," Josh agreed, and closed the car door.

Ten minutes later at his office, Carl went to the equipment room where Dub Oliver sometimes slept. He pulled open the bottom drawer of the safe, took out a shoe box, and opened it. "Oh, dear Lord, no," he moaned.

He let the box slide from his hands onto the floor. The pistol he had confiscated from Matthew Dawes was missing.

Nine

Viola Brown was picking string beans in her garden when the red Corvette drew to a stop in front of her house. Puzzled, she watched the driver get out and walk across the yard toward her. She didn't know anybody who drove a car like that. Then at the moment of recognition, her wizened black face broke into a wide smile. "Why, Joshua Collier! Aren't you the handsome sight. Come on over here."

She opened her arms and gave him a mighty hug, which Josh returned in kind. She smelled of pine-tar soap and tobacco, which reminded Josh of the present in his pocket. He pulled out a tin of Mail Pouch snuff. "For you, Viola."

She took the box, beaming anew. "Only sin I get to enjoy these days," she chuckled. "Thank you, Joshua."

He was happy the small gift pleased her. Viola Brown was one of his fonder memories of life in Seneca Falls.

After exchanging condolences about Stewart—his brother and her employer—they turned the conversation to happier memories. Eyeing the garden, he reminded her how years ago, when she spaded each spring, she would save the fat, bottomland worms she unearthed, so the town kids who fished from the riverbank behind her house would have fresh bait.

"Still do," she said, and pointed to the galvanized washtub filled with dirt and sitting beside the house.

In turn, she reminded him how he used to come snooping around every Monday, the day she did her baking, to find out if she had made any of the raisin pies she was famous for.

"Lordy, how you loved raisin pie!" she said, and her hefty body shook with laughter.

"Still do," he said.

She made a clicking sound with her tongue. "Well, if that's not the way of it. Here you come pay me a visit, and I haven't baked a pie in days." Her brow furrowed. "Got some applesauce cake. Would you settle for that?"

The talk of food reminded Josh that he hadn't eaten all day. "Viola, I'm famished."

She led him toward the house. "I'll put on a pot of tea. Mighty good with applesauce cake."

They chatted more about old times while he ate. She had dusted the cake with powdered sugar, just like Aunt Martha used to do, and he ate two huge pieces. When he finished he set his plate on the coffee table between them, thanked her again, and said, "Viola, this isn't just a social call. I have to leave this afternoon and would like to get a few things straight in my mind before then. Carl Travis says you might be able to help me."

Then he told her what they had discovered that morning at Dub's cabin.

He was not prepared for her reaction. For a long moment she just stared at him. There were no tears. But the anguish in her eyes telegraphed that Dub Oliver was more to Viola Brown than a mere boarder. After a moment she slumped back in the chair. "Oh, dear Lord, Joshua . . . what's happened to Dub?"

"I'm afraid no one can answer that yet, Viola. The sheriff's still searching. I'm sorry." He felt a surge of guilt for not having told her at once—and for telling her at all. He took slow drinks from the teacup, giving her time to adjust to the sorrowful news.

After a minute, he said, "Carl said you probably know Dub as well as anyone."

She nodded, but didn't speak. He wondered if he should leave.

She pushed up out of the chair and went to the kitchen. She

returned with the teapot and refilled their cups. He didn't want more tea, but accepted it, realizing that she was using the time to regain her composure. She took a magazine from a rack beside her chair, put it on the coffee table, and set the teapot on it. Then she settled back into her chair. "Dub and me . . . we're sort of family. We don't have folks to speak of. I've got a nephew down in Bluefield—Sonny, my brother Adam's boy. Adam, he's dead now. Dub, he's had no folks since he's a boy. Closest he's got now is Mr. Carl and me."

Josh was relieved that she had started talking. "Carl said Dub boards with you."

"Twenty-five years. Wintertimes, that is. Summers, he stays in that old hunting cabin up on Mount Canaan. Mr. Angus lets him live there for free."

Mr. Angus?

A scene from the distant past flashed through Josh's mind. Now he knew why the old logging road on Mount Canaan that morning had seemed vaguely familiar. The road past Dub's cabin was the same road he and Beth Munroe had taken one summer night to go skinny-dipping in a flooded mine pit on the back side of the Munroe estate.

" . . . up there in winter," Viola was saying.

"Huh? Oh, sorry . . . what did you say, Viola?"

"I said, it's too cold up there in winter. So Dub stays in town with me. Don't charge him nothin' for the room. He does handiwork for me for that. Digs the garden, cuts grass. Mr. Carl pays me for Dub's meals. Dub, he loves to eat. And I do love to cook for a man who loves to eat."

She cradled the warm cup in her hands without drinking. "Sure hope nothin' bad's got to him."

Josh said, "I remember he did handiwork for the Dunnings, too."

"All his life, seems like," Viola confirmed. "Long as me, anyway. Most times I tell him what needs doin'. Mr. Harold—you remember him, Mr. Stewart's daddy—he always let me handle chores around the manor. Mr. Harold never married again, you know. After Miss Jenny—your mama—left him, he just sort of gave up on ever'thing. Oh, he kept up a show of things, but his spirit was broke just the same. After while, got so he couldn't stand the sight of this town no more. When Mr. Harold finally moved away, Mr. Stewart—he was outta college by then—he let me run things just like before. Even after he and Miss Beth got married."

"Sheriff Hess says that Beth moved out of the manor some time ago."

"Five . . . six years back, at least. Should've done it long before that, for all they meant to each other. Never did understand that marriage. Seems I remember she was sweet on you there for a while."

"We were good friends," Josh replied.

"Uh huh. Well, anyway, Mr. Stewart and her went their own ways. Separate rooms long time before she finally left. She's living somewhere up East I hear."

"Washington," he said. "What happened between them?"

"Don't know. Didn't work out, I reckon. Turns out that way sometimes."

While they talked, Josh studied the well-packed magazine rack beside the chair. There were tattered copies of *National Geographic* and *Baptist Leader*, and several old copies of *Life*. Viola saw he was looking at the magazines. "They belong to Dub," she said. "Mr. Carl saves old magazines for him. Dub filches others from trash cans, wherever he can find them."

"Carl said he likes to look at the pictures."

"He likes to hear the words, too. Always bringin' more to me, pesterin' me to read to him. Like a little kid that way. Loves to hear all sorts of stories. Mostly, he likes the Bible."

She gave a reminiscent chuckle. "Wouldn't let him touch none of mine, though. Ever' time I read somethin' he really liked, he'd make me mark it for him. Then he'd tear it out and stuff it in his pocket. We've gone through three, four of his Bibles that way, maybe hundreds of magazines."

And that, Josh thought, explained the biblical collage pasted to Dub's cabin wall.

"Viola, do you have a key to the manor?"

"Got two. Sheriff Hess's got my front key. I still got the back one."

He glanced at his watch—three hours before he had to leave for Dulles. "Would you go up there with me?"

She shot him a wary look. "Now?"

"I don't have much time. You know that house better than anyone else in town. There are things I'd like to see before I leave."

She shook her head, hesitant. "I don't know, Joshua. Sheriff Hess said for me to make sure the place is cleaned up real good before anybody go up there. Lucy Boggs is gonna help me do it tomorrow."

"Viola, Sheriff Hess believes Dub killed Stewart."

For a moment it was as if she hadn't heard. Then, her eyes wide in dismay, she exclaimed, "He believe *what*?!"

Josh repeated the accusation. "They found Dub's bloody fingerprints at the manor. There's also . . ."

He hesitated.

"Also, what?" she prompted.

He took another approach. "Has Sheriff Hess warned you what to expect when you go to clean the manor?"

"Only that it's a mess."

No doubt, Josh thought. If he continued, he would be breaking his pledge to Hess. Somehow that didn't seem important now. "Viola, there are things about how Stewart died—how his body was found—that are pretty damned bizarre."

"What kind of things?"

"Things that Sheriff Hess and the state police are keeping to themselves. If you go to the manor with me, I think you'll see what I mean."

For a long moment she said nothing. Then she pushed up from the chair. "I'll get the key."

Ten

The back door opened onto a spacious laundry room. "Where's the kitchen?" Josh asked.

"This way," Viola said. She led the way down the long rear hallway to the other side of the manor.

Like in most antebellum mansions, where in later years the cooking facilities were moved from separate outbuildings into the great houses themselves, the kitchen in Twin Oaks was enormous. Overhanging racks, heavy with well-seasoned cast-iron skillets and sparkling copper cookware, were in easy reach from the huge electric range. An oversize refrigerator/freezer was situated next to a walk-in pantry. Polished oak storage cabinets for dishes, plates, and condiments encircled the room. Incongruous in this otherwise orderly setting, shoved against the counter beneath one row of cabinets, was the elongated harvest table upon which Stewart Dunning's body had been found. The burned-down candles that had bracketed his head were still seated in hardened wax. That end of the table and one of the overhead cabinet doors bore the darkened stains of dried blood. The stains on the cabinet had been dusted with a white powder that revealed the outline of a palm print.

Viola's eyes were fixed on the table. "They . . . they found Mr. Stewart . . . back here?"

"On that table. He was covered with a drape from the living room. His head was resting on a pillow from one of the chairs."

A visible tremor shot through her body. Josh wondered if he should have brought her, but it was too late to turn back now.

"Where's the office?" Josh asked.

She kept staring at the harvest table, as though rooted in place.

"Viola?" He touched her gently on the shoulder. "The office?"

After a moment she gave a slight nod, and then turned and led him through the formal dining room out into the hallway.

The walls of the ceramic-tiled foyer were adorned with a priceless assortment of Early American paintings. Josh recognized works by Benjamin West, Gilbert Stuart, and John Singleton Copley. Among them was a tempura landscape of dissimilar but distinctive style. Stepping closer he recognized the soaring peaks of Seneca Rocks standing guard over a lush forest of fall foliage. In the lower right corner the artist had added the initials *SD*. "Well, I'll be damned," he thought. He turned to Viola. "Stewart?"

She nodded. "Told me once it brought him peace. He should've done more of it."

At the far end of the foyer a wide red-carpeted staircase rose to a landing midway, then fanned out onto the upstairs hallways leading to the bedrooms in separate wings of the house. It reminded Josh, a movie buff since childhood, of a scene from *Gone with the Wind*. For a fleeting moment he imagined Beth Munroe descending that regal staircase for the final time and found perverse delight in the thought. Then he realized that his mother, too, had once descended that staircase for the final time. He didn't know how he felt about that.

Just past the staircase, Viola pointed. "Last door, down that way."

There were four rooms on the north side of the house. Josh opened the door that Viola indicated. After he paused a moment for his eyes to adjust, he went to the window and opened the drapes. The office was about what he had imagined. An oversize walnut desk and swivel chair stood near the rear wall facing the door. Two wing-back chairs with green satin seats and backs sat nearby.

Others like them were situated around the large room. Viola settled into one of the chairs while Josh inspected the room.

The walls, paneled in Old World knotty pine, were adorned with framed certificates, diplomas, awards, and keepsakes interspersed here and there with scores of photographs portraying Stewart Dunning in the company of Presidents Reagan and Bush, Chief Justice Rehnquist, Senators Dole and Ryan, Governor Kane, and an assortment of other conservative power brokers from the corporate and political worlds.

An oversize couch that matched the satin chairs sat against the wall opposite the desk. The right arm, seat cushion, and beige carpet below were splattered with bloodstains. Near the middle of the bloody cushion, a small hole bearing the frayed markings of Sheriff Hess's probing instruments was circled with chalk.

A pair of brown leather house slippers sat on the floor at the opposite end of the couch. Josh picked them up. There was no evidence of bloodstains on them. "Are these Stewart's?"

"Yes," Viola confirmed.

Josh thought back to the photographs of the murder scenes he had seen in Hess's office. "The only thing Stewart had on when he was found was a robe with Oriental markings."

"Kimono," Viola interjected. "He an' Miss Beth took a long vacation once, traveled all over the Far East. He got that kimono in Tokyo. Pure silk. He sure did like that robe."

"Sheriff Hess said you told him that Stewart often worked in the office here wearing that robe. Nothin' else."

She chuckled. "Well, far as I know, nothin' else. In summers, anyway. He never did like the air conditioner. Most times, he just opened a window."

Josh set the slippers back on the floor and checked the two large windows, one on each side of the desk. They were protected by heavy outer screens bolted into the frames. Anyone attempting to enter the office through one of the windows would have faced the formidable task of first removing one of those screens. He studied them more closely. Neither had been removed for some time.

He turned his attention to the wall opposite the doorway. It was decorated by an original Wyeth—earth tones and sky-blue pastels—probably tempura, he guessed. Strangely, it was the only painting in the office. He gave the frame a gentle tug. As he suspected, it swung open to reveal a wall safe. He pulled on the dial. The safe was locked. Hess had remarked that the safe had contained a large amount of cash. Had he found it open? Josh made a mental note to ask.

"Viola, did Dub know about this safe?"

She had been watching him with keen interest. "Don't know. Wouldn't think so, but don't know for sure."

A door near the couch led to a bathroom. Josh entered, looked around, and opened the shower stall. "Did Stewart use this shower often?" he called out to Viola.

"Not often," she called back. "Mostly he used the upstairs one. Sometimes he showered down here."

"The door is soap stained," he replied.

"Then he did," she said. "'Cause I keep it clean."

There were no towels on the rack nor any in the hamper.

He stepped back into the office, went to the desk, and studied the IBM personal computer that was sitting on an adjacent stand within easy reach from the swivel chair. A large hard drive, a separate drive for making backup disks, and a color monitor. With the exception of the dot-matrix printer (Josh's was laser), it was much like the setup in his apartment office in Santa Fe.

A wastebasket beside the stand contained a dozen or more tear strips from the edge of fan-folded computer paper. "How often is this wastebasket emptied, Viola?"

"Ever' day when I'm here. Did it Friday."

"Did Stewart have other household help?"

"Not much keepin' up to do, with just him livin' here. I do all the cookin', a bit of dustin'. Lucy Boggs comes up ever' few days to help do the heavy moppin' and scrubbin.' Other'n that, just me and Dub. Anyway, I'm the only one ever does the office cleanin'."

"And you're sure you emptied this basket last Friday?"

"I'm sure."

Well then, he thought, someone had used the printer since then.

Hess said the computer was on when he arrived at the murder scene, and he surmised that Stewart had been working the night he was killed. The tear strips in the wastebasket seemed to confirm that. Josh sat down in the desk chair, swiveled to the computer, and turned it on. He waited for the machine to boot up, and then typed a request for a directory of files on the hard disk. A message appeared on the monitor screen: DISK ERROR C: ABORT? RETRY? CANCEL?

That didn't make sense.

He rummaged through the desk and found the instruction manual containing the master disks that came with the computer. He removed the diagnostic disk from the folder and slid it into the disk drive slot and booted it up. At the beep indicating it was ready, he typed a command requesting an analysis of the hard disk. Moments later a different message appeared: C: NO FILES LISTED.

The first error message now made sense. Whatever had been stored in this computer had been erased. He checked the power cord and saw that it was plugged into a circuit strip that protected the unit against power surges. No electrical malfunction had caused the deletion. And the odds against it happening by accident were enormous.

There was a plastic case beside the computer marked "backup disks." Josh flipped open the lid. There were no disks in the case.

Josh switched off the computer and turned to speak to Viola. "Sheriff Hess says Stewart gave you that weekend off because he was going to be out of town. He told his secretary at the bank the same thing. Do you know any reason he'd do that?"

Viola shook her head. "Uh-uh. Sheriff Hess ask me about that, too. Mr. Stewart never did anythin' like that before."

"Do you know of any reason why Dub would have been up here at the manor that weekend?"

"Mowin' the grass. I sent him myself."

"Did Dub have a key to the manor?"

She patted the back door key in her pocket. "This one. He came by for it whenever he was to work up here."

"Why did he need a key?"

"So he could get in the kitchen. Mr. Stewart let Dub eat whatever he wanted from the fridge."

"I see," Josh said, with a sigh of resignation. "Then Dub must have been the only other person inside the manor that weekend."

"Uh-uh," Viola said, shifting her bulk in the chair.

"No?" Josh said, puzzled.

"Joshua, Dub didn't do harm to anybody up here." She gave a strong shake of her head to emphasize her conviction.

She was holding something back. "What is it, Viola? What makes you so positive?"

"Not gonna say any more about it," she replied. "But I'll tell you this. Dub Oliver, 'less Mr. Stewart or I asked him, never went anywhere in this house except the kitchen."

"But his prints were found here in the office, Viola."

"Maybe so. But he didn't do harm."

Josh stood and went to where she was sitting. He dropped to one knee, took her hand, and eyed her keenly. "Viola, you know something you're not telling me. Please, what is it?"

She shook her head.

"Viola, Dub may be in serious trouble, or . . . worse."

"Maybe. But I've said enough already."

She rose, and he stood too. She looked as if she had aged ten years since they had shared tea and cake barely an hour before. She gave him a melancholy smile. "You can take me home now."

He started to protest, "Viola . . ."

"Please, Joshua," she beseeched. "I'm awful tired."

Whatever she knew, it would have to wait. "Of course, Viola. I shouldn't have pried."

They relocked the back door and started for the car. Josh stopped. "One moment, Viola."

The doors to the garden barn were still open, just as they had been last night. He entered the barn and studied the floor. Fresh tire marks, with an inverted-V tread and center split, were plainly visible in the dry dirt. All-terrain tires, like those on any of a hundred or more vehicles in Seneca County. But the marks revealed something else. When the person who had been hiding here accelerated to try to run Josh down, the back *and* front tires had dug deeply into the dirt. The box-shaped vehicle that almost killed him had four-wheel drive.

He closed the barn doors, and drove Viola home.

Eleven

Carl Travis was taken aback. "Your old job?"

"Same pay," Josh said. "Five dollars a week . . . just to keep things legal."

Carl laughed. "And what makes you think you're worth five dollars a week as an investigative reporter?"

"Don't give me that Woodward-Bernstein crap," Josh retorted. "*All* reporters are investigative reporters—or should be. That's their job. Besides, what's so different about that and researching a book? I'm a writer. I dig for facts, try to match them against other facts, and keep at it until I come up with a denouement. I think this case could use a bit of independent digging for a denouement."

Carl tossed aside the article he had been editing. "I thought you had a flight to catch . . . work to do."

"There'll be other flights."

Carl regarded Josh as one might regard an errant child. "Have you really thought this through, son? You've got a life, you know—one that most people can only dream of. And this town and its people haven't been part of it for a long time. Now, all of a sudden, here you are wanting to put everything on hold, just because a grieving old woman thinks she knows more about criminology than the county sheriff and the FBI and the state police all put together?"

"I was there, Carl. I heard what she said, and I was watching her when she said it. Viola Brown saw something up there in the manor this afternoon that neither Hess nor the state police nor any of the rest of us can see. Legal or not, I'm not leaving here until I find out what it is."

"Josh—"

Josh raised a hand. "Carl, listen to me, please. Just this morning you were commiserating over what was happening in, as you put it, this 'tight little community.' Neither of us knows the answer to that question yet. But a long time ago you taught me never to overlook the story that's staring me right in the face. I believe there's a mighty big story staring us in the face right now. There's something going on in these mountains beyond what any of us have imagined. What, I don't know. But I intend to find out. Not just because of Viola, either. I've got other reasons."

Carl pondered this. "You been keeping something from me, Josh?"

Fair enough, Josh thought. If he couldn't trust Carl, who else was there? "This morning, before sunup, I was out on the veranda at Aunt Martha's. I spotted a light inside Twin Oaks and went to investigate. Whoever was there tried to run me down with a truck." He patted his sore leg. "I've got a cut—"

"Well dammit all," Carl broke in, "that was just plain stupid. Why didn't you call Hess, or me, even? Have you told him about this?"

Josh ignored the question. "There's more. Stewart's robe—the one he was wearing when he was found. Viola said Stewart wore it sometimes to work in his office late at night."

"So? Hess said the same thing."

"Yeah. Well, that robe—a Japanese kimono, really—was embroidered with a series of Oriental hieroglyphics."

"I saw the pictures. What're you getting at?"

"The robe was inside out, Carl. I don't think Stewart would have put it on that way."

Carl gave a perplexed look. "Inside out? What makes you say that?"

"Those dual-letter hieroglyphics across the chest are from the art of the Ainu—Japanese aborigines. They mean health and long life—somewhat ironic in this case. Anyway, many Ainu symbols are identical to ones found among Anasazi petroglyphs in New Mexico and Arizona. Anthropologists believe the two cultures evolved from a common root. You can look it up if you want, but I'm sure I'm right. Those symbols were backward on the robe Stewart was wearing. At first I thought Hess might have reversed the negative of that photo, but he said he hadn't. Other things in the picture bear him out—Stewart's watch on his left wrist, for example. No, that robe was inside out."

"But Hess didn't say anything about that. Doc either."

"What makes you believe either one of them would recognize it?"

It was a telling point.

"There's something else," Josh said. He hesitated, staring into the middle distance, deep within himself.

"What?" Carl prompted.

Josh looked back at the editor and shook his head. "I guess it sounds crazy, but I don't know. Something I've seen or heard just doesn't jibe. It's driving me nuts." He leaned forward to underscore his next words. "Carl, this is the first thing that's enthused me in months. I've got to stay on this story. I've got to figure it all out."

After a long moment, Carl turned to his desk, opened a drawer, took out a press card, and placed it in his typewriter. He typed *Joshua Chacón* in the appropriate space, withdrew the card, and signed and dated it. He handed the card to Josh. "You're on the payroll as of today. It's not going to make me any too popular with our good sheriff, you know."

"Does that bother you?"

"Not really."

"Thanks, Carl. You won't regret it."

"Just keep telling me that," Carl said.

He sat back and gave Josh a what-else look.

Josh placed the card in his shirt pocket. "I need to call the lady who handles my answering service, to let her know I'll be delayed. Is it okay to give her your phone numbers?"

"Absolutely."

"I didn't bring much with me. I'll need some slacks, a couple of shirts, and some socks and underwear."

"Toothman Dry Goods, right down the street."

Josh nodded. "Incidentally, did Hess tell you how he got into Stewart's safe?"

"It was open. But nothing was missing. Several thousand dollars in it, as I recall. It wasn't robbery, Josh."

"How about Stewart's computer?"

"Computer? Nothing. Except that it was on. What's his computer got to do with anything?"

"All the files were erased. The backup disks are missing."

"But Hess said nothing about that," Carl protested.

"What does Hess know about computers?" Josh said.

Another telling point, Carl thought, increasingly impressed.

"Another thing," Josh said. "Stewart wasn't the type to be careless with a safe. If it was open, he must have been working in his office that night alone, like Russ said, or . . ."

He paused, adjusting his thoughts to fit the premise.

"Or what?" Carl prompted.

"Or . . . he was with someone he knew well, and trusted."

Carl emitted a forlorn sigh. "Dub."

Josh disagreed. "I don't think so. I believe that whoever killed Stewart is the same person who erased his computer files. Dub might have been capable of pilfering the backup disks, but I doubt that he had the smarts to even turn on a computer, much less erase a hard drive."

"By God, you're right!" Carl said. After some thought he added, "But he was there, Josh. They found his prints in the office."

"Yes. And Viola said that Dub went nowhere in the manor except the kitchen, unless she or Stewart asked him. Which tells me that he must have seen or heard something to make him break that rule. My guess is, he heard Stewart's printer."

"Printer? I thought you said all the files were erased."

"They were. But before that, someone had used the printer." He told about the tear strips in the wastebasket, despite the fact that Viola had emptied it on Friday. "The printer's a dot-matrix. It would have made enough noise to be heard in other parts of the house."

"And you think that attracted Dub to the office?"

"It's only a guess."

"You know what you're implying, don't you?" Carl said.

"If Dub heard the printer, he just may have seen who was doing the printing."

Josh tapped the end of his nose. "Right on." He sat back in his chair. "Carl, Russ Hess to the contrary, I think there *is* something missing from that wall safe. And I'm willing to lay my Pulitzer against your pocket change that whatever it is, it's the key to all this."

"And the sacrificial trappings?" Carl asked.

Josh lifted his hands in a gesture of bewilderment. "I'm as stumped as the rest of you."

Carl contemplated this new spin Josh had put on things. In the course of twenty-four hours this virtual neophyte had developed viable theories far beyond anything Hess or any of the other professionals had come up with. After a while he asked, "What next?"

Josh stood and stretched long and hard. "Next, I'm going to go home and try to catch up on the sleep I didn't get last night. Tomorrow, I think it will be time to pay a visit to the big question mark in this puzzle."

"Angus Munroe," Carl submitted.

"Angus Munroe," Josh confirmed.

"He's not an easy man to get to. What makes you think he'll see you?"

Josh patted the press card in his pocket. "I think when Mr. Munroe hears about the story I'm working on, he'll be as curious about me as I am about him."

Twelve

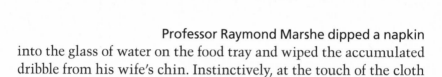

Professor Raymond Marshe dipped a napkin into the glass of water on the food tray and wiped the accumulated dribble from his wife's chin. Instinctively, at the touch of the cloth she opened her mouth.

"No, no, dear," he said, tenderly. "Lunch is over. I just want to clean you up a bit before I leave."

Throughout this visit to his wife's private room in Pennyrile Memorial Hospital in Morgantown, the professor had made it a point—as he had during all other visits—to talk to her, to recount favored memories, and to describe his ongoing activities, even though the nurses said she could no longer understand.

He folded the cloth and used the tip to clean the corners of her mouth. "I have a class at 2:30. Summer semester, you know. Saturdays are just as hectic as any other day."

Gloria Marshe kept her eyes, now sunken coals in a sallow face, fixed in a vacant stare at the wall behind her husband. He wondered if she could see the family photographs he had posted there along with the crucifix, or if she was lost in the visions of her mind, or if she was capable of thought at all.

He finished the improvised bath and pulled his chair closer to the bed. When he took his wife's frail hand in his, she did not respond. That caused him pain. It had been their final physical bond, the frail but reassuring squeeze signaling that she was aware of his presence. Then, two days ago, that, too, ended. He had wept that day, surprised at how easily the tears came. He had thought he could cry no more—that all his tears had been expended during those first agonizing days and nights after doctors explained to them Gloria's irreversible, debilitating illness. They had clung to each other so desperately then. Other times, always in the cloaking security of darkness, he would drive to the campus and slip unnoticed into the ivied chapel just off the quad. There, kneeling in homage to the God he had abandoned three decades before on discovering science, he prayed for a miracle that never came. Day by day he watched his wife deteriorate before his eyes—this vibrant woman who had hiked the continental divide with him; who had accompanied him on his geological expeditions into the Canaan wilderness; and who had never complained of the forty-pound backpacks or the frequent drenching from summer storms or the dreary nights when they had to make a cold camp.

Until two months ago, when it became necessary to commit her to Pennyrile, he had tended to her needs at home. And it was during that time that Rachel had become an unexpected blessing. Rachel, Gloria's brilliant but estranged daughter, who had transformed overnight into a stalwart helpmate available at any hour of day or night to nurture the woman whose heart she had broken so many years before.

If there was a silver lining to this otherwise ominous cloud, it was this—that Rachel had come home. If only she could have arrived while her mother was still aware, then the reconciliation could have been complete. Still, it was Rachel who, by moving into the house, made it possible for the professor to continue his work at the university. Moreover, during these otherwise cheerless days, stepfather and stepdaughter had come to know each other for the first time, often talking late into the night, establishing a rapport that Marshe had once deemed beyond possibility.

The professor gave his wife's hand a final squeeze and stood. "I must get back to the office, my dear. I have lecture notes to prepare. Rachel will be here later. And I'll be back this evening." He bent down and kissed her gently on the forehead. It was like pressing his lips to parched leather.

He had just pushed the down button at the elevator when the ward nurse hailed him. "Professor Marshe!"

He turned. "Yes?"

"Sir, Dr. Bradley would like you to stop by his office before you leave."

His stomach churned. He had hoped to avoid a confrontation today. He nodded and reluctantly headed to the administration office.

Dr. Joseph Bradley greeted him without rising from his desk. "Ah, yes. Come in, Professor."

The physician nodded to a Spanish-leather chair near the desk and began to search through a pile of file folders on his desk. Professor Marshe sat down and glanced around the spacious room, comparing it in his mind to his own uncarpeted cubbyhole at the university. The office was richly appointed, certainly more luxurious than one would expect to find in a small college-town hospital in impoverished Appalachia. He turned his attention back to the doctor and waited for what he knew would come. He thought of his class due to start in forty minutes and wondered if he should call and cancel it.

"Marshe . . . Marshe," Dr. Bradley intoned. "Ah, yes . . . here we are." He pulled one of the files and opened it on the desk. "Hmmm . . . hmmm. Yes. Well, Professor, there seems to be a problem with your account. Not a small one, I might add."

"I've assigned my insurance to the hospital. I—"

"Surely you understand that medical insurance doesn't begin to cover the costs of care such as your wife requires, Professor. We were led to believe that you would be able to meet your obligation. As it is, you are well over forty-thousand dollars in arrears."

For just two months! "Doctor, I've been making payments as best I can."

"I'm afraid that won't do. Pennyrile is not a charitable institution, Professor. Surely you have other assets. Investments? Your home? Relatives? Perhaps a second mortgage, or an assignment of property to the hospital . . ."

Marshe shook his head. The house had been mortgaged for medical bills months before. Stocks sold. Insurance cashed in. Savings depleted. "I'm afraid not."

"I see. Well, then I fear there's no recourse other than to make different arrangements. There's the sanitarium at Bardstown. They handle indigent cases. I will arrange to have Mrs. Marshe transferred at—"

"No!"

"Pardon?"

The professor sucked in a deep breath. "I . . . I'm sorry. I didn't mean to be so abrupt. It's, well, I have something pending that should pay off handsomely in a matter of days . . . perhaps hours. If you will just grant me some additional time I'm sure I can take care of everything."

"Everything, Professor?" The doctor gave him a skeptical look. "You realize that your wife may live for several months?"

"I understand. I can handle it."

"Hmmm."

Dr. Bradley closed the file. "Very well. We are not heartless here at Pennyrile. I will notify the cashier to expect a substantial payment on your bill not later than . . . let's say, three days from now. Otherwise, we will have to take other steps. Good day, Professor." The doctor turned his attention to other files on his desk.

Marshe rose. I wonder if the bastard expects me to genuflect, he thought. "Thank you, Doctor," he said, and left.

In a black funk, he walked across the parking lot. The sight of Dr. Bradley's mint-condition Mercedes 460L coupe in the chief-of-staff's reserved parking space didn't improve his spirits. Angry and frustrated, he opened the door of his eight-year-old Dodge sedan, slid into the frayed seat, and sat there gripping the steering wheel.

Not all of his ire was directed at medical arrogance and the ruinous system of health care Bradley represented. He thought of his telephone calls to Greenleaf, the last one just two mornings ago. The woman who had identified herself as Angus Munroe's secretary said that none of the Munroes were available. They were attending a funeral in Seneca Falls, she claimed. He didn't have to ask whose funeral. Everyone in the state knew that well enough. He left a message. It was urgent that he speak with Angus Munroe, he stressed. The woman promised to pass it on. But no one returned his call. He had decided to wait a few more days before calling again. But now, things had changed. Bradley was threatening to transfer Gloria to the state sanitarium. To banish her during her final days of life to a foul overcrowded ward filled with drunks and dope addicts and diseased whores and other human flotsam. He would never permit that. Never!

He started the car and drove northward across town to the university, and parked in his private spot behind Marron Hall. For a while he sat watching the mighty Monongahela flow past the campus, and he wistfully reflected how, unlike that of mere mortals, the life force of the great river seemed to surge onward forever.

He got to his classroom ten minutes late. For those students who remained, he conducted from rote an uninspiring lecture on the molecular composition of selenite as opposed to gypsum, and then left without allowing the usual period for questions.

His office was in the same building, three doors down from the classroom. He unlocked the door, dropped into the chair at his cluttered desk, and stared at the telephone. Munroe was ignoring him. Perhaps the Lord of Greenleaf considered a lowly professor too insignificant to accommodate with the courtesy of a return call. If he realized the reason for my calls, Marshe thought, he would be beating a path to my door.

He grabbed the phone and started to dial. He had entered the first three numbers when he spotted the package in his in basket. Campus mail wasn't delivered on Saturdays. Why hadn't he seen it yesterday? Then he remembered; he hadn't come to the office yesterday. He replaced the phone in the cradle and picked up the small cardboard box. It bore a hand-printed address to Prof. R. Marshe at his Marron Hall office. Puzzled, he took out his pocketknife, sliced through the strapping tape, and pulled back the top flap.

The explosion tore off both his hands, ripped open his chest, and turned his face into hamburger. The janitor who heard the blast and found the gruesome results called 911.

Throughout the remainder of that afternoon, coupled to alien machines in the intensive-care ward at Pennyrile Memorial Hospital, one floor below where his wife lay vegetating, Professor Raymond Marshe clung to the fragile threads of life. Shortly before midnight, with his stepdaughter at his bedside, he closed his eyes forever.

Thirteen

From Greenleaf, seventy-six-year-old Angus Munroe reigned over the largest privately owned conglomeration of deep-shaft coal mines, strip mines, sawmills, paper mills, and timberlands east of the Mississippi River. On this Saturday morning, his thoughts were not on his corporate empire. Seated beneath a striped garden umbrella at a wrought iron table on the grand west veranda of his home, he was poring over a score of musty books and pamphlets. He was deeply engrossed when his personal secretary, a middle-aged woman who seldom left the premises except when traveling with him—which was increasingly rare these days—approached. "Barlow just called, sir. There's a Mr. Chacón at the gatehouse asking to see you."

Angus Munroe glanced up over the spyglass he was using. "Chacón? Ah, yes." He sat back, recalling the phone conversation last evening. "Tell Barlow to pass him through. Have him join me here when he arrives at the house, and tell Lucille to prepare lunch for two."

"Yes sir." She turned to leave.

"And Mary . . ."

She stopped. "Yes sir."

"Would you please bring me F. G. Speck's book *The Iroquois*. You'll find it on the first shelf of my Seneca collection."

"Yes sir," she said, and left to assure that his orders were heeded.

Munroe paused in reflection. Joshua Chacón. He recalled the few times he had seen from afar the cinnamon-skinned young lad who had grown up in Seneca Falls as Joshua Collier and had overcome adversity to rise to the top of his profession. Two of a kind, he thought with a chuckle, recalling his own humble beginnings. He lowered his spyglass again and returned to his research.

Joshua Chacón had heard and read of the splendor of Greenleaf. But as he drove through the huge, electronically controlled iron gate, he realized that no description or series of photographs in *Architectural Digest* or *Town and Country*—both of which had featured the estate in their publications—could prepare one for the reality. Cresting the hill a mile into the wooded estate, Josh spotted the sprawling three-story, sixty-room manor house that dominated the Mount Canaan skyline. The original cardinal brick building—built during colonial times by Lord Fairfax, on land surveyed and platted by a young George Washington—had been a historical landmark for two centuries before Angus Munroe bought it as a gift for his bride. He added two wings—painstakingly constructed to conform to the original architecture—with stark high-rise chimneys and massive arched windows. Twice along the drive, Josh spotted Jeeps with armed drivers patrolling the perimeter. They must have been alerted by radio to give him safe passage. In the lush meadowland below the east wing of the mansion, he passed a green and white barn flanked by two broad paddocks. In the paddock nearer the road, someone was grooming a magnificent black horse. As Josh drove past he recognized the denim-clad groom as Constance Munroe. She glanced up at him briefly, made no sign of recognition, and returned to her chore.

Just off the west wing of the mansion, a flagstone veranda the size of a basketball court overlooked the broad panorama of Canaan Valley. It was to this veranda that Josh was escorted by the butler who met him at the door.

The silver-haired man seated on the sunny veranda rose with a spryness that belied his age. He was taller, up close, than Josh had imagined, and huskier. He was dressed in field khakis that had seen considerable wear. His lace-up boots were caked with dried mud. A leathery, deep-tanned complexion revealed him to be a man who spent much of his life outdoors. In a far corner of the veranda a crew-cut blonde man was scrutinizing Josh with great care. Josh recognized him as the bodyguard he had seen near Munroe at Stewart's funeral two days before. Although the man was well out of hearing range, Josh wondered what would happen if he made a sudden threatening move toward his host. He didn't care to find out.

"Ah, Mr. Chacón." Angus Munroe greeted his visitor with extended hand. "Welcome to Greenleaf."

Josh noted that his host's handshake was as firm as his voice was sonorous. "Mr. Munroe," he acknowledged. He wondered fleetingly if Munroe knew of the one-time torrid affair between his granddaughter and Josh. He pushed the thought aside and glanced at the mound of books on the table.

Munroe noticed. He picked up an object from the table and handed it to Josh. "You're an educated man, Mr. Chacón. What do you make of this? Careful, please."

The thin, unpolished stone was jet black. Two inches in length, it was crudely sculpted into what appeared to be the form of a bear. Josh studied it for a moment, wondering what was expected of him.

"Pure obsidian," Munroe said, relieving Josh of the stone. "Most likely some sort of talisman. The hole, here, suggests that it was worn around the wrist or neck, perhaps the ankle. It's quite rare for this part of the country, more likely to be found in your great Southwest, which causes one to wonder about its origin. I unearthed it at the river this morning. I've gathered quite a handsome collection over the years: arrowheads, lance points, flint knives, sharpening stones—some are currently on display in the Smithsonian. The Senecas were a great nation, you know. Remarkably advanced, relative to the other tribes that made up the Iroquois Confederacy. Still, they were not averse to fetishes." He placed the figurine back on the table. "But nothing like this . . . not that I've found before. I've been trying to identify it, as you can see."

"Yes, I see."

Munroe chuckled. "And you're probably quite bored. Of course, you did not request this meeting to hear a lecture about American Indian archaeology."

He moved toward a far table. "Come, let's sit over here. I was intrigued by your call last evening. I've ordered lunch for the two of us. Then we can talk in private."

The table nearest the veranda railing had been set for dining: saffron-hued linen tablecloth with matching napkins, a centerpiece of freshly cut flaxen Peace roses, and sterling silverware bearing the Munroe clan crest. As Josh took his chair, the veranda grew momentarily dark. He looked up to see a flotilla of giant cumulus clouds drifting across the sky, casting a ghostly convoy of shadows on the mansion and the verdant valley far below. On the far bank of the river, a dozen Herefords being fattened for market grazed in a fenced two-acre bluegrass pasture. It was an unusual sight for someone from the West, Josh mused. In New Mexico, it would take ten times that acreage of pastureland to serve the same number of cattle.

"Fascinating view, don't you agree?" Munroe said.

"I'd forgotten how green West Virginia is in summer," Josh replied.

"I can imagine," Munroe said. "That's one of the reasons I could seldom persuade my wife to travel with me. She couldn't bear to be separated from her beloved green hills."

He pushed an intercom button. A voice responded, "Yes sir?"

"We'll have lunch now, Morris. One moment, please."

He looked at Josh. "I drink only spring water. But we have anything you'd like. Some superb wines."

"Water's fine."

Munroe pushed the button again. "Water for both, Morris."

Munroe settled back and laced his fingers across his chest, his steel-gray eyes fixed on his visitor. Josh realized that he was being scrutinized.

"You bear a striking resemblance to your father, Mr. Chacón."

It was unexpected. "You knew him?"

"Estévan? Oh yes. Quite well. He was a remarkable young man. It was I who brought him to Seneca County, you know. I see by your expression that that surprises you."

"I'm afraid it does."

"Years ago, I used to spend a few weeks each fall elk hunting on the Jicarilla Apache Reservation in New Mexico. That's where I first heard of your father. He was working for Consolidated Uranium in Gallup. Brilliant mining engineer . . . brilliant. Despite his relative youth, no man in the country at that time knew more about strip mining. I had just opened operations on Mount Hazard. I bought out Estévan's contract with Consolidated and moved him here to take charge of my mine. He would have had a bright future in the organization, had it not been for . . ."

"Had it not been for my mother," Josh interjected bitterly.

"Your mother was a beautiful young woman, Mr. Chacón. A bit headstrong, perhaps, but that simply made her more attractive. Her misfortune was in meeting and marrying the wrong man first. Jennifer Collier was never meant to be a Dunning. She was too carefree, too vivacious for that stodgy clan. I think that in Estévan Chacón she found the kindred spirit she'd been looking for all her life. But nonetheless, it was a precarious affair—indeed, dangerous. Her social position, the racial implications. No offense, I'm simply stating facts as they existed. When I learned of it, I settled a year's wages on your father and urged him to leave West Virginia at once. I wasn't surprised when your mother followed."

"She deserted her own son," Josh said.

"Stewart. Yes. Sad, that. He was married to my granddaughter you know. He and I never cared much for one another, but I saw enough to know that the abandonment by his mother scarred him deeply. I've often wondered if that was the price the Dunnings extracted from Jennifer for her freedom."

He waited a moment, then, with a knowing look, said, "And I suspect that you have often wondered if she would have done the same to you, given the right circumstances."

Josh was visibly shaken.

"I see that I've upset you," Munroe added quickly. "Please forgive me. I can empathize with your feelings, believe me . . . Ah, our lunch has arrived."

The butler who had met Josh at the door arrived pushing a serving cart. He placed a basket of poppy-seed rolls and an iced bowl of butter pats on the table. Then he set a small green salad at Josh's place, lifted the silver cover from a luncheon plate, and placed the plate beside the salad. Josh welcomed the interruption. He concentrated his gaze on the plate, unwilling to pursue the painful subject of his parents any longer. Somehow, he had to regain control of this conversation.

"Shad roe," Munroe said.

Josh glanced up. "Pardon?"

"Shad roe. I have it delivered fresh from Richmond each day during the season. Lucille, my cook, flours it and then sautés it lightly in butter. I think you'll find it delicious."

"I'm sure I will."

The butler tonged ice into their glasses, filled them with water, and set the pitcher on the table. "Will that be all, sir?"

"Yes, Morris, thank you," Munroe replied. "Please see to it that we are not disturbed. No calls."

"Yes sir," the butler said, and left.

Josh ate his food mechanically, barely tasting it. He was anxious to get to the real purpose of his visit.

Munroe took a roll from the bread basket and broke it. "Now, let's see if I understand correctly your call of last evening. You say you're working on a book about the potential hazard created by the Waste Isolation Pilot Plant in New Mexico. And you're interested in the similarity, from an environmental-impact viewpoint, between that project and the reclaimed mine pits here in Seneca County. Is that correct?"

"That's right," Josh said, pleased with this new turn in the conversation, "I believe there's a reasonable basis for comparison."

"I see."

Munroe began to butter the roll. "Now, Mr. Chacón, in all frankness, isn't your real purpose in coming here to satisfy your curiosity about whether or not I had Stewart Dunning killed?"

Only by quick reflex did Josh manage to keep from dropping his fork. Damn! He was beginning to understand how this unusual man had managed to build a private corporate empire before his fortieth birthday. He gave a quick glance to the crew-cut man in the far corner.

Munroe noticed. "Don't mind Max. He's quite loyal."

No doubt, Josh thought. He ended the charade of eating

and pushed his plate aside. "Yes, Mr. Munroe, that's exactly why I'm here."

Munroe smiled. "Very well. Now we can speak candidly. Of course I know of the rumors and speculations regarding me and the unfortunate Mr. Dunning. But tell me, as one not fettered by the parochial viewpoint, what do you think I had to gain by Dunning's death?" He continued to eat.

"Riddance of a threat," Josh replied. "Possibly the first serious one you've faced in years. Stewart was beginning to make headway in his anti-strip-mining campaign. A ban would have halted your Mount Hazard mining operation, not to mention your lucrative garbage-pit contracts."

Munroe took the last bite from his plate. "Superb roe. I'm sorry you didn't seem to enjoy it."

Josh said nothing.

Munroe dabbed his mouth with a napkin and pushed back from the table. He took two oversize cigars from his shirt pocket and offered one to Josh. "*Partagas*. Finest Dominican."

Josh declined.

A sudden reflection of sunlight from one of the windows above the veranda caused Josh to look up. Someone was rearranging a venetian blind. He wondered if it might be Beth.

Munroe removed the wrapping from one of the cigars, licked it on all sides, bit off the end, and lighted it with a kitchen match from a receptacle on the table. When the cigar was drawing to his satisfaction, he said, "You and I are a breed apart around here, Mr. Chacón. Outsiders. Blessed with the capability to see beyond the Alleghenies, so to speak. You've been back in Seneca Falls now, how long . . . two days is it? Before that, I doubt you seldom gave the place a second thought. So I think it safe to surmise that whatever suspicions you harbor about my involvement in your brother's death have been fostered by the locals."

He paused long enough to let that point take root. "No West Virginia legislature will ban strip mining of coal, Mr. Chacón . . . *ever*. Just as Kentucky will never ban the distillation of bourbon, or North Carolina the growing of tobacco—both of which are products, as you know, that also have been labeled threats to the public health. Permit me to state some facts."

He ticked off points on his fingers. "First, during the past two decades strip mining has become the leading method of coal mining in the world. Today, it accounts for 60 percent of all coal produced in the United States. Those are not figures to be dismissed lightly.

"Second, strip mining has produced the greatest financial boon this state has ever experienced. Last year the taxes generated by my Mount Hazard operation alone repaved a hundred miles of highways, financed construction of a children's wing at the Henry Sites Memorial Hospital, equipped the new technical-vocational school in Seneca Falls with state-of-the art computers, and paid for a 9 percent increase in teachers' salaries. And that was just in Seneca County.

"Third, strip mining is responsible for the most important advance in miners' welfare since the discovery of coal; it has brought the miner up out of the deep mines into the sunlight. All you need do is read the Department of Interior studies for the past decade comparing the incidence of black lung disease, crippling accidents, and other causes of death in deep mines to the relative safety of the above-ground mines, to understand the significance of that.

"Fourth, as to what you call the lucrative garbage-pit contracts: America is drowning in its own garbage, Mr. Chacón. Sites for urban landfills are becoming nearly impossible to find. Right now, in some eastern states, landfill sites are costing a half -million dollars an acre. What is so wrong, I ask you, with restoring mined-out pits with a base of solid waste, where the cost is only two thousand dollars an acre. Right here in Seneca County there are enough pits to satisfy the needs of a city the size of Philadelphia for the next decade. And there are thousands of pits available throughout the country that can be filled with waste and converted to tillable acreage. I can show you examples within five miles of where you sit that are producing some of the finest pine saplings and seed grasses to be found."

"What about leaching?" Josh asked.

"Ah, leaching," Munroe said with a flourish of his cigar. "The favorite whipping boy of the environmentalists. One thing you must keep in mind, Mr. Chacón—and I'm sure that a man of your intellect knows this already—is that things are never as bad as the environmentalists claim. *Never.* Granted, there are problems with leaching. But no more so from waste-filled pits than from any other reclaimed pit. But you can be assured that a solution will be found. Meanwhile, mine owners must see to it that their side of the story receives equal billing with that of the Jeremiahs. No small task, given the increasingly hostile media. But of this I can assure you, the legislature will never vote to send men back underground for the benefit of a few fanatical trout fishermen."

He knocked ash from the Partagas into an oversize ashtray on the table. "Now, a personal note. I do not need to eliminate my adversaries by felonious means. In my time I've handled far more dangerous, and considerably more intelligent, adversaries than Stewart Dunning. Indeed, I was looking forward to any encounter he wished to initiate. There are few pleasures in life more satisfying than putting one over on a Dunning." He made a wry face. "There are reasons you would agree, I believe."

A veiled reference to Beth, Josh recognized. Munroe knew about their affair.

Munroe continued, "One last point—an important one, I submit. Dull as he may have been in some matters, Stewart was no fool. He knew the facts about mining as well as I. In my opinion, his strip-mine tirades were grandstand gestures to attract like-minded media to foster his future political ambitions. Indeed, despite what others may tell you, I'm yet to be convinced that his death was connected in any way to the mining issue."

Munroe sat back with the air of a man satisfied that he had presented irrefutable arguments.

Josh pondered his next move. If Munroe was dissembling, it was a masterful performance. Yet, no man could have achieved the prominence he had without being just that—a masterful performer. Josh decided on a bold gamble. Once again, he would be breaking his word to Hess. But circumstances warranted it. Carefully watching Munroe's reaction, he asked, "What's your theory about the way Stewart's body was found?"

"I don't follow you."

In for a penny, in for a pound, Josh thought. "The pagan trappings."

Munroe stopped the cigar halfway to his mouth. "Pagan trappings?"

"The altar, the shroud, the candles . . ."

"Mr. Chacón, what *are* you talking about?"

It was the question of a man whose bewilderment was sincere. Josh decided to go all the way. He described in macabre detail where and how Stewart Dunning's body had been found.

Munroe hung on every word. When Josh finished the ghoulish description, Munroe stubbed the Partagas in the ashtray, rose, and stepped to the veranda railing. He stood there several minutes, his back turned to Josh, silently looking out over the valley and the rolling hills beyond. After a moment he asked, "Tell me. Were there traces of salt found on that shroud?"

What a strange question, Josh thought.

"Salt? I have no idea. Why do you ask?"

Again, there was a leaden silence before Munroe answered. "I have lived in these hills over a half century, Mr. Chacón. I never had the advantage of a formal education. Nonetheless, I am an educated man. I have read the classics and have studied the major philosophers, some in their native languages. I sit on the board of regents at the university. I am a director of the Center for Appalachian Studies. I have both financed and personally conducted exhaustive research into the cultures of those who have inhabited these mountains and valleys, from prehistoric times to our contemporary era. During all that time, folklore and legend to the contrary, neither I nor any of my colleagues have ever been able to substantiate what you have just told me."

Josh stood and went to the railing. "I'm afraid I don't understand."

Munroe turned to face him. "Mr. Chacón, you have just described the ritual of sin eating."

Fourteen

Viola Brown twisted her handkerchief nervously as she contemplated Josh's question. She had been frying a pork chop for her supper when he called and asked if he could come right over. She had turned off the burner and set the skillet aside and went to the front window. For no accountable reason—perhaps it was the urgency in Josh's voice—she was nervous about this meeting. When at last the red Corvette pulled up to the curb, she stepped out onto the porch and met him with an offer for him to join her for supper. He declined, stating that he wanted to get right down to business. Now, seated in her living room, she grappled with the dilemma of how, or whether, to answer the question he had just asked her.

"Viola," Josh insisted, "It's very important."

She studied her hands, not responding.

Josh had been stunned at the sight of her. Her eyes were bloodshot. Her face was swollen. She dabbed at her nose with the handkerchief she kept folded in her hand, explaining in a hoarse voice that she hadn't been sleeping well lately, what with all the horrible things going on in Seneca Falls these days, and it had lowered her resistance and she'd caught a summer cold.

Josh inched forward to the edge of the couch. "Viola, please . . . did Dub ever say anything to you about sin eating?"

She shook her head. "No, Joshua, he never said anything like that to me."

He gave her a skeptical look.

"Oh, Joshua, do we really have to talk about things like that?"

"Yes," Josh emphasized, "we really must talk about things like that."

"I told you the truth. Dub never said anything to me about . . ." She paused. "It's just that . . . well, I don't want to say anything to put a blight on Dub. Some folks around here take a low view of other folks' beliefs."

Josh waited, hoping the silence would urge her on.

Viola gave her nose another dab. Then, with a sigh of resignation, she let her hands rest in her lap. "You remember Sam Grokie . . . lived up around Spring Run?"

"Grokie? No, should I?"

"Old man. Been a miner all his life. Anyway, six summers ago Sam was diggin' coal out of a shaft near his home. No one'd worked it for years. Roof timbers were rotten —same in all those old mines up there. When he was comin' out, one of 'em gave way. Fell on him and busted him up awful bad."

"Excuse me, Viola. What does all this have to do with Dub?"

"You ask me to tell," she admonished him. "Now I'm tellin'."

"Sorry. Go ahead."

"Sam, he got that beam off him and started makin' his way out to the highway. Crawled the last half mile or so on his hands and knees. Coal trucker found him lyin' on the road and got him to the hospital. He was bleeding bad. His head, here"—she laid her hand on her right temple—"was all swelled up, purple splotched and yellow like. Doc Townsend didn't know if Sam'd make it or not. They bedded him out on the ward. Just pulled a curtain 'round him. Sam didn't have no folks, so I used to go up nights and help take care of him. That's where I was, one night late, sleepin' in a chair, when somethin' woke me up. And there was Brother Dowell standin' there with his hand—"

"Excuse me," Josh interrupted. "Brother Dowell?"

"Preacher," she explained. "Had a no-denomination church up on Mount Hazard. Passed away last summer."

"I see," Josh said, steeling himself for yet another story about an idiosyncratic preacher in this heartland of the Bible Belt.

"Well," Viola continued, "Brother Dowell was standin' there with his hand on Sam's head. And he was prayin' in the other tongue."

"Other tongue?" Josh said. "You mean, speaking in tongues?"

"It's a gift of the Holy Spirit, Joshua."

"Yes, I understand. Please go on."

"Brother Dowell, he was prayin' in the Spirit. Beautiful words. I never heard words like that before. Couldn't understand 'em. 'Course, he was talkin' to the Lord, not to me.

"Anyway, when I sat up, Brother Dowell looked right at me. But he kept on prayin', all the time keepin' his hand on Sam's head. When he quit he told me it'd be best if I didn't mention him bein' there. Said other preachers around town get riled when they hear he's been prayin' over folks like that. I told him not to worry, that I wouldn't do or say anything to cause him any trouble, seein' as how he was the only preacher around here cared enough to come see Sam in the first place." She paused, then added wistfully, "He was a fine man, Brother Dowell."

"He must have been," Josh agreed.

"Couple of nights later Sam turned real bad. Doc Townsend said he might not make it to mornin'. I didn't know who else to call except Brother Dowell. He came right off, about midnight as I remember. Sam already had the rattles by then. Brother Dowell laid his Bible open on the bed. He took a bottle of oil outta his pocket and put some on his finger and made a cross on Sam's forehead. Then he pulled down the sheets and made another one on his chest. Then he prayed again in the unknown tongue. When he got done he put his hand on my shoulder and said Sam could pass over now in pure peace with the Lord. Then he pulled up a chair and we both sat there through the night.

"Come mornin'—I'd dozed off—I woke up and saw Sam starin' straight at me. 'Viola,' he say, 'I'm mighty hungry.' Woke Brother Dowell up too. He got a real odd look on his face. He stood up and laid his hand over on Sam and said, 'Praise the Lord!' Then he left without another word. Few days later they let Sam go home."

She grew silent, twisting the handkerchief in her hand.

Josh let the silence grow for a while. So far, nothing related to his query. He said, "There's got to be more, Viola. Dub, remember?"

"Alice Herkimer—you remember her?"

Josh thought back. "Herkimer . . . elderly lady. Lived alone on a farm out near Dorcas? Used to hold an ice cream social for the high school senior class every summer?"

"That's the one. She died alone, too. One day Sam Grokie come to town to see me. Said Brother Dowell wanted to talk to him before they buried Miss Alice. He was frettin' about it, said he wouldn't go unless I went with him. Sonny—my nephew—was livin' here then. He drove us up to Mount Hazard. Sonny couldn't stay. Brother Dowell said he'd drive us home.

"There wasn't any office in the church, so we sat out on the wooden pews while we talked. Brother Dowell wasn't taken too highly with me bein' there. Sam told him either I stayed or we'd both leave. Brother Dowell finally said he knew I was a believer, so it was all right. Then he said some mighty peculiar things to Sam. He told Sam that on that last night he came to the hospital he had said the prayer for the dead over him. Said it was the 'final cleansin'.' Said that even though Sam had lived, far as the church was concerned, he was dead. Said that since Sam's sins had been wiped away that night, and since he didn't exist no more in the eyes of the church, he couldn't commit more sin. Fact was, he said Sam could take other folks' sins off their souls now, so they could go to heaven—even dead folks. And he told Sam that's what he had to do for Miss Alice."

She gave Josh an imploring look, as if questioning whether to continue.

"Please go on."

Viola cleared her throat. "Brother Dowell explained that Miss Alice died without the final cleansin'. Then he drove us to the Herkimer farm. Some of Brother Dowell's flock were waitin' on the porch. Mr. Jason—he was her only livin' kin, but he's dead now, too—he was there. All those folks got up and followed us in the house. Miss Alice was laid out on a table in the front room. She was covered with a blanket up to her chin. Her head was on a pillow, restin' between two candles."

Galvanized now, Josh was hanging onto every word.

"Mr. Jason lit those two candles. Then he went to the kitchen. When he come back he put a slice of bread on the blanket coverin' Miss Alice. Then he took a pinch of salt and sprinkled it over the bread."

Salt! Josh thought with a start. Angus Munroe had asked if salt had been found on the drapery covering Stewart Dunning.

"When Mr. Jason stepped back, Brother Dowell took Sam by the arm and led him to where Miss Alice lay. He whispered something to Sam, and Sam picked up the bread and ate it.

"Brother Dowell say, 'Amen.' All the other folks did too. Then Mr. Jason took some money outta his pocket and handed it to Sam. After that, Brother Dowell drove Sam and me home. He told us never to say anything about what happened. Said most folks don't understand such things and would be awful upset about it."

She leaned her head against the back of the chair, weary.

Guessing what was coming next, Josh said, "Viola. Was Dub there that day?"

She nodded. "Dub was a member of Brother Dowell's flock. He was at the cleansin' that day. And least one other time that I know of. But he never said anything to me about it . . . like you ask if he did. We never talked about it at all."

After a short silence she said, "I knew why Dub's handprints were on that kitchen cabinet at the mansion the minute I saw them. That's where the salt's kept. He was doin' the only thing for Mr. Stewart he knew to do."

Josh sat back, his mind filled with the images she had provoked. "Yes, I understand now. And it explains a lot of things." After a while he stood and placed his hand on her shoulder. "You've been a big help, Viola. I'm sorry I interrupted your supper."

"It'll still be good." She pushed up out of the chair to accompany him to the door.

He was almost to his car when he turned and looked back. Viola was still standing in the doorway. He went back to the house. "Viola, you told me that whenever Dub went up to do chores at Twin Oaks he'd stop by here first to get the key to the manor."

"That's right."

"And he'd bring it back, same day?"

"Uh-huh. Always kept it here with me nights."

"Then you must have seen Dub soon after he found Stewart's body."

She didn't answer. He could tell something was troubling her.

"What is it, Viola?"

"Dub didn't use the key that weekend. He came by for it, but he told me later that he didn't use it."

"But he was inside the manor."

"I know he was. I could tell that. It's just that, well I never knew Dub to lie."

That gave Josh something to think about.

"Viola," he said, "did Dub show up any night that weekend in bloody clothes?"

"No . . . I'd've seen that right off. He keeps extra work clothes in that big laundry room at the mansion, though, just off the back porch. He could change clothes anytime he wanted."

"I see." Josh considered that for a moment. "Carl says that Dub has a habit of pilfering . . . collecting things."

"Anything that catches his eye, almost."

"Does he keep things like that in his room here?"

"My, my, does he ever. I'm always tossin' things out, all the time."

"Did he bring anything out of the ordinary here that weekend?"

"What kind of thing?"

"Computer disk. Small plastic case, about the size of a deck of cards, but much thinner—like this." He held a thumb and finger about an eighth of an inch apart. "Thin strip of metal on one end."

"If he did, I didn't see it. Want me to go look around his room?"

"Later. Whenever you get a chance. Call me if you find anything like that. Thanks again, Viola."

He went to the Corvette and drove off in a hurry, anxious to get to Carl Travis's office.

Fifteen

From the window of her sitting room, Constance Munroe had an unobstructed view of Greenleaf's sprawling west veranda, one floor below. Earlier that morning, after Joshua drove past the stables, she had suspended her grooming job in the paddock and slipped up the back way to her suite. She arranged the venetian miniblind so that she could watch the meeting between Angus and his visitor, without them being able to see her.

She thought about that now as she removed her saffron peignoir from the hanger and laid it on the bed. Joshua Collier—now Joshua Chacón—had matured into a handsome man with professionally styled hair and a slender physique. He was indeed his father's son, she thought, remembering the swarthy Latino, Estévan Chacón, who had cuckolded the pompous Harold Dunning and stolen his wife years ago. Harold, the heir to the Dunning fortune, fled Seneca County in humiliation.

She removed her clothing and stepped in front of the full-length mirror beside her closet door. Sliding her hands slowly down over her hips, she turned to view herself from one side, then the other. She was proud of her body. It had served her well, and would still.

That morning on the veranda Angus handled Joshua with captivating charm, as she had seen him handle so many others during the years she had lived at Greenleaf. First, the younger man was led to admire Angus's collection of flints. Then they had dined (Joshua barely touched his food) and chatted until Angus, the perfect host, moved slightly away so his cigar would not annoy his visitor. It all appeared amicable, so under control. There was nothing to worry about. Then came that sudden look of stupefaction on Angus's face, and he rose and stepped to the railing. From the way he stood looking out over the valley, from the set of his shoulders, she could tell that he had been taken by utter surprise. How she wished at that moment she could have overheard what Joshua had said to rattle him so? Tonight, she intended to find out.

She sat down at her dressing table and ran a brush through her hair until the ebony sheen of the morning returned. She refreshed her lipstick, blotted it, and then sprayed a faint mist of Boucheron at the base of her throat and behind her ears. She surveyed her face in the mirror. Pleased, she went to the bed and slipped into the gossamer peignoir and stepped out into the hallway.

The door to David's suite was ajar. Through the opening she could see her husband sprawled, fully clothed, on his back on the couch. A rasping snore kept cadence with the labored rise and fall of his chest. His left arm, sleeve rolled above the elbow, dangled onto the floor. She looked for the needle and spotted it on the rug beside his hand. She pulled the door shut and continued down the long hallway.

Angus Munroe took the key from the pocket of his night robe and unlocked the door to Greenleaf's master suite. He stepped inside, relocked the door behind him, and switched on the lights. No other person was allowed entry to this suite, with the exception of the elderly maid whose sole duty was to care for it daily. He looked around the sitting room for a moment before entering the bedroom. As always, he inspected the vanity first. The tortoise-shell brush and comb were in place. The hand-cut crystal atomizer with the squeeze-bulb dispenser and golden tassel sat beside the cloisonné jewelry case. The sterling silver hand mirror inscribed with the initial *N* was freshly polished, its glass face spotless. Everything was in order, just as Nan had left it.

Against the far wall, positioned between lofty arched windows framed by cerulean drapes, was the bed—a four-poster fashioned from solid walnut. A single satin-encased pillow lay at the head, where the patchwork quilt was neatly folded back. Beside the bed, a Morocco-leather chair sat in the same spot it had occupied for thirty years. Angus sat down in the chair and gazed longingly at the old four-poster.

They had enjoyed twenty-eight years together, he and the plain, straw-blonde girl who married him, a penniless young miner who had just emigrated from Scotland. Twenty-eight wonderful years. First, in the small house they rented on Mountain View Street; then in the larger one on Grove Avenue; finally, in Greenleaf, his present to her after the patent attorney for Dixon Coal Company informed him that the safety adapter he had invented for deep-mine elevator brakes would make him rich beyond his dreams. In this grand four-poster they had shared the remaining years of their lovemaking, never tiring of one another. In this bed their son, David, was born. And in this bed his beloved Nan had spent the final months of her life, never once uttering a bitter word as she was wasting away, while he took every moment of the day and night he could spare to be at her side.

On the morning she died he proclaimed that no one would occupy this suite again as long as he lived. And no one had, not even himself. Still, he came here each night before retiring to spend a few moments in quiet reflection, sitting in the same chair he had sat in during those final anguishing months three decades ago.

At last he rose, laid his hand for a moment on the soft pillow that had last cradled Nan Helmick Munroe's head. Then he left, locking the suite behind him.

His own suite was straight across the hallway. The heady aroma of Boucheron struck him when he entered.

"Good evening, Connie," he said into the darkness.

"I swear, Angus," his daughter-in-law replied, "sometimes I think you have the eyes of a panther."

"Just as you have the *soul* of the animal, my dear."

"Oh, Angus, you're cruel."

She switched on the lamp and rose to greet him. Instead of going to her, he went to his own chair and put his feet up on the ottoman. Not to be deterred, she went to him, sat on the floor near the chair, and laid her head in his lap. "You seem troubled."

He ran a hand through her hair. "Dean Stoval called me this evening. Seems there was a bizarre attempt on the life of one of the university faculty this afternoon. Man named Marshe. Do you know him?"

She kept her face away from him. "I don't think so. Was he . . . killed?"

"He's not expected to live. Mary tells me that a man by that name has called here several times recently."

"Marshe?" She raised her head, her brow furrowed in thought. "Oh yes, now I remember. He's a geologist or surveyor or something like that. He's been working near some of our reclaimed pits on Mount Hazard. He was hired by the state, though, not us. I suppose he wanted to talk about that."

"I see."

She stood, went to the chair where she'd been sitting when he entered, and turned off the light. Then she lifted the peignoir over her head and let it drop to the floor. At that moment, as if orchestrated, the moon drifted from behind an eclipsing cloud, illuminating her body in incandescent gold.

"You are quite beautiful, my dear," Angus said, approvingly.

She came to him and took his hand. "Come."

She led him to the bedroom. "It's been too long," she said, loosening the sash on his robe.

Afterward, he lay on his back, his hands clasped behind his head. She lay with her head on his chest. "I never know if I've pleased you," she said.

"You always please me."

She ran her hand up and down his thigh. "And you're a better lover than any other dozen men put together. I've never known anyone like you."

"Thank you. You lie as splendidly as you make love."

She slapped him playfully on the chest. "Oh, Angus."

After a moment she said, "How was your meeting with Joshua Collier this morning?"

"Chacón? A most unusual young man. Absolutely convinced I had his brother killed. He revealed the damndest thing."

"Oh?"

He told the story quickly. How Stewart's body was surrounded by paraphernalia, the meaning of which was unrecognized by the authorities, but which was eerily suggestive to anyone who had studied the unconfirmed ritual of sin eating.

She gave an involuntary tremor. "How barbaric."

"Most religious practices are barbaric, my dear. Except those you personally subscribe to, of course."

"Did you convince him?"

"Of my innocence? I'm not at all sure that I did. He's a persistent young man. Obviously intelligent, despite his amateurish comportment today. I suspect he will be here until his curiosity is satisfied."

She lay there a few minutes longer, then started to get up. Except on the rare occasions when he asked her to remain, she always returned to her own room after one of their assignations.

"There's something else," he said. "Secretary of the Interior Mulhaney is arriving in Charleston Monday. You've met him, I'm sure."

"Oh, yes. Quickest zipper on Capitol Hill. Has a pool of secretaries on his staff who can't even spell, much less type."

Angus chuckled. "Ostensibly he's making a quick survey of the timber industry in the Potomac Highlands. But Senator Ryan has tipped me that he's actually coming to assess the strength of the anti-strip-mining sentiment that Stewart Dunning churned up."

"Is it something to worry about?"

"I don't think so. But with this new administration you never know. They are environmentalist to the core, so it's best to keep as many options in our favor as possible. I'm offering the secretary the use of my hunting lodge. Ryan says he has expressed a keen interest in having you dine there with him."

He had worked it in so smoothly that it took a moment for her to comprehend. "Dine with him? Mulhaney? No, thank you!"

"It would be good for business, my dear. I'd take it as a personal favor if you would be particularly nice to him."

She raised herself on one elbow and searched his face in the pale light. "For God's sake, Angus. You must be kidding. The man is abominable, he's perverted, he—"

"I would never kid about such a thing, Connie."

Genuinely angry now, she flung her legs over the side of the bed and sat up. "You bastard! You make me so goddamned mad. Why do I let you do these things to me?"

"Because, my dear, you know full well that I will never leave Greenleaf to a weaseling junkie. How, then, will you ever secure it, unless from me?"

He rolled onto his side. "Now, please return to your room. I'm suddenly very sleepy."

She stalked out of the room. Down the hallway, her husband stood slumped against the doorsill of his suite, his bloodshot eyes fixed on her like those of a scourged animal. She stopped and turned to face him, for a long moment offering him a close-up view of her sumptuous nakedness. Then, with a snort of contempt, she entered her own suite and slammed the door behind her.

Forty-five minutes later she exited the massive gates of Greenleaf and turned the blue Rolls convertible north toward Davistown. Martin's Texaco station might still be open. If not, there was a pay phone at the all-night market at the Fox and Ox Camp farther down the road. She opened the glove compartment and took out three quarters from the change holder. She thought for a moment, and then took out a dozen more. This call might take a while. It was time for Manny Marconi to know about Joshua Chacón.

Sixteen

Sheriff Russell Hess appeared oblivious to the odor of scorched coffee that permeated his office. "Sin eating? Speaking in tongues? What the hell are you two talking about?"

Carl Travis frowned. He wished he hadn't insisted to Josh that they inform Hess at once of what Josh had learned from Viola Brown. The sheriff had been a pain in the ass ever since he learned that Josh had remained in Seneca Falls to work on the Dunning case for the *Ledger*. Carl hoped that sharing this latest finding might appease him. Hess wasn't acting appeased.

"Glossolalia," Carl replied. "One Corinthians 14:2: 'For he that speaketh in an unknown tongue speaketh not unto men, but unto God.' It's controversial in most major denominations, but to the charismatic believer it's a gift of the Holy Spirit. As to sin eating—certainly you've heard of it."

"Sure I've heard of it," Hess replied. "And it's a bunch of hokum."

"Maybe," Carl concurred. "But sin eating is a long-rumored phenomenon in Appalachia. Some sociologists believe it springs from an ancient rite of savage tribes that slaughtered an animal on a dead member's grave in the belief that it would take on the sins of the deceased. Granted, I've never known of a verified case in West Virginia, but I don't think we can dismiss Viola's story out of hand."

"Bullshit!" Hess protested.

Carl was exasperated. "Oh, for God's sake, Russ, quit belly-aching for once and help us think this thing through. And turn off that damned coffeepot!"

Hess stiffened, started to respond, but didn't. He got up and switched off the offensive pot.

Josh was surprised at the authority in the old editor's tone. When Hess returned to his chair, Carl said, "For my part, I think Viola's revelation explains a lot of things."

"Such as?" Hess demanded.

"Such as why Stewart was found laid out the way he was."

"It also explains Dub's fingerprints," Josh added. "When he found Stewart dead he did the only thing he knew to do. He carried the body to the kitchen—he was strong enough. He recreated the setting he'd seen Brother Dowell's flock use, and gave Stewart posthumous absolution. Viola confirmed that the kitchen cabinet where Dub's prints were found is where the bread or the salt is kept. That should be easy to check out."

"And it *will* check out," Carl submitted. "Which puts every-one back to square one in the search for Stewart's killer."

Hess leaned forward. "Explains this! Explains that! What're you two using for brains—pea soup? So Oliver lays Stewart out on a table and leaves his prints all over the place. Haven't you guys ever heard of establishing an alibi? All he had to do was say, 'Hey, fellows, I was eating Stewart's sins.' Pretty convenient, huh? Well, you guys can swallow that hillbilly voodoo if you want, but it doesn't cut any mustard with me. Dub Oliver *was* and *is* the number one suspect in Stewart's murder. That's how I see it, that's how the FBI lab sees it, and that's how the state police see it. And until something a hell of a lot more convincing than what I've heard here tonight comes along to change my mind, that's how it is."

"And just what was Dub's motive, Russ?" Carl asked.

"Who knows? Fit of rage? Rubout for a few trinkets? I don't see him as a saint, like you guys obviously do."

Carl shook his head. "Russ, you're giving Dub more credit

than he deserves. He could never have devised such a plan. Never. What about the computer erasure?"

"*Stewart* was working at the computer, damn it. So, Dub didn't turn it off. Maybe he didn't know how. But there was one hell of a storm that weekend, remember? You ever hear of computer crash? A stroke of lightning, a power surge—they tell me that's all it takes. Surely your star reporter here can set you straight on that."

Carl waited for Josh to respond. Josh said nothing.

Hess splayed his hands on his desk with a show of impatience. "I don't think there's anything else to discuss," he said, and stood.

It was obviously a dismissal. Carl and Josh rose. "We'll keep in touch," Carl said.

"Yeah. Do that," Hess replied.

Back at the car, Carl gave Josh a puzzled look. "Did you actually buy Russ's computer theory?"

Josh started the engine and pulled out onto Virginia Avenue. "You want to go home or back to your office?"

"Home. I've had enough for today. Answer my question."

"You know as well as I do that when a computer crashes you lose whatever document you're working on at the time. You seldom lose what's stored in internal files. Besides that, the computer in Stewart's office was plugged into a high-quality surge protector. I checked. Nothing less that a direct lightning hit could have caused it to crash, and there's no evidence of that. That computer was deliberately erased by someone who knew what he was doing. And he made doubly sure there were no files left by taking the backup disks, too."

"Then why didn't you call Russ's hand back there instead of letting me sit there like an idiot?"

Josh laughed. "Sorry about that. Obviously, Hess is hostile to our ideas. For the time being, I think it's best to let him believe what he wants to believe."

After a moment, Carl said, "Josh, there's something I haven't told you."

"Oh?"

"That night Dawes came to give me a shellacking, I kept the pistol he dropped. I put it in the file cabinet in the equipment room. Yesterday, when we got back from Mount Canaan, I checked to see if it was still there. It wasn't. That's the room where Dub sleeps sometimes."

Josh thought a moment. "What caliber was it?"

"Twenty-two. Smith and Wesson, short barrel."

"Loaded?"

"I had removed the bullets. They're missing too."

"Have you told Russ about this?"

"Not yet," Carl admitted.

"Then that makes two of us that are playing games with our good sheriff. Can you continue to sit on it for a while? Until we sort some of this stuff out."

"I guess so. For a while. Speaking of sorting out stuff, have you ever figured out what it was about Stewart's office that's driving you nuts?"

"I think so. Remember I told you about Stewart's robe being on backward. Stewart wouldn't have put it on that way. I believe Dub did it."

"Dub? But that means . . ."

"Yeah," Josh said. "It means Stewart was naked when he was killed."

Seventeen

Rachel Bond climbed the long stairway to the second floor of Marron Hall, walked down the corridor past the empty classrooms, and placed the key into the lock of an office door. It wouldn't open. She looked at her watch: 7:44 a.m. The department secretary . . . what was her name? . . . Petri. Yes, Mrs. Petri should be arriving in a few minutes. Rachel sat in one of the chrome and plastic chairs in the hallway, placed her backpack on the floor beside her, and waited.

After ten minutes the self-service elevator at the end of the hall whined to a start. Moments later the door to the cage opened, and the department secretary stepped out. She was a frumpish, heavyset woman with a sluggish gait. She hadn't climbed the stairway to the upper floor since the doctor who kept insisting that she get exercise had dropped dead of a heart attack while jogging around the campus. Spotting the blue-jeans-clad woman seated at the end of the hallway, she wondered why a student would be here this early on a Monday morning.

"May I help you, Miss?"

Rachel stood. "Mrs. Petri, I'm Rachel Bond, Professor Marshe's stepdaughter."

"Oh, Miss Bond, yes," Mrs. Petri acknowledged. "I've heard the professor speak of you. I'm surprised to see you. I'm so sorry about your stepfather . . . so well liked . . . horrible tragedy, just horrible . . . why would anyone . . . did you just get in from Nevada?"

"Arizona," Rachel said. "No. I've been home for a while, helping with Mother. Mrs. Petri, I tried to get into the professor's office. The key doesn't work."

"Well, yes, FBI agents have been here all hours of the day and night since . . . it happened. It's a federal case, you know . . . letter bomb and all. Crudely made. Amateurish is how the agent described it. They're questioning all of the professor's students, past and present, especially those he graded low."

"Yes. I can see why. The key, Mrs. Petri?"

"They didn't release the office back to us until late last evening. Dean Stoval thought it best to change the lock."

"I'd like to get in."

Mrs. Petri made a clucking noise with her tongue. "I'm not sure that would be wise, my dear. Not at all. It hasn't been cleaned yet, you see. Perhaps I can hurry them up and you can come back tomorrow."

"No. You see, he kept his personal files here," Rachel lied. "The funeral director demands to see the insurance papers before . . . Well, I can't wait until tomorrow."

"Oh, my. Yes, I *do* understand." She gave the situation thought. "Very well, come with me, dear."

Mrs. Petri led the way to her own office. Inside, she worked with the combination lock on the heavy file cabinet behind her desk and pulled open the top drawer. She took out a key and handed it to Rachel. "Perhaps I should go with you."

"No . . . no, thank you. I'll be all right. It might take a while. I'll just gather some of his personal stuff while I'm here."

"Well, if you say so. Just remember to return the key to me before you leave."

"Yes. Thanks, Mrs. Petri."

Rachel walked down the hall, unlocked the door, stepped into the office, and froze. What the bomb had not destroyed, the investigators had. Desk, bookcases, and the computer on which the professor stored lesson plans—all were beyond salvage. But that wasn't what shocked her. What shocked her were the walls, ceiling, and floor splattered with dried blood and bits of leathery skin particles. It was all that remained of a human being, she reflected, except for the mangled corpse that was being reduced to ashes and bone fragments in the Garden of Peace Crematorium at this very moment. God, how could he have survived the horrible mutilation to his body for as long as he had? But he had hung on, in and out of a coma, suspended in a twilight zone between life and death. And during one final moment of lucidity he had whispered to her.

She pulled from her pocket the Kleenex box fragment on which she had written his barely decipherable, broken words: "Geomorph . . . ology . . . Earth Sci . . . ence . . ."

Now, she rifled the desk drawers, carefully scanning every folder, every scrap of paper. She did the same to the file cabinets and the miscellaneous magazines piled on an end table near the couch. Nothing.

With a frown, she turned to the bookcase that took up one entire wall. It was a mess. Some volumes lay blown apart on the shelves. Others were scattered around the floor. She searched each shelf in turn. Dropping to her knees, she culled through those on the floor.

"Damn!"

Frustrated, she stood and yanked the remaining books from the shelves and flung them to the floor. When all were down, she kicked among them, sending some flying across the room. She was about to admit defeat when a large tome she had kicked against the door caught her eye. She picked it up. *Geomorphology of Earth Science.* Certainly a publication few persons outside the profession would take from the shelf. Her pulse quickening, she turned to the inside back cover. Taped inside, where it couldn't have been seen when the book was shelved, was a thin plastic computer disk. Or, she noted with sinking spirits, what remained of one. Rock fragments that had once been part of a collection of exotic stones on Professor Marshe's desk had been propelled like shrapnel through the book's binding, destroying the disk.

She shoved the shattered disk into her backpack. Then she remembered something Professor Marshe had once told her. Something about a newspaper editor in Seneca Falls—a man who knew everything about everyone in the county. What was the editor's name? She wished she'd written it down. Well, there couldn't be too many newspapers in a small town like that. Her watch said 8:22. She could be there by noon.

She stood and gathered a few of the professor's personal items, shoved them into the backpack with the demolished disk, and left.

Eighteen

Viola Brown dumped the box of odds and ends she had gathered in Dub's bedroom onto the bed so she could sift through them one by one. She clucked her tongue at the sight. What compulsion drove that good-hearted man to collect such useless rubbish? There were a pair of pliers so rusted the jaws wouldn't open, a metal beer-can opener, a length of nylon string with a broken fishing lure still attached, two dirty soda pop bottles, matchbook covers, outdated coupons from cereal boxes, and much more.

In winter, when Dub roomed here, this clearing out had been a weekly ritual. Each time she cleaned his room she would discard most of the junk he had collected over the past week. In the beginning, she had placed it all on the back porch for him to look through, just in case there was anything he really wanted. However, he never paid it any attention, so she simply started throwing it away. If he cared, he never mentioned it. It was clear that his joy was in collecting, not keeping.

Today the cleaning chore had another purpose. Although Dub had moved back to his cabin in May, he still came by from time to time to change clothes or to pick up the key to Twin Oaks, or sometimes just to get a good meal. Occasionally, he would spend the night. He hadn't done that for a while. Still, she knew that

Joshua had been right in suggesting that because Dub had returned the key to the manor to her every evening that fatal weekend, she must have seen him soon after he had performed the copycat ritual of absolution over Stewart's body. Now she was looking for the small plastic case Joshua had wondered about, whatever it might be.

As was her custom, she had probed every nook and cranny in the room, searching under the bed, behind the dresser, on all the closet shelves, and in the pockets of all his clothing. She even felt around inside his shoes. Nothing. Except the usual garbage. *His* usual garbage. This stinking . . . irritating . . . useless damned garbage!

"Oh, Dub . . . Dub," she moaned, feeling hot tears on her cheeks, "what has happened to you?"

With a bitter flourish, she shoved all the stuff back into the box.

For a long while she sat there looking around the room. It was hard to believe he might not be moving back in here this winter, or any winter ever again. Would they ever again spend long evenings beside the fireplace with Dub listening with childlike fascination while she read and reread his beloved biblical passages? Would he ever again bring a magazine to her and ask her to explain what this or that photograph meant? And what real joy would there be now in spending a day in the kitchen making chicken and dumplings or ham hocks and lima beans or fried corn bread or chocolate steam cake, unless Dub was there to make it all worthwhile? Would she have to get rid of everything? The clothing? The old magazines? The cutout pictures taped to the wall? The wooden crosses he had carved? The pain of such thoughts became unbearable.

Viola rose and pushed the box to the foot of the bed. She would take care of it later. She went to the door and started to turn off the light when something caught her eye—a strange shadow on the wall. It had not been there before. Curious, she turned and looked around the room again. Nothing she saw could be causing it. Then she glanced up, and spotted it. She could make out the outline of a small object inside the frosted ceiling light fixture.

She went to the kitchen for the stool with the fold-out ladder attachment. Back in Dub's room, she balanced herself carefully on a rung of the ladder, unscrewed the frosted glass, and lowered it gently. Resting inside the hollow of the glass was an ornate ring.

She stepped down from the ladder, sat on the side of the bed, and studied the find. The finely etched silver setting was mounted with a lustrous turquoise stone a quarter inch wide and nearly twice as long. Something was terribly wrong. Dub had never taken anything of real value before. And he had taken unusual steps to hide this ring. Why?

Then another thought hit her. She had changed the bulb in this room recently. When? She tried to remember. Yes, it was the day she called Dub to get himself up to Twin Oaks to mow the lawn. The weekend Stewart was murdered! And a week later, Dub was missing. That meant he had to have hidden the ring in the light fixture one evening when he came by to return the key that fatal weekend. Almost surely he had taken it from the manor. An icy tremor shot through her. What did it all mean? It was too confusing to try to figure out.

Viola wondered what to do next. Go to Sheriff Hess? That might be the lawful thing to do, but it didn't appeal to her. She had never been comfortable around the sheriff. Mr. Carl? She trusted him completely. Or, perhaps, Joshua? She looked at the ring again. It wasn't what Joshua had asked her to look for. It might mean something to him, or it might not. Still, for some reason she couldn't explain, he was the one she felt closest to these bewildering days.

She made her decision. She would take the ring to Joshua.

Nineteen

The fat man loosened his tie another inch, then yanked a paper napkin out of the dispenser and mopped the perspiration that poured down his face. His seersucker suit jacket was soaked through at the armpits. "Five thirty in the damned morning, and already I'm sweatin' like a stuck pig," he griped. He grabbed a fly-specked menu from between the sugar bowl and the napkin dispenser and read the hand-printed note, "Trucker's Special," clipped on the front. "White beans and molasses with fried bread?" he exclaimed, his voice like a foghorn. "What the shit kinda chow is that?"

The smaller man seated across from the fat man gave a wary glance around the room. "Keep your voice down, Mike," he admonished. "Manny doesn't want us calling any more attention to ourselves down here than we have to." He blew his breath onto steel-rimmed glasses, wiped them with a handkerchief, slipped them on, and studied the bill of fare for the Mount Hazard Café.

Undaunted, Mike "Fat Man" Santino tossed the hand-printed breakfast menu onto the sticky Formica table in disgust. "All I want's a couple of cheeseburgers." He made no effort to control his foghorn voice. "Don't these stupid hillbillies know what a god-damn cheeseburger is?"

From a table near the front window, two truck drivers, grimy with coal dust, shot sour glances at the boisterous fat man.

Joe Bartelli put the steelrims back into his pocket, leaned across the table, and fixed the fat man with a cold stare. "Mike, I'm not asking now—I'm telling. Zip your lip or I'll personally see to it that your stay on this mountain is permanent. You get my drift?"

Santino blanched. He knew from long association with Joe Bartelli that the little man didn't make idle threats.

"Hey, Joe, sure," Santino responded in softer tones. "Keep your shirt on, okay? I guess I'm just wired, that's all. I been drivin' all night, I'm tired, I'm starvin'. What's worse, I can't get this shit with Tommy outta my mind. Busted outta four schools in six months. It's drivin' Madge and me up the walls. What the hell is it with kids these days, huh?"

"Little Joe" Bartelli made no comment. Bellyaching about his punk kid was broken record with Santino these days and Bartelli was getting sick of it. He thanked God that he had never gotten hooked up with any broad for keeps.

Santino gave a quick glance around the room. Lowering his voice even more, he said, "Another thing, what's with Manny makin' us haul ass down to this God-forsaken hole to do a job that any button man who's made his bones could do? What's his point?"

"He sent us because this is not—" Bartelli sat up abruptly. "Put a lid on it. Here comes the waitress."

The woman in the soiled apron assured them that the café did, indeed, serve cheeseburgers at this time of the morning. "Lotsa truckers work all night. This is suppertime for them."

Bartelli smiled his thanks. He ordered black coffee, a single slice of whole wheat toast, and jelly. Santino ordered two cheese-burgers with fries and iced tea.

"Sweetened or unsweetened?" the girl asked, shoving her pencil back behind her ear. It was a common question in Appalachia, where most restaurants routinely sweetened tea unless asked not to.

Santino gave her a dumb look.

"You want sugar in your tea?" Bartelli said, knowing it was a superfluous question.

"Shit yes," Santino exclaimed.

The girl frowned and went to fill the order.

The Mount Hazard Café was a lonesome truck stop situated at a cinder-paved pulloff midway between Munroe Mining Corporation's Mount Hazard strip pits and the Potomac Light and Power Company's massive tristate generating plant twenty-three miles away. Truckers who shuttled thousands of tons of coal around-the-clock from the mines to the power plant's insatiable furnaces often stopped for coffee, a quick snack, or a few minutes of rest from the monotonous drudgery of their jobs. On this predawn morning, Joe Bartelli and Mike Santino were seated at a remote corner table Bartelli had selected on entering. The truckers by the window were the only other patrons in the café. In this relative seclusion, Bartelli explained things to Santino again. Lately the fat man required repeated explanations. That worried Bartelli.

After the waitress left, he said, "Now get it straight in your head, Mike. This is *not* a button job. Manny wants us to put the fear of God in this guy, mess him up a bit if necessary, but just enough to scare him back out West where he came from. No rods, no shivs. Understand?"

"Why so goddamned finicky? Manny goin' soft or somethin'?"

Bartelli shot the fat man an acid look. "Manny Marconi sweats more brains through his hatband every day than you'll have in a lifetime. The guy we're looking for is a celebrity. He writes books. He's won the Pulitzer Prize. We waste him, and these hills would be crawling with nosey reporters from all over the country. Remember the Bolles hit in Arizona? Manny doesn't want that kind of publicity down here. That make sense?"

Santino shrugged. "If you say so. How we gonna recognize this guy?"

Bartelli pulled a piece of slick paper from his pocket and unfolded it on the table. It was a cover from *Newsweek* magazine. "This is the guy. He's operating out of Seneca Falls. Has an aunt there who runs a hardware store. Manny says he's driving a Corvette, red, with an Avis emblem on the rear bumper. There's not a hell of a lot of Corvettes in this nowhere neck of the woods. We should be able to spot him, no problem." He refolded the *Newsweek* cover and put it back in his pocket. "Any questions?"

"Nah," Santino replied. "I'll just follow your lead, Joe."

"Yeah. You do that, Mike."

Their order came. Santino finished off both his burgers and all the fries by the time Bartelli ate his slice of toast. The fat man gave a belch, reached into his pocket, and fished out a pill case. He downed a couple of brown capsules with a gulp of tea.

"What's that you're taking?" Bartelli asked, concerned.

Santino looked at the label. "Something Madge picked up. Helps me control my appetite."

Bartelli chuckled. He put a moderate tip on the table paid the bill at the register, and then left with Santino.

The sun was just rising above the tree line when they walked out into the parking lot to their black Oldsmobile sedan. They started to get into the car when a gruff voice called out, "Hey, fat man!"

On the driver's side, Santino looked around. The two truckers from the café were approaching him menacingly. The burlier one was carrying a tire iron. "Yeah, you . . . you tub of lard," the man said. "Got a burr up your ass for 'stupid hillbillies,' huh? Let's see how loud you can bad-mouth without any teeth."

The man swung the tire iron in a savage arc toward Santino's head. With a sudden ferocity that belied his girth, Santino caught the trucker's arm in midswing and gave it a violent twist. There was an audible snap. The trucker screamed and fell to his knees, his arm dangling at his side. Santino grabbed the second trucker, slammed him backward against the hood of the Olds, and rammed the barrel of a snub-nose .38 revolver a full inch up the man's nostril.

"How 'bout you, Turdface," Santino said. "You wanta play tough guy too?"

The man's nose gushed blood, and his coal-grimy face was streaked with tears of pain. Santino rammed the gun again. "I asked you a question, goddamn it!"

The hapless man slowly moved his head from side to side.

Santino didn't move. Bartelli grabbed the fat man's arm. "That's enough, Mike."

Santino gave the gun a twist. "I oughta spread this cocksucker's brains all over this hill."

"I said, *enough!*" Bartelli commanded.

Santino withdrew the revolver roughly. He yanked out the trucker's shirttail, cleaned the gun on it, and then shoved the weapon back in his shoulder holster.

The man grabbed his nose and bent forward, sobbing. Bartelli shook him by the shoulder. "Now listen carefully. You hearing me!?"

The man nodded.

"You and your friend got hurt working on your truck, understand? One word of what happened here gets out to anyone, and the fat man here is coming back for you. That happens, and you're history. You get my drift?"

"Ye . . . yes . . . yes sir!"

Bartelli shoved the man away from him.

"Let's get the hell out of here, Mike."

They sped away, kicking up a shower of flying cinders. Behind the wheel, Santino looked exhilarated. Bartelli sat looking glumly out the window. If the incident at the café queered things, Manny would have their heads on a platter. And it was all Mike's fault. The fat man was becoming unpredictable, almost uncontrollable. Something would have to be done about that. Soon.

Twenty

The Hunter's Grill at the Fox and Ox Camp was secluded in a deep-wooded cove on the west bank of the Potomac, ten miles upriver from Seneca Falls. Despite its rustic ambience, the popular eatery attracted patrons from three states for evening dining. The luncheon crowd was sparse. At twenty minutes past two, Joshua Chacón sat alone at a round oak table on the grill's elevated redwood patio that overlooked the river's "shoot the rapids," zipping along on the boiling waters within twenty feet of where Josh sat. But on this sweltering afternoon he was not watching the boaters. He was concentrating on the patrons who walked through the circular bar on their way to the patio. A moisture-conditioned breeze rising from the water, plus a broad canopy of giant elms, made the open dining area the coolest section of the old restaurant.

Josh had been surprised to find Coors beer on the wine list and had ordered a bottle to enjoy while waiting. He had just poured the last of it into his glass when a slender young woman dressed in casual western garb came through the double doors, paused, and looked around. Spotting him, she made for his table.

He sized her up as she crossed the patio. With a little care she could be quite pretty. Her rich auburn hair, brushed back into a pony tail, was held in place by a leather barrette secured with a wooden peg. Her stone-washed jeans were cuffed over rawhide boots. She wore a white short-sleeve blouse with pearl snap buttons on the front and at both pockets. A thin copper bracelet encircled her left wrist. She wore no other jewelry. All told, she would have been more in place among the ancient adobe compounds in Santa Fe or Taos than in the Potomac Highlands of West Virginia.

He rose when she reached the table. "Miss Bond?"

She extended her hand. "Please call me Rachel, Mr. Chacón."

He took the proffered hand. "And I'm Josh."

This close he could see the lines of strain that marred her face. Otherwise a warm, friendly face, he thought. He judged her to be in her midtwenties, twenty-seven at most. "I'm sorry about your stepfather, Rachel. Carl Travis told me what happened."

He held a chair for her.

"Thank you," she said, and sat down. "I recognized you from your photo on your book jackets." She smiled. "Even without the suit."

He laughed. He was wearing jeans and a short-sleeve blue knit polo shirt opened wide at the collar. "Plague of the nonfiction writer," he said. "Our publishers expect us to appear more dignified than the mere storytellers."

She joined in the laugh. "I had no idea you were from around here until Mr. Travis told me. That's a plus for the natives. I just finished *Cargo of Shame*. It made my blood boil, just as it was supposed to do."

In spite of himself, he was flattered. It was the first time since he had arrived in Seneca Falls that anyone had mentioned actually reading one of his books. He thanked her warmly. "It's always a pleasure to meet a reader."

"Oh, I'm more than that. I'm a fan. I used *Evil Witness* for a text in my classes. What are you working on now?"

"Oh, I've got a couple of works in progress," he lied, unwilling to spoil the illusion by admitting he had no idea what to do next. He deflected the conversation. "You're a teacher?"

"*Was*. Adjunct professor in English lit. at the University of Arizona . . . three semesters. It didn't last."

He wanted to ask why it didn't last, but decided against it.

"Can I order you something? I'm afraid I ate earlier. I wasn't expecting a late luncheon date."

She smiled. "I'm really not hungry, but is that actually a Coors?"

"None other. Would you like one?"

She said yes, and he ordered two more bottles.

A sudden "YAH-H-H-H!" caused him to turn toward the river. A kayaker, oar held defiantly over his head, was shooting the rapids, negotiating the dangerous shoals with whoops and body movements.

"Crazy nut!" Josh exclaimed. "Those are class four waters, at least." He turned back to see Rachel staring at him with ardent curiosity.

She reddened and lowered her eyes. "Are you a white-water enthusiast?" she asked, making hurried conversation.

"Oh no. I've floated the San Juan in Utah a couple of times. Pretty tame compared to this."

The beer arrived and he poured for her. "Carl suggested that I meet you here rather than in town. I take it he explained our relationship."

"Yes. He's quite thrilled to have a Pulitzer Prize–winning writer on his staff."

"Oh, well, the pay is right," Josh said, and it brought another laugh from her. He was glad, even though it was clear that laughter was coming hard to her.

She moistened dry lips with her tongue and glanced apprehensively around the patio.

Understanding, Josh nodded toward the cascading water. "I think that will mute our conversation."

She nodded. "Did Mr. Travis tell you why he wanted us to meet?"

"You're trying to find out who killed your stepfather; I'm trying to find out who killed my brother. Carl says there was a connection between them."

"There was."

"And you believe it may have had something to do with their murders?"

She took a drink of her beer and cupped her hands around the cold glass. "I don't know much. Just what Raymond told me."

"Raymond? Professor Marshe?"

"Yes. You'll have to take my word for it, I'm afraid."

"Fair enough."

"He was . . . well, wary of me at first. We'd never met, you know. But he sensed that I was on a guilt trip."

"Guilt trip?" Josh said.

"I'd been away from home for years—since I was fifteen. We lived in Golden, just outside Denver. After my father died my mother and I . . . well, we didn't see eye to eye. I moved to Phoenix. I had enough sense to stay in school; I waited tables to work my way through college. When my mother remarried, she made overtures . . . but I just didn't care to get it started again. I didn't know she was so desperately ill." She gave Josh a plaintive look. "Truly I didn't. When I heard about it I caught the next plane here. But she was beyond recognizing anyone by then. That hurts . . . a lot."

"I understand," Josh said.

"Thank you."

She grew silent. He let her have the time. After a moment she leaned back, seemingly more at ease now with her story. "Raymond and I finally established a rapport. I think he felt sorry for me, the prodigal daughter and all. One night—it had been particularly hard on him at the hospital that day—he came to my room and asked if he could confide in me. He said there was something I should know. Looking back at that night, I've often wondered if he had a premonition that something was going to happen to him. Anyway, that's when he told me about Senator Dunning.

"Raymond gave up a good job with the University of Colorado to take a teaching job at West Virginia University. He was well established in Denver, in line for chairman of the geology department. He tossed all that away. Took a huge cut in salary to move."

"Why?"

"For no good reason that I ever knew. Mom was always agreeable, whatever he wanted . . . you know. Anyway, soon after he got to Morgantown he began moonlighting as a surveyor. Nothing steady. No contracts. Freelancing, I guess you'd call it."

"What was he surveying for?"

"Coal. He traveled all over the state, plotting sites and taking core samples. He used a university rig, truck mounted for mobility. He took the samples back to the geology lab at the university to analyze.

"About six months ago, he got a state contract that called for him to concentrate on Seneca County. He was to report any serious leaching problem, hazardous waste—that sort of thing. Evidently certain legislators in Charleston weren't convinced that the cities shipping their garbage to Seneca County were all that dependable, especially because it wouldn't be rivers in their cities that would catch on fire if things went sour.

"Then, about three months ago, the chairman of the senate committee who hired him—"

"Let me guess," Josh said, beginning to see where this conversation was leading. "Senator Stewart Dunning."

"The same," Rachel confirmed. "Senator Dunning wanted Raymond to take on a confidential job. Raymond objected. He explained that he couldn't afford to take time off from teaching to do more than what the state contract required. The senator offered to double his fee out of his own pocket. He said Raymond could continue to collect the state payment, too, but didn't have to do the work. Raymond was reluctant, but my mother was critically ill. The bills were crushing him. Her medical coverage ran out months before. The hospital was being a real bastard about a couple of overdue payments. He'd already mortgaged the house, cashed in all his life insurance policies, used up all his loan potential at the banks . . ."

"I understand," Josh said.

"Anyway, Raymond finally agreed."

A light breeze from the river lifted a corner of the tablecloth. Rachel brushed it back in place, and gazed out over the waters to the steep woodlands beyond. Josh let her use the silence for a few moments to collect her thoughts, and then prompted her to take up the story. "He finally agreed . . . to what, exactly?"

"I don't know."

"You don't *know*?"

She nodded. "All he told me was that soon after he started working with Dunning, he recognized that he was sitting on a gold mine—a bonanza that could keep my mother in relative comfort for as long as she lived. During his last meeting with the senator, Raymond demanded more money. Dunning was furious. He made threats. Raymond took them seriously. On the drive home that night he made up his mind to stay away from the senator for a while, to give him time to cool down." She looked aside in reflection. "Then, Dunning was murdered. Raymond figured the threat was gone, and relaxed. It was a fatal mistake."

"You mean you believe that Stewart set up his murder?"

"Who else?" she replied, her voice coarse with anger.

"And he never told you what it was he and Stewart were working on?"

"No."

"I don't understand. Why would he tell you all that he had done, and then leave out the most important part?"

"He was trying to justify himself to me. I think he felt that if I knew too much, I'd be in jeopardy too. There's something else. It could be important."

"I'm listening."

She described the professor's final hours in the hospital. "He was fighting desperately to stay alive. I was with him when he died. Sometimes, just before death, a dying person will have a brief period of lucidity."

"Not all that uncommon, I've heard."

"It was difficult for him to speak. He had me lean over him, then he whispered about a book in his office, something hidden there. I found the book and what was hidden in it." She reached into her pocket and withdrew the shattered computer disk. "But I don't think it will be of much use to us."

He took the disk and studied it, frowning. "No, I'm afraid it won't. You have no idea what was on it?"

"No. Only that Raymond said it was important."

"And that's all he said?"

"All except . . . it sounded like 'Pyahga.'"

"Pyahga? What does it mean?"

"I don't know. It's the last thing he said before he died."

Josh pondered the story, trying to mesh these pieces of the puzzle with the other pieces he had collected. "Rachel, at any time during your conversations, did the professor mention anything about Stewart's computer?"

She shot him a questioning look. "Computer?"

"Those times he was at Twin Oaks, did he mention anything

to you about Stewart using his computer, perhaps to print out new instructions for the professor, or whatever?"

"No. I'm afraid I don't understand."

"Stewart's computer was on when they found his body. The authorities believe it was because he was working at it just before he was killed. I have other ideas about it."

"Oh? Such as?"

"I believe that whoever killed Stewart deleted the files on his computer. What you've just told me seems to fit in with that theory. There was something stored there that the killer didn't want found."

Rachel said, "You mean . . . whatever it was that Raymond and the senator were working on?"

"That's exactly what I mean."

Josh's thoughts turned to Dub Oliver. Hess was convinced that Dub had killed Stewart. And, there was the pistol Carl had hidden where Dub could easily have found it. But that was circumstantial, at best. Also, Josh couldn't comprehend Dub erasing Stewart's computer. He *could* comprehend the benign kleptomaniac purloining the backup disks as an afterthought, after finding and removing Stewart's body from the office for the bizarre ritual of absolution. Could it be possible that somewhere in Dub's collection of junk there existed a computer disk that explained Professor Marshe's association with Stewart? Josh had asked Viola to search through Dub's things in her home. Evidently she had found nothing worth reporting. But that wasn't Dub's only cache.

An idea took shape in Josh's mind. "I think I'll take a ride to check something out. Does Carl have your number, just in case?"

"Yes, but I'm not going back home just yet. I have a room in the lodge here. Room fourteen, if you need to call me."

"What about your mother?"

"She's in an irreversible coma. She could go tomorrow or live for months, even years. I call the hospital every day and go back to the house every few days to sort through Raymond's belongings, but right now my priority is to do whatever I can to learn why he was murdered. It's the least I can do for either of them now, or for myself."

"Would you like to ride along with me, then?"

She declined. "I'm going to soak in a scalding tub, then take a nap." She thought a moment. "How about tonight? Dinner, my treat. I'll even wear makeup, if I brought any."

"Now there's an offer I can't refuse. Eightish?" The word had no sooner left his mouth than he wished it hadn't.

"If that means eight o'clock, it's a date."

He smiled at her good nature. "Sorry about that. It's one of the hazards of living in Santa Fe. Shall I pick you up?"

"No. I have Raymond's car. Anyway, why not eat here, unless you know somewhere better?"

"Here is fine."

He pushed his chair back, stood, and left the table. She followed. They stopped at the cashier's desk in the bar, where he paid the bill. Then he escorted her through the lobby and down the connecting corridor to her room. He thanked her for confiding in him. "By the way, don't bother with the makeup. You don't need it."

She smiled at the compliment. "Well, thank you kindly, sir."

He went to the parking lot, revved up the Corvette, and pulled out onto the road toward Mount Canaan. Neither he nor Rachel had noticed the two men who watched them intently from a window table in the bar—one obese and sweating profusely, the other small and wiry and wearing steel-rimmed glasses. The two men followed Josh to the parking lot.

Twenty-one

The old logging road was still muddy from the recent rains. Josh pulled to a stop on the last ridge overlooking the narrow glen and let the engine of the Corvette idle. From this vantage, he had a sweeping view of Dub's cabin and its surroundings. The forest was so thick here that only random shafts of sunlight penetrated the canopy of trees and reached the ground.

Hess claimed that he had searched the valley and hills on all sides of the cabin, and found no signs of Dub or an intruder. Well, Hess or no Hess, there certainly had been an intruder.

Josh thought about the scorched oil lamp with the charred wick still extended in the burn position. Dub had worked all that day at the *Ledger* before hitchhiking back to the cabin late in the afternoon. He had eaten a tin-can supper (the bean juice in the can was still fresh), and was looking by lamplight at the photos in an old issue of *Life* magazine when he was shot. Later, the lamp had burned out from fuel exhaustion. All things considered, whoever ransacked the cabin must have left the lamp burning, and then he tried to burn the cabin. Why? Hess's theory was that the fire was intended to burn Dub. Josh disagreed. More likely it was because the intruder hadn't found what he was searching for, and the fire was an attempt to destroy whatever that was. How could someone have done all that, at night yet, when erasing tracks would have been virtually impossible without leaving a trace of how he entered and left this valley? Even more baffling— what had happened to Dub?

Josh pondered it all for a moment before filing it away to be considered later.

Shifting the Corvette into gear, he drove down the final descent from the ridge and parked in the large yard at the rear of the cabin. He left the car and walked around to where the front bordered the creek. The door was secured with a heavy padlock, and the windows were boarded over. Hess's work, Josh thought. It didn't matter. The intruder had probed every nook and cranny inside the cabin. Odds were that he had been searching for the same thing Josh hoped to find. But because of darkness, or lack of forethought, the intruder hadn't disturbed the throng of trash barrels and crates outside. Well, a kleptomaniac will stash loot in the most unlikely place, and the outside of the cabin offered fertile hiding spots.

He went to the nearest trash barrel, bent down, and started pulling out old bottles, empty cans, pieces of rags, engine parts, hubcaps, tableware, and other junk—some of it eroded by the rust of decades. In thirty minutes he had sifted through less than half the barrel. His arms were grimy all the way up to the sleeves of his polo shirt.

He wiped the sweat from his eyes and straightened up to rest his back. Somewhere in one of the high oaks the bark of a gray squirrel competed with the raucous cry of two blue jays fighting for scraps beneath the tree. He listened to the sounds of the forest for a moment, and then looked around at the score or more of other barrels, crates, and discarded kitchen appliances sitting around the yard. At the rate he was going, he would be here for days. He stepped back, placed his foot on the top of the barrel, and shoved it over onto the ground. Grasping the bottom, he tugged and rolled it around until the remaining contents fell out. He kicked and poked through the pile. It was much faster this way.

"Uh oh," he muttered aloud, staring at one item in the rubbish. He knelt and picked up a pearl-handled .22 revolver. The good Reverend Dawes's pistol, he mused. There were no shells in the cylinder. He sniffed at the muzzle. It hadn't been fired in weeks. Just another bauble for Dub's purloined collection, he concluded. He put the gun aside to return to Carl later.

He searched through a second barrel, and a third, but found nothing resembling a computer disk. He went around to the other side of the cabin where the crates were stacked high against the wall. He was so engrossed in the task that he didn't notice the creatures of the forest suddenly cease their chatter. In the stillness, a large car approached down the dirt lane and pulled to a stop behind the Corvette.

The slam of a car door caught Josh's attention. He stepped around to the rear of the cabin to see two men emerge from a black Oldsmobile sedan and walk toward him. The larger of the two, an obese man dressed in a blue-striped seersucker suit, stared at him with a sinister leer. The smaller man, wearing a tan silk jacket and matching slacks, pulled a sheet of paper from his pocket, adjusted his steel-rimmed glasses, and studied the paper. Josh recognized what the man was looking at—the old *Newsweek* cover bearing his photograph. At once he was filled with a foreboding sense of being in the wrong place at the wrong time.

The little man with the glasses looked from the photo to Josh. "Mr. Joshua Chacón?" he asked.

Josh said nothing. The man had his picture. He knew who he was.

The man smiled and folded the photo and put it back in his pocket. "Mr. Chacón, we have a message for you."

"Oh? From whom?"

The fat man snorted. "From *whom*, yet. How 'bout that, Joe? Manny's sure got this guy pegged, all right. We're talkin' to one of them high and mighty eggheads here."

The man with the steel-rimmed glasses gave the fat man a sharp look. If the fat man noticed, he made no sign of it.

Steelrims turned his attention back to Josh. "Let's just say, from someone who has your best interest at heart. Someone who believes it would be much healthier for you if you would return to Santa Fe. Like today. We have instructions to escort you to Dulles and put you on the first available plane for New Mexico. I will personally guarantee your safety if you come with us now."

Josh glanced toward the cars. He had left the keys in the Corvette, but the Olds was parked snug against its rear bumper. Still, there was a good three yards between the front of the Corvette and the cabin. Plenty of room to maneuver, if he could get to the car.

"All my things are in Seneca Falls," he protested.

"Your aunt can mail them to you."

Whoever they were, they knew a lot about him. Josh gave a sigh of resignation. "Guess I have no choi—"

He made a sudden lurch forward, thrust his hands against the two men's chests, and pushed hard. The small man lost his balance and fell. The fat man took a couple of unsteady steps backward. Josh wheeled and made a dash for the Corvette. He had just reached the door when he felt the fat man's vise-like grip on his shoulder. Who would have thought that tub of lard could move so quickly? Josh struggled to break free. The fat man gave a throaty laugh and pinioned Josh's arms as tightly as if they had been strapped into a straitjacket.

Steelrims rose from the ground, dusted himself casually, and came to where the fat man held Josh immobilized. "I'm sorry you did that, Mr. Chacón. I thought we had an understanding."

Steelrims reached into his back pocket, pulled out a leather glove, and placed it on his right hand. Josh saw the blow coming and turned his head. Steelrims's fist struck him a glancing blow on the temple.

"Damn it, Mike, hold his head."

The fat man pulled Josh's arms tighter behind his back, laced one of his huge arms around them, and grasped Josh's head with his free hand. The next blow caught Josh squarely on his left cheek, splitting it to the bone. A starburst of light exploded in his vision. Addled, he realized that another blow like that would put him out.

Suddenly, the fat man's grip went loose and Josh dropped to the ground. Through blurred eyes he saw the fat man being hurled backward into a stack of crates beside the cabin. The crates came tumbling down, pelting the fat man with bottles, cans, and other rubble.

"Joe!" Fat Man shouted. "Shoot the son of a bitch!"

Josh looked around to see Dub Oliver grab the pickaxe that hung on the cabin wall.

Steelrims's pistol roared.

Dub stumbled to one knee. From that position he swung the pickaxe broadside, striking Steelrims in the chest and stomach.

Without a word, the little man crumpled to the ground like a rag doll and lay there not moving.

Regaining his balance, the fat man pushed the crates off himself, stared at his friend on the ground for a moment, and then focused on the unexpected intruder. "Why you son of a bitch!" He shoved his hand beneath his coat where the butt of a revolver was clearly visible.

Struggling to his feet, Dub twisted the pickaxe a quarter-turn and swung it with all his might. The steel point penetrated the fat man's hand, holster, and shoulder and impaled him to the cabin wall. Flopping like a bloated fish on the end of a harpoon, he screamed through the scarlet froth that spewed from his mouth, while Dub sank to the ground and lay on his back, unmoving.

Six feet away, Steelrims rose to a sitting position, gasping for breath. After a full minute he got to his feet and looked around at the carnage. Mike's screams had subsided into piteous moans. The ground beneath him was saturated with blood.

Grabbing his pistol from the ground, Steelrims stepped over to where Dub lay and put two more bullets into his chest. Then he turned to Josh.

Still dazed from the blows, Josh was sitting on the ground, arms limp at his sides. Steelrims cocked the pistol and aimed it point-blank at Josh's head. "Too bad, Mr. Chacón. I liked your books."

There was a sharp crack of gunfire.

Josh flinched. He instantly realized he would not have been able to flinch, had a bullet entered his brain. He opened his eyes. Steelrims's pistol lay at his feet. Hands drenched with blood, Steelrims clawed at his throat. Slowly, he sank to one knee, then toppled over onto the ground as the dregs of his life pumped out between his fingers.

Twenty-two

A thousand demons pounded anvils in Josh's brain. He leaned his head back against the seat in Hess's patrol car and held the bandage tighter against his face to staunch the blood. He looked toward the sheriff.

Hess had propped his Winchester .270 rifle against the cabin wall and was now on his knees opening Dub's shirt.

"Is he still alive?" Josh managed to call out.

"Barely," Hess called back.

Hess removed gauze compresses from his first-aid kit and taped them over wounds in Dub's chest and neck. Then he stood, pushed some of the fallen crates aside, and approached the side of the cabin where the fat man hung suspended by the pickaxe. He brushed away a swarm of flies that were feeding on froth dripping from the fat man's mouth and placed a finger against his carotid artery. He turned toward the patrol car and shook his head.

Hess frisked the fat man and lifted his wallet. He grabbed the rifle, went to where the little man lay face down in the dirt, and retrieved his wallet too. He tossed both wallets onto the hood of the patrol car, and returned the rifle to the rack beside the driver's seat. "You all right, Chacón?"

"Oh sure. Never felt better."

"Atta boy."

The sheriff's flippant tone irritated Josh. "How long you been watching us?"

"Long enough to see that goon start to blow your brains out. I enjoyed that part."

"You lousy bastard! How'd you know I was here, anyway?"

"Watch your lip, Chacón. I know where you've been every minute since Stewart's funeral. Classy dish you were hitting on, back at the Fox and Ox."

Josh ignored the gibe. "You've been following me?"

"Lucky for you, wouldn't you say?"

There was no rebuttal to that. Josh realized that, due to weird twist of fate, he now owed his life to a man he despised.

"Whose pearl-handle is that on the ground?" Hess asked.

"Carl's. Dub pilfered it. It's not loaded."

"Interesting." Hess looked again toward the weapon.

"I've got to take it back to Carl."

"You won't take it anywhere," Hess replied.

He looked at the driver's license in one of the wallets. "Michael R. Santino." He picked up the other wallet. "Joseph P. Bartelli. Friends of yours, Chacón?"

"I never saw or heard of either one of them before today."

"Why'd they wanta kill you?"

"I don't think they did, not at first anyway. They said it would be unhealthy for me to stick around here, and said they'd been ordered to take me to Dulles and put me on a plane for New Mexico."

"Ordered? Who ordered?"

"Your guess is as good as mine."

Hess replaced the licenses and tossed the wallets into the backseat of the car. "Then you must have pissed off somebody around here real bad. Somebody rich and powerful. Goons like those two don't come cheap. I don't suppose you've got any ideas about that?"

Josh shook his head. The reflex action caused it to throb even worse. He grimaced. "No . . . no idea."

"Uh-huh," Hess said, skeptically. "Well, maybe you *shouldn't* stick around. Next time, I might miss."

From the distance came the undulating wail of a siren. Minutes later, Deputy Sheriff Bob Mares came barreling down the dirt road in his patrol car with all lights flashing. He slid his car to a jarring stop beside Hess's and jumped out with his pistol drawn.

Hess shook his head, disgusted. "Put that damn gun away, Bob. Where's the ambulance?"

Mares holstered the gun sheepishly. "On the way. I brought Doc with me."

An ashen-faced, portly man emerged from the patrol car, pushed his wind-whipped hair out of his eyes, and glared furiously at Mares. Then he went to where Dub lay and checked the fallen man's vital signs. "Not good," Dr. Linton Sites said. "Not good at all." He checked the compresses Hess had applied. "Where the hell is that ambulance?"

"Be here soon," Hess replied.

The physician went to the fat man, then to the little man on the ground. He confirmed what Josh and Hess already knew. Both of the strangers were dead. "It's pretty obvious what killed them."

A second siren signaled the approach of the ambulance Mares had summoned from Davistown. Dr. Sites glanced toward the road. "About time."

He turned his attention to Josh. "You need stitches, son. And antibiotics. He's in no shape to drive, Russ. I'm going to take him back in the ambulance with Dub. I'll send a meat wagon up for those two."

As the ambulance pulled to a stop, Dr. Sites helped Josh out of the patrol car.

"What about my car?" Josh asked.

"I'll have the hearse bring an extra driver," the doctor replied.

"Hey, Doc," Hess said, as he and Mares helped strap Dub to a stretcher. "Tell Travis to get up here with his camera. This is front page stuff for the *News* and the *Post*."

Dr. Sites smiled. "Almost forgot there's an election coming up, Russ."

"I didn't," Sheriff Russell Hess replied.

Carl Travis switched on his desk light and made a closer examination of the turquoise ring Viola Brown had just brought to his office. "Joshua ask me to look for somethin' else, but this the only strange thing I come across," she said. "Dub had it hid up in the light, on the ceiling." She explained that she had changed the bulb on the Friday before the weekend that Stewart Dunning was murdered. "Wasn't there then. Dub had to've put it there that weekend. I tried to find Joshua, but couldn't. So I thought I best bring it to you."

Carl was no connoisseur, but he recognized the lustrous aquamarine gemstone as a fine piece of jewelry. The silver setting was Indian made, surely.

"You think he picked it up at Twin Oaks?" Carl asked.

"Don't know where else. That's the only place he was over that weekend, up there doin' yard work. He musta hid it when he came by to drop off the key. He's always puttin' something in his room, or takin' something out to take up to the cabin with him."

Carl switched off the desk light. "Well, I don't know, Viola. It might be important, or it might not. I know it's not what Josh had in mind."

He handed the ring back to her. "Why don't you just hold on to it, and next time I see him I'll tell him about it. He'll probably want to take a look at it, at least."

She put the ring in her pocket and got up. "Whatever you say, Mr. Carl."

"You need a ride home?"

She rose from the chair. "No thanks. I need the walk. Besides, I gotta pick up some things at the A and P."

"I'll be in touch," Carl promised.

After she left, he sat for a moment wondering where Josh could be. He was eager to know how the meeting with Rachel Bond went.

He picked up the list of ads that had been called in since Monday and carried them to the composition room. Miss Angie was at the computer, typing the classifieds and moving them to the proper category.

"More work," Carl said, dropping the new call-in ads into her in basket.

"That's what pays the bills," she said, cheerfully.

He started to return to his office but stopped short. "Miss Angie, how long have you been doing that?"

She gave him a puzzled look. "Doing what?"

"Taking your ring off like that when you type?"

Miss Angie's high-cluster princess ring, which her Navy-officer brother had bought for her years ago in Hong Kong, was lying on the table beside the keyboard.

"Why, my goodness, Mr. Travis, over thirty years, I guess. I always take off my larger rings when I type."

Well, I'll be a son of a bitch, Carl thought. With a flourish, he lifted her hand and kissed it. "Miss Angie, you're a sweetheart!"

She stared, agape, as he hurried back toward his office. "Now what on earth was that all about?" she asked herself.

At his desk he looked at the phone, wondering where to call. He had to get in touch with Josh right away. If what he suspected was correct, it put a whole new light on things. The Fox and Ox Camp, he thought. That's where Josh and Rachel were to meet. And she had mentioned she was staying at the lodge there. Perhaps she would know where Josh went. He reached for the phone, just as it rang.

He picked it up, hoping it might be Josh. "Travis."

It was Dr. Sites calling to relate the carnage that had taken place at Dub's cabin. "Hess wants you to get up there ASAP with your camera."

To Carl's anxious query, Sites gave assurances that Josh was banged up, but coping well. "Just needs a few stitches and a good night's sleep." Only then did Carl grab his 35-mm Pentax from the shelf beside his desk and run for his Buick.

Twenty-three

Groggy from the sleeping pill Dr. Sites had given him, Josh tried to make out the features of the person who was sitting on the bed and dabbing his face with a washcloth. His cheek was afire. He reached up and grabbed a wrist. "Damn it, that hurts!"

"Don't be such a baby," Rachel said, freeing herself from his grip. "This bandage needs changing."

He blinked several times to bring the room into focus and saw they were alone. "What time is it? What are you doing here, anyway?"

"It's ten after eight. I came to find out why you broke our dinner date last night."

"Last night? You mean I've been out since yesterday?"

"That's right." She yanked a piece of tape from his jaw.

"Agggh! Hey, Doc'll do that later."

"*I'll* do it now," she said, firmly. "Don't worry. I'm a registered nurse."

She lifted the blood-encrusted bandage off his cheek and felt around the sutured wound. "Not bad. You're going to have a scar, but that'll just make you more fascinating."

"You think I'm fascinating?"

"Just hold still."

She cut a long strip of gauze and folded it into a square pad.

"Your aunt had everything we need in her medicine cabinet. She's a sweet lady." She opened a bottle of hydrogen peroxide.

He gave up and lay back and let her tend to him. "What do you mean, nurse? I thought you were a teacher."

"It didn't work out," she said, swabbing his cheek.

"You said that before. Why didn't it work out?"

"I got tired of baby-sitting so many college students who knew nothing about literature and cared less. I could have dealt with that—and perhaps could have taught some of them to care—if they had been capable of constructing a simple English sentence. I had neither the time nor the desire to teach things they should have learned in grade school."

"Not even about us Literary Lions?" he quipped.

She laughed. "You know, I once had a senior whose name was Dorothy Parker. No kidding, that was her real name. The first day of class I mentioned to her that she had a famous name. She gushed, 'Oh, yes, I know.' Later I learned she was in Little Theater on campus and her name was plastered on all the quad billboards. She didn't have the slightest idea who the Dorothy Parker was."

He joined her laughter.

"Anyway, soon after that I quit trying to be Mr. Chips and switched to nursing."

"Back to college?"

"Phoenix General. I already had a degree, so it didn't take long to get my license. That's where I stayed—until I learned about Mother and came back here. I should have done that sooner." She touched his cheek. "Was this because of what I told you?"

"Uh-uh. Those guys were from out of state. Whoever sent them had to set it up days ago. I just met you yesterday."

She taped the bandage in place, letting her hand linger on his face a bit longer than necessary. "I'm glad. I couldn't bear it if you got hurt because of me."

Just then a ray of sunshine fell across the bed, illuminating her face. He reached up and touched her hair. "Do you know that your hair glistens like burnished copper in the sun?"

She smiled. "I hope it—"

There was a rap on the door. "Everybody decent?" a familiar voice called.

Josh shrugged and lay back. "Come on in, Carl."

The editor entered, accompanied by Viola Brown and Aunt Martha.

Martha gave a cluck of her tongue. "Might as well roll your bed out in Main Street, all the traffic you're getting." She saw that the new bandage was in place and picked up the pan holding the discarded one. "You ready for breakfast? I'll bring it up."

"I'm ready, but I'm going down, just as soon as I get some privacy to put on my clothes."

"Then I'll get back to the store," she said. "Holler when you get downstairs."

Breathing hard from the climb up the steps, Viola dropped onto the low couch. Josh turned to her. "How's Dub, Viola?"

"Holding on. One of them bullets tore up his throat. Doc says he may never talk again. Also got an old wound in his temple. Mr. Carl says that's where he was shot that night in his cabin. But Dub always was a hoss, strong inside and out. I say he'll be all right. 'Specially since Miss Rachel's gonna help nurse him."

"Oh?"

"He needs round-the-clock care," Carl explained.

"It's the least I can do," Rachel said. She rose from the bed. "And I better get to it."

"Hey," Josh said. "You still owe me a dinner."

"Sure. Now that I know you didn't ditch me on purpose. You know where to find me." She blew him a kiss, and left.

"Nice lady, that," Carl said. He pulled a chair to the bed. "Hope you feel better than you look."

Josh's face clouded. "Men were killed up there, Carl."

"With good reason, from what I hear."

"Yeah, I guess so. Where the hell did Dub come from anyway?"

"From the looks of his clothes, he'd been hiding in one of those old mine shafts just above his place. Guess he came down to the cabin for food. In the nick of time, I'd say."

"No argument there," Josh agreed.

After a moment, he asked, "Carl, is there a pay phone in town? I need to make a private call."

"What kind of question is that? You know you can use my office in private anytime you want."

Josh shook his head. "I need to call someone whose phone might be tapped. I don't want anyone to be able to trace it to you or to Aunt Martha."

"Most intriguing," Carl said. "Something to do with what happened yesterday?"

"Maybe."

"The most private public phone's down at the park. Northeast corner of the little league field."

"Good. Now, if you guys will let me get dressed . . ."

"In a minute. First, Viola has something to show you. She couldn't find you yesterday so she came to me. Viola."

The hefty black woman retrieved the turquoise ring from her blouse pocket and handed it to Carl. Carl dropped it into Josh's hand. A strange look crossed Josh's face. He shifted to one side and held the stone up to the sunlight streaming through the window. "Where did you get this?"

Viola explained how she found the ring while searching Dub's room. "Like you asked me to do. It was up in the light fixture. He had to've put it there sometime over that weekend Mr. Stewart was killed. Wasn't there when I changed the bulb that Friday."

Carl said, "I didn't give it much thought when Viola first showed it to me. Then something happened that made me think about it a lot."

He told how Miss Angie always removed her rings when typing. "Hell, it's logical, come to think of it. Does that suggest anything to you?"

"Stewart's computer," Josh replied. "Are you saying that's where Dub found this ring?"

"Where else? Given the circumstances, Dub could only have picked it up sometime that weekend. And we know that's the only time he was in Stewart's office."

"This is a woman's ring, Carl."

"Precisely. You always suspected that someone messed with Stewart's computer that night. For the sake of assumption let's say it was a woman, maybe even someone at Stewart's invitation. For whatever reason, isn't it likely that if she were wearing a ring like that, she would have taken it off while using the keyboard? And then simply forgot it when she left."

"Or when she fled," Josh said.

"Yes . . . maybe when she fled," Carl agreed.

Carl nodded toward the ring. "Looks like the sort of jewelry that comes from out in your part of the country. Navajo, maybe?"

"Zuni," Josh said. "Solid silver mounting, turquoise gemstone. It's genuine reservation pawn. Not cheap."

He spoke with authority, and a curious tone of lament.

Carl caught it right off. "What are you trying to tell us, Josh?"

"Huh? Oh, nothing really. It's just that I've seen rings like this before. Up around Gallup. Sometimes at the Indian Village at the state fair in Albuquerque. They're pretty rare, mostly collector's items these days."

He looked over at Viola. "Thanks, Viola. It might be important or might not. I'll let you know. Now, both of you, get out of here and let me get dressed, okay? I'm hungry. And I want to get over to the park and make a phone call."

Carl stood and helped Viola up off the floor-hugging couch. "I'll be in my office. Come see me later."

"I'll do that."

After they left, Josh sat on the side of the bed twisting the blue-green ring over and over in his hand. He hadn't lied to them. He *had* seen rings like this before. But he wasn't ready to tell them that he had seen this particular ring one summer night long ago, when he and the lovely blonde girl wearing it had gone skinny-dipping in a flooded mine pit on the back side of her grandfather's estate.

Twenty-four

The outside phone, mounted in a truncated acoustic shell, was far enough removed from other areas of the park to be relatively private. Josh took out the roll of quarters Aunt Martha had sold him from the store's antiquated cash register. His grandfather's cash register, he recalled with an ache, realizing that just as he could not remember his parents, he had never known any of his grandparents.

He opened the roll of quarters and dialed the District of Columbia telephone number that was etched in his memory. At the operator's instruction, he deposited the appropriate number of coins and listened for the ring. He hoped he was calling early enough to catch his man at home. A familiar voice came through the receiver. "Hello."

"Don't say my name," Josh cautioned. "Do you recognize my voice?"

"Yes."

"Is your phone safe?"

"Who knows?"

"How long would it take you to get to one that is?"

"Ten, twelve minutes."

"I need to talk to you. Do you remember the number I gave you?"

"I've got it."

"Good. When I hang up, go to a safe phone and call that number. Use the code name you used before. The woman who answers will tell you how to call me. I'll be waiting. Okay?"

"Okay."

Josh hung up the phone, waited a couple of seconds, and then dialed his number in Santa Fe. Annie Zah answered. He explained the situation and gave the number of the pay phone he was using. He started to hang up, but then thought of something else. "Annie, another favor. You remember Vicki Armijo?"

"The gal who was gonna cook steaks for you. Sure."

"That's her. She's a journalist, damned good one too—"

"I've seen her on the tube."

"Right. After you give the other guy my number here, call Vicki and ask her to run a name check on a Dr. Raymond Marshe. He's . . . he *was* a geology professor at the University of Colorado in Denver, and later at West Virginia University. I'd like to know Marshe's reputation among his colleagues, his competency in his field, that sort of thing. Vicki may be able to get some information from Mel Simmons, the guy I went spelunking with. Will you do that for me?"

"No sweat. Want her to call you?"

"Yes, at Carl Travis's number. If I'm not there, have her give Carl the message."

"Will do."

"Thanks, Annie."

He put the phone back in the cradle and waited.

Slow minutes passed. He was concentrating so hard on his watch that he didn't see the young boy walk up. He just appeared, dressed in a little league baseball uniform. His fielder's glove was tucked under his arm, and he was fingering a quarter in one hand. The boy stared at Josh and the phone, his eyes posing a question. After a moment he said, "Hey, Mister, I gotta call my mom to come pick me up."

Damn! The last thing Josh wanted now was for this phone to be busy. He thought about offering the kid money to wait. But he would probably stand right there, listening to every word.

"Tell you what," Josh said, pulling his money clip from his pocket. "See that red Corvette parked beside that big oak tree over there? I'm afraid I left it unlocked. I'll give you two bucks to guard it while I'm waiting for a phone call. It shouldn't be more than a few minutes. You can sit in it if you like."

The boy went bug-eyed at the sight of the sleek new sports car. "Hey! You got a deal, Mister."

Josh peeled off two ones. The boy grabbed them and made a beeline for the car. Josh returned to waiting.

Two minutes later the phone jangled. Josh picked it up in mid-ring. "Hello."

"*Oye! Compadre! Cómo estás?*"

"Sorry, Ramón. Still don't speak the lingo."

"You said you were going to take a course."

"I never got around to it."

"How sad. Still a coconut—brown on the outside, white on the inside. Hang your head."

Though it was said in good humor, it disturbed Josh. He hadn't called Ramón Torres to bemoan his identity crisis. He made no response.

Torres must have sensed it. "Okay, amigo. I see by the area code that you're just over the hill. What's up?"

"Ramón, when you were with the bureau, did you ever hear of anyone in the rackets called Manny?"

"Manny? Perhaps. I need more than that, though."

"He had a couple of hoods named Mike Santino and Joe Bartelli working for him."

There was a long silence on the line and Josh wondered if the connection had been broken.

"Manny 'The Man' Marconi," Torres said at last. "*Capo mafioso*—Pennsylvania, western New York state, Jersey. *Capo regime* for the Bono family in the Big Apple for twenty years before that. Marconi started his own family when the old man died. Operates out of Philly. Josh, are you mixed up with that bastard?" Torres's concern registered clearly through the phone.

"Looks that way. I didn't know it before yesterday. I need to know more about Marconi. Does he have anything to do with solid-waste-disposal contracts in his area of operations? Is there any known connection between him and a big shot here named Angus Munroe?"

"Angus Munroe? The coal-mine mogul?"

"That's the one. Is there any way you can get that sort of information?"

"I still got friends on both sides of the street. I'll check around. But I gotta warn you, Marconi plays hard ball."

"Tell me about it!" Josh exclaimed, wincing at the throb in his cheek. He looked at his watch. "Look, it's 9:30. I need a half hour to let people here know I'll be gone overnight. I can be there by 1:30 at the latest. Can you get the info by then?"

"I can try. No need for you to make the trip, though. I can call you."

Josh fingered the turquoise ring in his pocket. "No. I have another reason for coming to Washington. I'll see you at 1:30. Usual location. Okay?"

"I'll be there. Adios, amigo."

Two hours later, his stomach queasy from the narrow twisting roads he'd had to negotiate when leaving Seneca Falls, Josh descended the eastern slopes of the Appalachian chain into Virginia and turned onto Interstate 66 toward Washington. Almost anywhere in the Southwest he would have been able to make a 145-mile drive like this in two and a half hours, max. In these eastern mountains, if the weather cooperated, and if there weren't too many coal trucks lumbering along the two-lane Appalachian blacktops, it was a grueling three- to four-hour trip.

As he drove, he thought about the man he was going to meet.

Within five years after graduating magna cum laude from Columbia Law School, Ramón Torres was recognized as a rising star in the Federal Bureau of Investigation. Then, during the final year of J. Edgar Hoover's reign, the special agent in charge of the FBI field office in Miami retired. He strongly recommended Ramón Torres as his replacement. The recommendation was approved all the way up the hierarchy to the director's office. Hoover vetoed it. Although no reason was given, it was widely known that the aging director preferred Anglo candidates as agents-in-charge. Angered by the slight, Torres resigned and went into private law practice.

Years later, when Josh was gathering material for *Evil Witness*, he received an anonymous note in the mail: "If you want the real lowdown on the witness protection program, talk to ex-FBI agent Ramón Torres, now living in Washington, D.C."

Josh and the old FBI agent established a warm rapport from the start. With a promise of anonymity, Torres supplied the fertile material that made the book possible. Even so, although the book garnered critical acclaim, it didn't catch on with the general public until—in a major faux pas—the United States attorney general called a press conference to denounce the book and its author. Overnight, the midlist, slow mover became a national best seller.

Josh chuckled at the memory.

At 1:15 Josh poked along through irritating bumper-to-bumper afternoon traffic crossing the Theodore Roosevelt Memorial Bridge. At Twenty-third Street he exited south. Parking spaces around the Lincoln Memorial were filled. He circled the memorial twice, and then turned off onto Independence Avenue. Near the District of Columbia War Memorial he spotted a space reserved for maintenance vehicles. He pulled into it, fished out the press card Carl had issued him, placed it in conspicuous view on the dash, and walked toward the site where he would meet the FBI agent.

At Constitution Gardens he spotted Torres sitting on a shaded bench near a food vending cart. During their meetings on *Evil Witness,* Josh had objected to this place as being too public. Ramón Torres had laughed. "You don't understand Washington. This is fine." Josh had deferred to the ex-agent's judgment.

Now, he was surprised to see how his friend had aged. Rumpled as ever, Torres was wearing the same sweat-soiled straw hat he had worn when they first met. However, the unruly tufts of hair protruding from beneath the brim were much grayer than before. His bronzed face, more deeply lined now, reminded Josh of the parched countenances of timeless old men who were fixtures in every pueblo in New Mexico.

Torres's wide smile on first sighting Josh faded to a frown. "*Madre de Dios!*" he exclaimed. "What happened to you?"

"Long story," Josh replied. He removed his sunglasses. The left side of his bandaged face was discolored a sickening purple. His eye was swollen almost shut.

"You got no business driving in that condition," Torres admonished.

"I'm okay," Josh lied. In fact his head was throbbing. He fished out a pill case and shook three aspirins and an antibiotic capsule into his hand. He didn't want to take them on an empty stomach. "You hungry . . . want something to drink?"

Torres glanced at the hand-printed menu posted on the front of the nearby vending cart. "Diet Coke," he said.

Josh bought a Coney Island hot dog, a Pepsi, and a Diet Coke and then sat beside Torres. "Your money's still drawing interest," he said in prelude.

"You don't owe me any money," Torres barked. "Case closed!"

When *Evil Witness* hit the best-seller list, Josh started salting away a portion of the royalties in a special account earmarked for Torres in Santa Fe National Bank. Torres had refused to take it.

"It'll be there when you need it," Josh said.

"Humph!"

Josh downed the pills with a swig of Pepsi and started on the hot dog. Between bites, he told Torres about the bloody scene at Dub Oliver's cabin, and the events leading to it, underscoring the possible connection between the murders of Stewart Dunning and Professor Raymond Marshe.

Torres emitted a low whistle between his teeth. "Holy tamale! Ritual sacrifice. Sin eating. Letter bombing. I can see it now. 'The Appalachian Murders' . . . no, 'Murder in Appalachia.' What do you think?"

It was said in jest, but Josh suspected that Torres was serious. Sooner or later, everyone an author knows gets around to telling him what he should really be writing. He said, "I don't know. Maybe."

"You never told me you had a gringo brother. I've been wondering why a guy who has so many pesos in the bank he's trying to give them away would run around the country playing Sam Spade. To avenge blood? Is that it?"

"That's as good an explanation as any, I guess."

"Okay, I can buy that, up to a point." Torres paused. "You know, I can understand how you guys managed to get Santino. Marconi should have put him under years ago. The Fat Man was a real hothead, lost his balance wheel somewhere along the way. That type usually drops his guard once too often. But Bartelli . . ."

He shook his head. "I never figured anyone would take out Little Joe except maybe one of his own. And he got it from a hick county sheriff. You better warn your friend that he's gonna be on Manny's shit list."

"He's not my friend, but I'll warn him, little good that it'll do."

"Bullheaded, huh?"

"From the original mold."

"I know the type," Torres said.

Josh wadded his napkin and tossed it into a waste receptacle near the bench. "What about Marconi? Did you turn up anything?"

"More than I figured I would, considering the time you gave me."

Torres finished the Diet Coke, crushed the can in his hand, and held onto it. "Dope peddling, prostitution, and numbers—Marconi controls it all in his territory. As for this solid-waste business, those are legitimate contracts between Munroe Mining Corporation and the cities involved. But Marconi's got his hooks into that, too—especially in Philly. He has a lot of city pols in his pocket, but his hold on the trash business is through the sanitation union. He's controlled that from day one. Nowadays, most trash is culled for recycling. What's left goes to processing plants where it's dumped down a large chute into a compacting machine the size of a house. It's got a name, but I don't remember it. Anyway, the compactor compresses the stuff and wires it into bales—just like a hay baler does with loose hay.

"Those bales are trucked to the nearest railhead where they're loaded onto boxcars for shipment over the Appalachians to a switching yard in Cumberland, Maryland. Then they're shunted onto a spur line running down to the Munroe operation in Seneca County, West Virginia . . . Mount Something-or-other."

"Mount Hazard."

"Yeah. That's where the bales are off-loaded onto trucks and hauled right down into the belly of those played out strip pits for burial."

Torres paused. Led by a green-coated guide from one of the tour buses parked along Seventeenth Street, a group of Japanese tourists passed near the bench. The old FBI agent waited.

When the tourists had passed, Torres shifted on the bench. "Now, everything I've told you so far is from the sunny side of the street. A guy still active with the bureau owes me, if you know what I mean."

Josh nodded.

"But what I'm going to tell you next is from the shady side," Torres said. "Don't ask me how I got it."

Not once in all their prior collaboration had Josh ever pried into the source of Torres's information. Nonetheless, he said, "I won't."

Torres said, "For the past couple of months, Marconi has been doing some serious head-to-head negotiating with Munroe."

"What kind of negotiating?"

"My man couldn't—or wouldn't—say. I got my ideas. But whatever's going on, you can bet your next royalty statement that it's not on the up-and-up."

"You've got your ideas? What ideas?" Josh asked.

"Marconi runs a disposal racket for all the East Coast families. Toss a few offed stiffs into that compactor, and they become part and parcel of yesterday's milk cartons and tin cans. Then the bales are shipped to a remote disposal pit."

"On Mount Hazard."

"Think about it."

Josh did. "It just doesn't make sense, Ramón. Why would a self-made billionaire like Angus Munroe get down in the sewer with a scumball like Marconi?"

"You got any kids?" Torres asked.

"I'm not married," Josh replied, puzzled at the question.

"That's not what I asked."

"I don't have any kids," Josh said.

"I do," Torres said. "I'm not married either, never have been. But I've got a son. Fine young man, about your age. He's a math teacher at Cornell. He's one of the few things I've done right in this world. A father will do almost anything for his kids."

"Ramón, what in the hell are you trying to say?"

"I'm trying to tell you why Angus Munroe would get down in the sewer with a scumball like Manny Marconi. Munroe's got a son."

"David . . . yes."

"Well, David Munroe has a giant monkey on his back. The guy I talked to said Marconi holds about a quarter million in IOUs from David and a few of his high-flying friends—for the white stuff. Now, you know and I know that no pusher lets go of that much powder on credit, unless there's a reason. David was set up. Marconi let David have fixes for chits. Then he encouraged him to talk his pals into jumping onto the gravy train. David took the bait. And in legalese, my friend, that makes David Munroe a dealer. That fact is Marconi's ace in the hole in dealing with the father."

"Nope, still doesn't fit," Josh replied. "Angus Munroe could buy off a quarter-million-dollars' worth of chits with petty cash. It doesn't ring true."

"Think again, amigo. Marconi doesn't give a damn about the cash. He's not about to let go of those chits. My hunch is that in exchange for access to the remotest pits, he offered not to make a federal case—and I use that term literally—out of David Munroe's drug dealings with his buddies. The old man is trying to keep his only son and heir out of the federal slammer."

It had a feasible ring to it. "That's all he gets out of the deal?" Josh asked. "A security blanket for David?"

"That, and Marconi makes sure Munroe has no union trouble at the mines."

"In West Virginia? He can reach that far?"

"There's no evidence that Marconi controls the mine unions there. Most likely he's got a quid pro quo with whoever does. That's the way those things work."

Josh had suspected that Angus Munroe was implicated one way or another. Now, for reasons he didn't understand, he found himself saddened by Torres's revelations. "Then your theory is that Dunning and Marshe were killed to keep them from exposing the Marconi–Munroe unholy alliance—whatever it is."

"Right or wrong, that's how I see it," Torres replied.

"Then the question is which one had them killed—Angus or Marconi?"

"Hits like that are not exactly Marconi's style. Still, I'd say the killer was whoever feared that Dunning and Marshe were getting close to the truth."

"Or had already found the truth," Josh said.

"Yeah. That too."

Josh thought for a moment. "Whatever they found, I believe evidence of it was stashed in Stewart's office at Twin Oaks where he was killed. Whoever killed him was trying to find it."

"Could be. But you realize it's all conjecture. There's nothing that any prosecutor would take to court."

"I don't give a damn about prosecutors or courts. I just want to know the truth."

Josh let what he had heard soak in for a while. "Was there anything else?"

"That's it. Except for a word of advice." He didn't wait for Josh's approval. "From what you told me about what happened to you on the mountain, I figure Manny Marconi was giving you a chance to get out of all this and go home. If he'd wanted you dead, you wouldn't be here talking to me now. Then your friend Oliver and that sharpshooter sheriff you're not so fond of changed the game plan. Still, it might not be too late for you to get out with no more than that memento you're going to have on your face for the rest of your life. That's my advice. As an old friend, I'm telling you, get out of it. Tell that sheriff what you've learned—just keep my name out of it—and let him do the job the county pays him to do. If he's got any brains at all he'll know who to call on for help."

"I'll think about it," Josh said, knowing he wouldn't. He sensed that Torres knew it too. He stood. "Once again I don't know how to thank you."

Ramón got to his feet and pushed his hat back so he could see Josh better. "How much did you say is in that bank account you got earmarked for me?"

"Forty thousand. More, considering interest. I can get it to you by wire today."

Torres shook his head. "I've got a good pension; my son's doing fine for himself. You familiar with the Boys Ranch in New Mexico?"

"Yes."

"They take throwaway kids—kids whose families can't take care of them—and give them a home and an education. Black, brown, white—no difference to them. How about donating it there? In both our names."

"Consider it done." Josh made a mental note to call his bank just as soon as he got back to Seneca Falls.

"You said you were staying the night. I've got an extra bed."

"Thanks, but I've got to pay a visit to someone else here. What's the best route to Georgetown?"

Torres nodded toward the Lincoln Memorial. "Seventeenth Street north to Twenty-nine West, then follow the signs. You can't miss it."

Josh reached out to shake hands, but to his surprise Torres grasped him by the shoulders and pulled him close. "Take care, my young friend. You're traveling a road that would make angels tremble."

"Maybe," Josh said. "But I've got to see where it leads."

"Then carry a gun. I can get one for you."

Josh shook his head. "I'd just shoot myself in the foot."

"Okay. Then carry a pickaxe."

Josh laughed.

"One last thing, amigo," Torres said. "Don't take my ribbing about you being a coconut too seriously. But remember, the blood of conquistadors flows in your veins. Never be ashamed of it."

"I'll remember that, Ramón." He gave the old FBI agent a warm hug, and left.

At the Corvette, there was a ticket on the windshield, taped right over the spot where the press card was visible on the dash. So much for the power of the media, he thought. He stuffed the ticket in his pocket, got in the car, and headed toward Seventeenth Street.

Twenty-five

Russell Hess initialed his approval of the draft report he had dictated about the deaths of Joseph Bartelli and Michael Santino. He didn't bother reading it. He was confident that Agnes Thompson had expressed his thoughts on paper with far more clarity and impact than he had orally. Earlier, when she first came to work as a shared secretary between his office and the office of the county clerk, he had resented her editorial corrections, and told her so. Subsequently, she typed his correspondence exactly as he dictated it. The contrast was painful. After a few weeks he suggested that perhaps every now and then she might change a word or two where she thought it appropriate. She accepted that as an apology, and thereafter things were fine between them.

He added a note at the bottom of the draft asking Agnes to make extra copies for the upcoming inquest and then tossed the papers into his out basket. He sat for a moment looking at the letter lying on his desk calendar. It had arrived that morning from Colonel Gene Gregory, Commandant of State Police. He picked it up and read the final paragraph again, for the third time since he had opened it:

> For the time being, this office will support
> your theory that Senator Dunning died at the
> hands of Mr. Dub Oliver, motive undetermined.

However, I must emphasize that, considering
the circumstances of Mr. Oliver's disappearance,
significant questions remain regarding his sole
culpability for the act. I strongly advise you to
assign the utmost priority to continuing the
investigation of this matter.

He tossed the letter back on his desk. "Bullshit."

"I strongly advise . . . the utmost priority . . ."

Who the hell did Gregory think he was talking to—one of his detachment corporals who couldn't find his ass with four hands without a field directive from Charleston?

He got up and poured himself a cup of coffee, tasted it, and spit it into the wastebasket, now cursing Mares. The deputy made coffee like he did everything else—half-assed. He rinsed the pot and cleaned the basket with a paper towel. He put two level scoops of fresh grounds in the basket, measured three standard cups of cold water into the pot, put it together, and plugged it in. Then he went back to his desk to wait.

"Assign the utmost priority . . ."

Well, Dub Oliver was no longer missing. Still, according to Doc Sites, it might be days before Oliver was moved from intensive care. Even then he might not be able to speak. There would be no chance to question him any time soon, utmost priority or not.

And who was Gregory trying to kid, anyway? He knew, as well as anyone else in the Potomac Highlands with half a brain, who was behind Dunning's murder. Angus Munroe had paid Dub Oliver to kill Stewart. Then Munroe had taken the extra precaution of trying to silence Dub. But the state police would never make those accusations. They wanted Sheriff Russell Hess to take that fall. Well, hell would freeze over first.

The coffee quit perking and he got up and filled his cup again. He took a sip. Perfect. He took the cup back to his desk and turned his thoughts to the two stiffs up in the hospital morgue. Santino and Bartelli. Had Angus brought them in to do the job on Chacón? Moreover, had the two thugs come in earlier to do a job on Dub? If so, they'd sure made a mess of it. And how had they carried off that botched hit without leaving a tire track or footprint on a road or anywhere else in the valley? He leaned back in his chair to think about that.

And how about Chacón? What did Munroe have against him? Was he pissed after all these years that a greaser had been banging his granddaughter? That was a bit farfetched. Whatever else Angus Munroe was, he was not a bigot. Whatever the reason, Hess thought, it's a damned good thing I got curious when I saw them tailing Chacón from the Fox and Ox Camp that day, or the half-breed Mex would be dead meat now.

As always when he thought about Chacón for long, he felt his blood pressure rise. That little guy—Bartelli—was getting ready to blow Chacón's brains out. Well, why not, considering what had happened to the Santino. He thought about the fat man, pinned to the cabin wall with a pickaxe. He gave an involuntary tremor. What a stinking way to die. Hanging there watching your blood spurt out like a geyser.

If only I'd waited ten more seconds before shooting Bartelli, Chacón would be . . .

He savored the unfinished thought for a moment, and then dismissed it. Unprofessional.

Still, Chacón was a thorn in the side. Carl was responsible for that, giving him that damned press card. Hess had made a strenuous protest of that to the county attorney. All legal, the attorney said, as long as Chacón was officially on Travis's payroll. Well, Carl would get his comeuppance for that little charade someday.

He swiveled around to look at the blown-up map of Seneca County that covered half the back wall between the two windows. He was still studying it when Agnes came in to check his out basket.

"Looking for fishing holes?" she asked.

Hess smiled without turning around. You could always count on Agnes Thompson for an irreverent quip. Somehow it didn't bother him as much as it would have coming from anyone else.

"Agnes, you come from up around Mount Canaan don't you?"

"Yokum's Hollow. Why?"

"Yokum's Hollow," Hess repeated. He stood and stepped closer to the map.

"You won't find it by name." She came around the desk and stretched upward to put a finger on the map. "Here. On Patterson Creek."

Distracted by her heady perfume he looked down at her for a moment. In the clear light of the windows her red hair gleamed like a new penny. With her arm raised, her blouse was pulled revealingly tight. Why hadn't he noticed her figure before? He cleared his throat and looked back at the map. She was pointing to a valley well back from the main highway.

"That's about, what . . . four miles past the turnoff to Dub Oliver's cabin?" Hess asked.

"Just about. He lived in this hollow down here, on Mohawk Creek."

Hess studied the two locations. "Let's say you wanted to get into one of those hollows without leaving a trace of how you did it. What would you do? Hire a hot-air balloon to drop you in?"

She laughed, and lowered her arm. "Hardly. I'd do what Daddy Heckum always did."

She was referring to her father.

Judd Heckum was a legend in Seneca County. For as long as he lived, every year in mid-December he would drive his vintage Ford pickup truck to Gresham Brother's Wholesale Grocers in Cumberland and buy a couple of hundred pounds of hard candy and a case of paper bags. Then, a couple of days before the schools let out for Christmas vacation, he would make the rounds of playgrounds, passing out sacks of candy to the children, some of whom would get no other present. For fifty-five years, generations of Seneca County schoolchildren had stood by the roadside during Christmas week, waiting for the sight of Daddy Heckum's old red pickup truck.

"Oh?" Hess said. "And just what did Daddy Heckum do?"

"Winters can get pretty nasty up on the mountain. Every few years the road into Yokum's Hollow would become impassable. When that happened Daddy Heckum would park his truck just off the main highway, here,"—she pointed to the map—"about two miles from home. He'd pull on his rubber boots and wade up Patterson Creek all the way to the house, and then wade back out next morning. I used to do it myself, to get to the road to catch the school bus. None of those creeks up there are more than a foot deep, at most."

He stared at her, then back at the map as if seeing it for the first time. "Well, I'll be a son of a bitch!"

It startled her. "What did I do?"

He smiled down at her. "What you did, Agnes, is solve a puzzle that's been bugging the hell out of me and everyone else who's been wrestling with it. Damn . . . if you weren't a married woman, I'd kiss you."

She shot him a suggestive look. "Why let that stop you?"

She stood her ground, her eyes locked onto his. He gave a nervous cough and went back to the desk and sat down. "Uh, thanks, Agnes. You've been a great help."

She gave a girlish laugh. "Well, if you ever need anything else, just give me a call."

She went to the door, paused, and turned back to him. "*Anything at all,*" she said, and left.

He stared after her for several seconds. Had he been missing something here? He had always thought that Agnes and George Thompson had as good a marriage as anyone could. Of course, George—head coach of the Seneca Falls Vikings—was gone a lot, traveling with the team to away-from-home games. Hess leaned back in his chair and gazed at the ceiling, wondering what the coach's out-of-town schedule would be this fall. After a moment he shook his head and sat forward. This was distracting. He'd have to think it through later.

He picked up the phone and dialed the *Seneca Falls Ledger*. Carl Travis answered.

"Carl . . . Hess. Get over here. Bring Chacón if you want."

Travis wasn't surprised at the summons. Hess seldom visited the *Ledger*. Whenever he came across something he thought might interest the press, he would beckon Carl to the sheriff's office.

"Josh isn't here, Russ. He's in Washington."

"Washington? Is the bastard hightailing it home already? He's supposed to be here for the inquest Monday."

"No, damn it, he's not hightailing. He's just gone for the night. Now what's so important for me to drop everything and come see you?"

Gone for the night? In Washington? Hess mused. Figures. That's where Beth lives.

"It's about Dub," Hess said. "I'll tell you when you get here."

He hung up, his thoughts now on Joshua Chacón and Beth Munroe Dunning, together in Washington.

And his black funk returned in spades.

Twenty-six

As he drove toward Georgetown, Josh thought about Torres's parting words: "Remember, the blood of conquistadors flows in your veins. Never be ashamed of it."

He had never been ashamed of it, had never resented reminders of his ethnic heritage. Not as a child, when Stewart Dunning berated him as a "greaser"; not now, during this visit to Seneca Falls, when Russell Hess exuded bigotry with every word between them. He owed his fortitude to Aunt Martha. She had instilled in him the strength of character that sustained him through all the intolerance. Still, he knew that Torres had spoken the truth. He was, indeed, a "coconut." Born of an Anglo mother, raised by an Anglo aunt, educated in Anglo schools, he had grown up brown on the outside, white on the inside. Even after he learned his true heritage and moved to the land of his father, where he was surrounded by a rich Hispanic culture, he continued to gravitate toward the Anglo lifestyles that were most familiar to him. In time, he began to experience a sense of detachment, to question who he really was, and where he really belonged. Annie Zah diagnosed it first. "You're a one-man ethnic war zone," she said to him once.

"So what's the cure?" he asked, half seriously.

"Stop eating steak every night at the Bull Ring. Grab a bowl of posole at Garcia's. Move out of that ivory tower in the foothills, and get a place on Canyon Road. Learn the language. Discard those ivory-skinned bimbos and try cinnamon. You might learn something."

"I'll think about it," he said.

It was soon after that exchange with Annie that Vicki Armijo came into his life. She called from Albuquerque asking to tape an interview with him for ¡Colores!, a documentary program highlighting New Mexico culture and personalities. "It will be in English," she said.

"I see you've done your homework," he said.

"Oh, I hope I didn't offend . . ."

He laughed. "Not at all."

They discussed the planned format. Finally, reluctantly, he agreed. He didn't like playing the media game—didn't like being on display. He had suffered through previous interviews, often with reporters who obviously had never read a word he wrote, only by reminding himself that publicity sold books.

Vicki Armijo was to other reporters he'd dealt with as diamonds were to glass. Pretty, vivacious, witty, and articulate, she possessed an unexpected quality that put him at ease. She had no ulterior agenda, and was not waiting to pounce with loaded questions at the first sign of a crack in his armor. Without his asking, she offered him script approval before the cameras rolled. He was grateful.

The taping took three weeks. By the end of the first week they were dating, and by the end of the second, she was staying overnight in his new apartment on Canyon Road instead of returning to her own. Later, neither of them could recall who instigated their intimacy. It was mutual, a shared unfolding of ardor between two people who respected, admired, and enjoyed each other.

She was the first to mention love.

Love? He thought about that. One night, snuggled beside him in bed, she revealed that her feeling for him was more than a passing affair. It confused him. She was one of the few women in his life of late that he was as happy to see in his bed in the morning as he had been the night before. No, that wasn't true. She was the *only* one. All others he shooed out the door as soon after sex as possible, feigning late-night work to be finished, or an early next-day appointment. Not so with Vicki. He held her close until he drifted off to sleep, content that she would still be there come dawn.

Was that love? He couldn't bring himself to voice it. She sensed his ambivalence, and it brought things to a head.

On the afternoon he was packing to attend Stewart's funeral, she revealed that she had been offered a job in Wichita. It had stunned him, and his countenance had given him away. She had wanted to talk then about their relationship.

He'd asked for a continuance: "I'll be gone just a couple of days. Can it wait?"

She had said it could. But her point was made. She may not be in his life much longer.

The implication of their parting conversation was not pleasant. He was still thinking about it when he turned onto the leafy suburban street in Georgetown where Beth Munroe Dunning lived.

Now, another woman took center stage in his thoughts.

Twenty-seven

The red brick town house situated on a corner lot was straight out of a scene from *The Exorcist*. Stately elms lined the front and side. The front rooms abutted the sidewalk. A black wrought iron gate guarded the descending driveway. Josh found a parking space in the next block, stepped out of his car, and started toward the house. Then, remembering he was still in Washington, he went back and locked the Corvette.

He climbed the eight stone steps and reached for the brass knocker on the ornate oak door. Then he spotted the intercom mounted on the wall. He supposed the knocker was for show. When he pushed the intercom call button a muted three-note tone sounded on the other side of the door. Moments later a female voice responded through the speaker, "May I help you?"

The voice was heavy with an accent he couldn't place. "I'd like to see Mrs. Dunning. My name is Joshua Chacón."

"Mrs. Dunning is not available. If you will leave your—"

Just then a voice he would never fail to recognize broke in. "Josh! Is that really you?"

"It's really me, Beth."

"Well for . . . ! Ingrid, please show the gentleman to the sitting room. Josh, I'm drying my hair. Help yourself to the bar. I'll be down in a jiffy."

There was a sound of a latch being thrown. The door swung open to reveal a plump, gray-haired woman wearing a wide-brimmed hat and holding a purse. Obviously, she was about to leave the premises. At the sight of his bandaged face, her eyes narrowed in suspicion, leaving no doubt of her dislike of giving entrance to someone who appeared to have been involved in a street brawl.

"This way, sir," she said coolly.

She led Josh down a richly appointed foyer to a spacious room at the rear of the house, motioned for him to sit, and pushed an intercom button. "Madame . . . perhaps I should stay."

"No," Beth's voice responded though the speaker. "Mr. Chacón is an old friend. Have a good evening, Ingrid."

"Thank you, madame."

The woman turned a rheostat to start a Casablanca fan mounted high in the ceiling. Then, giving Josh a final sober once-over, she nodded curtly and left.

Josh surveyed the room. Sunlight filtering through wide jalousie windows accented the floral patterns of the wicker furniture. The handwoven accent rug on the floor was quintessential Appalachian craftsmanship. Silver-framed photographs adorning the grand piano, the walnut bar, and the walls bore witness to Beth Munroe Dunning's lofty standing in the elite sphere of Washington political society. There was Beth receiving a plaque from George Bush in the Rose Garden; Beth, Barbara Bush, and Nancy Reagan arm in arm beneath a banner proclaiming "Just Say No"; Beth, Jesse Helms, and Ambassador Bruce from the Court of Saint James, resplendent in formal wear; and Beth and Robert Byrd absorbed in conversation, seemingly unaware of the camera. Josh leaned closer to read the caption beneath this last photo: "Senator Robert Byrd and fellow West Virginian, Mrs. Elizabeth Dunning, at the White House reception honoring HRH The Duke of Wales and Princess . . ."

Josh was amused. In all their young life together, he had never heard Beth referred to as "Elizabeth."

He looked around the room for a photograph of a Munroe or a Dunning. Other than those of Beth, there were none.

He felt a tap on his shoulder. He turned and there she was,

that ten-megawatt smile as bewitching as ever. Then the smile faded and she did a double take.

"Josh!" She touched his cheek, gently. "Darling, whatever happened to you? You didn't have that in church last week."

She *had* noticed him.

"I had a run-in with a couple of guys who work for Manny Marconi." He watched for any sign that she recognized the name. If she did, she was a brilliant actress. She responded with a puzzled look. He grasped her hands and stepped back. "I'll tell you all about it later. Right now, let me look at you."

"Oh, I'm a mess," she complained. "I just got out of the shower. There's a reception for President and Mrs. Clinton tonight at the British Embassy."

"Ah, then you hobnob with Democrats too."

She laughed. "Wherever it's at, darling." She made a face. "But if I'd known you were going to be here I'd have passed it up. I do wish you'd given me warning, so I could have prettied up."

As far as he was concerned there was no way could she have improved on what he saw. Her blow-dried blonde tresses, slightly moist around the edges, were still pure gold. She had slipped into white woolen peg-cuffed slacks belted at her narrow waist by a matching belt. A half bra, more suitable for the evening gown he assumed she would wear later that evening, was visible beneath her pink silk blouse. Surely she could still fit into the clothing she wore in high school. He noticed the fluffy pink mules that adorned her feet and realized why she'd been able to slip up on him.

"I don't think your housekeeper approves of me," he said.

"Don't mind Ingrid. She's overprotective. You haven't kissed me yet."

He leaned down to give her a gentle buss. But she threw her arms around his neck and fixed her lips to his in an ardent kiss, and memories of impassioned trysts came flooding back as if they had happened yesterday.

Breathless moments later, she broke off the embrace with a nervous laugh. "Well . . . how about that? Shades of Make Out Point, huh? Hey, you didn't make yourself a drink."

She stepped back and went to the bar. "What can I fix for you?

Surely you don't still drink bourbon and Coke. Yuck!" She laughed at the memory.

"Sometimes. But I'd better not. I'm taking antibiotics, and I've got a long drive back."

"Oh?" Her disappointment showed. "You're not staying?"

"I think not."

She made herself a martini on the rocks, wrapped a napkin around the glass, and sat on the sofa. She patted the pillow next to her, and he sat down. She sipped her drink and fixed her iceberg-blue eyes on him above the glass. "Perhaps I can change your mind," she said. "Did you ever think about this moment, Josh? Wonder what it would be like? Our meeting again?"

It was as if she could see into his mind. He had thought about it for years, had been so obsessed with the memory of her, the scent of her, the taste of her, that it affected everything he did. The ghost of her was always there, night and day, wherever he went. At work. At play. When he ate. When he slept. When he was with other women.

That last thought was unexpected. Annie Zah had chastised him repeatedly for his frivolous run-on affairs and for being unable to make a commitment. Not until this moment did he realize why he was like that. Beth Munroe was always there, always between him and those other women, always the comparison against which all the others paled.

"I've thought about it," he said.

"So have I, Josh . . . so have I." She took a hefty drink from her glass. "You never knew, but I went to Santa Fe once, to find you."

The disclosure took him aback. He started to respond but she stopped him. "Please don't say anything. Let me finish telling it now, or I won't be able to do it at all."

She lowered her eyes. "It was a couple of years after you had left Seneca Falls. Granddad Angus has friends in New Mexico. They were able to trace you. I flew out to Albuquerque, rented a car, and drove up to Santa Fe. I stayed at La Fonda. I sat in that small park—the plaza across from the Palace of the Governors—all that next day, thinking . . . no, *hoping* that you would walk by and we could meet by 'accident.' Of course, you didn't. Next day I drove by your place a dozen times, promising myself each time that I'd stop. But I didn't. I couldn't bring myself to do it. I flew home that night."

"But why didn't you call? I was still in the book then."

"I don't know. I guess I was afraid of how you might react." Her eyes filled with tears, and her face contorted in anger. "That bitch! That lousy bitch!"

"Beth! Who are you talking about?"

She downed the rest of the martini in a gulp, holding the glass so tightly that her fingers were bloodless. "Constance," she said, spitting the word out as if it fouled her mouth to speak it. "My dear, sweet, conniving mother."

She got up and went to the bar and made herself a stronger drink. She returned to the sofa, sitting with her legs crossed in front of her, Buddha style. "We had it all, Josh, you and I, before . . . before she ruined it."

"Ruined it? Connie? How, for God's sake? You just walked out of my life. Cold. Not so much as a by-your-leave."

"She threatened to tell you about . . . about me and my father."

"Your father?"

"I was fourteen . . . he was drunk . . . I didn't know . . ." She took a large gulp of her drink. "It only happened once. He tried again. I told him that if he ever touched me again I'd tell Granddad Angus. It startled him. But he knew I was serious, and he knew Granddad Angus would kill him . . . literally kill him. He never bothered me after that."

Her face betrayed her anguish. "Do you understand now, Josh? Why I could never . . ."

Josh stood and went to the bar. "I believe I *will* have that drink."

He filled a glass half full with bourbon, then added ice without mix. He took it to the sofa and sat down again. "If your mother was going to tell me, she must have known. How could she have tolerated such a thing?"

"She didn't know until much later. We had one of our furious shouting matches one day and I blurted it out, hoping it would hurt her. She was shocked, but she wasn't hurt. I could see the wheels spinning in her brain, and I knew she was filing it away for future use, just as she did everything she saw or heard."

For the first time since she began the confession, she turned to look at him. "And she did use it. Oh, how she used it! She didn't give a damn about our affair in the beginning. She figured you were just another boy that I'd tire of and toss over. I can't blame her. I guess I thought the same, at first. If anyone had told me back then that I'd fall in love with Joshua Collier, I would have laughed in his face. But I did, Josh. Oh God, I did! I fell deeply, passionately in love with you. Constance sensed it, and it was the one thing she couldn't tolerate . . ."

"Because of Stewart Dunning," he said, downing half his drink in one swallow.

"Yes. She didn't care about me, personally. But I was her key to the Dunning fortune. She planned it from the day I was born. Power—that was . . . *is* her god. And a Munroe-Dunning merger would create the most powerful mining cartel in the country. So she decided to use the powerful ammunition I'd given her to get rid of you."

"And you married Stewart."

She produced a humorless chuckle. "Oh yes. I married Stewart."

They lapsed into silence. Josh felt the bourbon working on his brain. He had never been a straight-whiskey man and was beginning to regret this deviation from his usual watered-down version of a highball. He went to the bar and poured what remained of the drink down the drain and filled the glass with plain seltzer. Then he remembered the ring in his pocket, and his purpose in coming here. The thought disgusted him. Swayed by her warm greeting, he had become lost in the past, and had joined her in an emotional flashback when he should have gotten down to business the moment he arrived. Feeling like a fraud, he returned to the couch, sat down, and took out the ring, hoping she wouldn't recognize it. "Beth, I—"

"Where in the world did you find that?!" she exclaimed.

She set her drink on the glass-top coffee table and took the ring from him. She turned it over and over in her hand, gazing at it fondly, as one might gaze upon a lost treasure unexpectedly returned.

His heart sank. "Where did you leave it?"

"Leave it? I didn't leave it anywhere. It was never mine to leave."

"You were wearing it that night at the flooded pit, the night we went swimming."

"And nothing else, as I recall." She shot him a coy smile.

His face remained a sober mask.

Her smile faded. "I think I've missed something. What's going on here, Josh?"

He told her where and how Viola Brown found the ring, and how the circumstances left no doubt that Dub Oliver had picked it up in Stewart's office the weekend Stewart was murdered. He told her a little about the subsequent investigation, without going into detail. He didn't tell her what had happened to Mike Santino or Joe Bartelli, or mention the meeting today with Ramón Torres.

When he finished, she said, "I think I'm getting the picture now. You believe I had something to do with Stewart's death, don't you?"

His silence was answer enough.

"And I thought you came to renew an old acquaintance. Stupid me, huh?"

For a while there was no sound in the room except the whir of the Casablanca fan. Then Beth continued, "Why are you doing this, Josh? What the hell do you care what happened to Stewart? He was never a brother to you. Not when you were kids, not later. When stories about you started appearing in all the newspapers, he wouldn't allow them in his sight. When you made the cover of *Newsweek*, he canceled his subscription. He was obsessed with you. Know why? He told me once. It wasn't because of you and me. He knew about our affair from the beginning, and it meant nothing to him. No, he hated you because the mother that bore both of you deserted him and loved you. He could never come to terms with that. It drove him to rage. He hated you . . . and he envied you."

Envied me? Stewart Dunning? Josh thought back over the years to the contemptuous insults and slurs he had suffered from his half brother. Never, in all those painful times, had he suspected envy.

"As for Stewart's murder," Beth continued, "I wasn't even in the country that weekend. I was on a private yacht five miles off Cape Cod with Senator . . . with a friend. If it becomes necessary, I can get that verified.

"And this . . ." She held up the ring. "It never belonged to me. It was my Grandmother Munroe's. Granddad Munroe bought it for her during one of his trips to New Mexico, years before I was born. He let me wear it a few times . . . only a few. The last time I saw it, it was in Grandmother's jewelry case in Greenleaf. And that was years ago. I have no idea how it got from there to Stewart's office in Twin Oaks."

She laid the ring on the table and picked up her drink.

Her explanation had been straightforward, from the heart. Once again he concluded that if she was not being truthful, she was a brilliant performer. Still, how else to explain the ring?

He asked, "Did you and Stewart have a prenuptial agreement?"

"To protect whom?" she replied with a callous laugh. "No, we didn't. Stewart and I were going to start divorce proceedings next month. We both agreed not to ask for a settlement."

"Divorce? You mean you agreed to forfeit all claim to the Dunning estate?"

"He had nothing I wanted. Connie was furious, as I knew she would be."

"She knew?"

"Oh, yes. That was the most delicious part about it—watching her face when I broke the news."

News indeed, Josh thought. How convenient that Stewart had died before the divorce took place. Beth remained his heir.

"Why the divorce? Mutual?"

"Mutual, yes. As to why . . ." She paused. "I wasn't the Dunning he wanted in his bed."

It took a moment to register. "Bed . . . you mean, Connie?"

"She initiated it, right after she learned that Stewart and I were breaking up. It had always been her way of holding on to men she might want to use in the future. I think Stewart saw through that. But his brains were all in his balls where women were concerned. And, whatever else she is, Constance is all woman."

Josh tried to get it all together in his mind. Never in his most creative moments, he mused, could he have devised a convoluted plot like this.

Another thought struck him. "Beth, does your mother know anything about computers?"

"Computers?"

"IBM . . . Apple . . . you know."

"I don't think she could put one together, if that's what you mean. But she uses one. Granddad Angus appointed Constance his business manager about six years ago. She has a desktop PC for drafting interoffice memos, analyzing productivity—that sort of thing. Mary Henson, Granddad Angus's secretary, does all the finish work. Why?"

"Just curious."

He pondered this new thread in the enigma he was trying to unravel, then set his glass on the coffee table, and started to rise. "I think I better hit the road."

"Oh, no . . . not just yet."

She pulled him back to the couch, set her drink aside, and moved closer. "We don't have a flooded mine pit around here," she said, huskily. "But I do have an enormous Jacuzzi upstairs. We can improvise."

Since the day he had left her, his most erotic fantasies evolved around her, tormenting him days and night on end. No other woman ever aroused him as she had. No other woman consumed his total being as she had.

Why, then, did he feel nothing now?

Something in his eyes signaled it to her. Her face clouded, and she moved away.

He took her hand in his. "I'm sorry, Beth."

She pulled her hand away and retrieved her drink. "Is it because of my father?"

"No."

"I see. Well, so much for a girl's ego."

There was no easy way to depart now. "I know the way out," he said, standing.

"You forgot this." She picked up the ring and handed it to him.

He hesitated. "I would leave it with you, but it's evidence."

She nodded.

He put the ring in his pocket, and leaned over, and kissed her gently on the cheek. "Goodbye, Beth."

When she heard the front door close, she laid her head back on the cushion and fixed clouded eyes on the whirling fan blades.

After a long while, she went to the bar and fixed another martini. Then she went back to the sofa, picked up the phone, and dialed. A man answered. She said, "Sir Henry . . . Beth. I'm terribly sorry to call so late. But I've developed a splitting headache. I'm afraid I won't be able to attend the reception with you tonight."

After the regrets and the thank yous, she hung up, waited a few seconds, and dialed again. To the woman who answered she said, "Margo . . . Beth. I . . . need company tonight."

"My dear, are you all right? You sound dispirited."

"Just lonesome."

"Oh, yes. Well, we all understand that feeling, don't we? Let me see now . . ." There was a lengthy pause. "Ah, I see that Maurice is available tonight. If I recall, you were quite fond of Maurice."

"Yes. But not tonight. Is . . . I'm sorry, I can't remember his name. That lovely young man from Juárez, with the . . . uh, bronzed complexion . . . ?"

"Armando? I am so sorry. He has an engagement this evening. But I'm sure Maurice—"

"No. Armando. I'll triple the fee."

"Oh, my. I see. Well, in that case I'm sure it can be arranged. Are you *sure* you are all right?"

"I'm all right," Beth snapped.

"Very well. What time shall I tell Armando to be there, my dear?"

"As soon as he can. The door's unlocked. Tell him to come upstairs."

She put the phone down and tossed off the rest of the martini, tasting the salt of her tears in the gin. Then she stood and removed her clothing, dropping each piece in a trail along the floor as she went upstairs to the turn on the Jacuzzi.

Twenty-eight

Rachel Bond parked across the street from the Ledger Building, stepped from her vehicle, and waited for an oncoming car to pass by. She spotted Carl Travis standing at his office window while he munched an apple and watched the afternoon rush hour traffic. Rush hour traffic in Seneca Falls meant any time there were six cars on Main Street at the same time. Carl waved her up to his office.

When she entered the office he greeted her, then said, "I tried to call you at the motel earlier. No answer." He motioned her to a chair and offered her a Winesap from the basket on his desk. "It's all I have to offer, I'm afraid."

She thanked him but declined. "I haven't been at the motel. After my shift at the hospital with Dub, I drove around, trying to think things through." She sat down.

"Any luck?" he asked, and dropped into his swivel chair.

"I'm not sure. Just an idea. That's why I came to see you. Have you heard from Josh?"

"No. That's why I called you. I thought he may have gotten in touch with you."

"Oh, I don't think he'd call me and not you."

Carl gave her a wry smile. "I think he'd call you instead of me anytime he could."

She smiled, but said nothing.

Carl took the last two bites of the apple and tossed the core into the wastebasket beside his desk. "You said you had an idea?"

"Yes. When I was teaching at the University of Arizona—before I switched to nursing—I had a friend who wrote romance novels—Dottie Mason. You may have heard of her."

Carl chuckled. "Queen of the bodice rippers? Who hasn't? *Today Show*. Letterman. Eight million paperbacks in print . . . something like that. Absolutely wretched writing."

"I agree. Dottie did, too, by the way. Her academic essays were superb. But she wasn't stuffy about her novels. She was a professional—a bread-and-butter writer. She knew her readers, and she wrote for them. But that's not the point."

She shifted on the couch and crossed her booted legs at the ankles. "I was trying to write a novel at the time—all English teachers attempt that sooner or later. Few succeed. Anyway, Dottie was giving me pointers. Through no fault of hers it didn't work out, and I finally gave it up. But along the way, I got to know her and her work habits pretty well. She composed on a computer, and she always made backups on floppy disks."

"That's standard practice," Carl said. "We do the same here, on tape."

"Yes. But she always made *two* backups. One to keep in her office files for ready reference, and one to store in her safe-deposit box at her bank, just in case. It came to me this morning that Raymond once mentioned doing the same with his lecture notes. He was the most organized man I ever saw. His computer was destroyed in the explosion. But I got to wondering if he stored anything in his safe-deposit box that might shed some light on his murder. I stopped at a gas station and called his bank to ask if I could get into his box."

"And?"

"And . . . no way. His and Mom's signatures are the only ones on the account. He's dead, Mom's incompetent."

"Did your mother designate a power of attorney?"

"No."

"A living will?"

"Yes. But technically she's not in a terminal condition. As far as the bank's concerned, she's still owner of the box."

"How about the courts? You could be appointed her guardian with a durable power of attorney."

"That's what the bank said. They also said it could take two or three weeks."

Carl rocked back in his chair. "That's what they said, did they?" He thought for a minute and then swiveled toward his desk and pushed his intercom.

Angie's voice responded, "Yes."

"Miss Angie," Carl said, "see if you can get Chief Justice Crockett in Charleston on the phone. If he's not in, leave a message for him to call me just as soon as he can. It's important."

"Yes sir."

Carl turned back toward the couch. "It's a long shot. But if I know Judge Crockett like I think I do, it's not going to take any two or three weeks before that bank gives you access to your step-father's safe-deposit box. Not at all."

Twenty-nine

Late afternoon traffic outbound from the District of Columbia rivaled that in Los Angeles. Josh chafed at the snail's-pace progress, knowing that he would face another slow-down on the corkscrew roads from the eastern foothills of the Appalachians all the way to Seneca Falls. His stomach was also sending distress signals, reminding him that his only meal that day had been the hot dog he ate while talking to Ramón Torres.

Just past the Beltway, he pulled into a Texaco Food Mart, filled the Corvette with premium unleaded, and picked out two prepackaged ham-and-cheese sandwiches and a pint of chocolate milk. He paid for it all with his credit card and then pulled back onto Interstate 66.

On this stretch of highway, the traffic was light. Risking another ticket, he set the cruise control on seventy-five miles per hour. It was the only opportunity he would have to make good time before he reached the tortuous mountain roads.

He ate while he drove, using the time to sift through the pieces of the puzzle that Ramón Torres had supplied, trying to determine where they fit, or if they fit at all. Angus Munroe and Manny Marconi—the entrepreneur and the crook. Conspirators in racketeering, drug dealing, and—if Torres was right—murder. Then, there was the ring. Surely Dub had picked it up in Stewart's office on the night of the murder. It led to Josh's suspicion of Beth.

Beth. He grimaced at the thought of their parting today. He had hurt her. And lied to her. For fifteen years she had haunted his memory while he told himself he was struggling to forget. Now he realized that he'd been deceiving himself. He had not tried to forget. He had done everything to keep the memory of her, the desire for her, alive. Then this afternoon she offered herself to him, and he couldn't respond. In that moment of insight, he realized that for all those painful years, he had been obsessed with yesterday's memory. How different things appeared in the light of today's reality. He had told her he was sorry, but he had been dissembling. He wasn't sorry. He was elated. The onus had been lifted from him.

He recalled what Beth told him about the ring, and his thoughts shifted to her mother. Was Constance Munroe a party to the conspiracy? If so, why was she drawn into it? To protect her husband, just as Angus's motive was to protect his son? What was the significance of the affair Beth revealed? Constance and Stewart. Spider and fly. Had Stewart become entangled in her web, or had he merely played along? Had it been Constance who left the ring in Stewart's office that weekend? Had she been there when Stewart was murdered? Had Dub seen her there? Did she know he had seen her? Could that account for the attempt on Dub's life?

Something had been gnawing at him about Dub for days. Something Hess had said. Viola's bombshell about Dub's cursory knowledge of sin eating seemed to explain his presence in Stewart's office that fateful night, and the bizarre ritual that followed. To Josh and Carl, it justified a conclusion that Dub was not involved in the murder—that the simple giant had offered Stewart the only absolution he knew to give. Hess had dismissed that idea with contempt: "So Oliver laid Stewart out on a table and left his prints all over the place. Haven't you guys ever heard of establishing an alibi? All he had to do was say, 'Hey, fellows, I was eating Stewart's sins.' Pretty convenient, huh?"

Could Hess be right? Had Dub, for reasons of his own, or on behalf of another, killed Stewart? Had he acted on orders from Angus? Or perhaps from Constance? There was a new twist.

Could it be that Constance Munroe had some power over Dub? Enough to make him commit murder? Had she tried to silence him afterward?

He was beginning to get a headache. There was much still unresolved. And not a solid clue in sight.

The long shadows had come and gone by the time he crossed the Appalachians and turned onto Route 55 toward Seneca Falls. A hunter's moon appeared from behind a wooded hill, casting a ghostly half light across the winding blacktop. It reminded him of a scene from Noyes's "The Highwayman." He wondered if Rachel liked Noyes. He wondered why he was wondering about Rachel. Moments later his headlights illuminated a sign indicating the turnoff to the Fox and Ox Camp, where she was staying. For a brief moment he thought about turning toward the camp. Just as quickly, he dismissed the idea. If he went to her he might not get back to Seneca Falls tonight. And he wanted to talk to Carl as soon as possible.

It was past nine o'clock when he crossed the town bridge onto Main Street and pulled to a stop in front of the Ledger Building. The office was dark. Carl had gone home for the night. He decided to stop at Aunt Martha's and call ahead before going to the editor's house.

At the hardware store, he pulled into the alleyway to park in his usual place beneath the outside stairs. There was a car in the space. Whose? Aunt Martha had no car. He flicked the lights on high beam and recognized the green Buick station wagon at once. Was Carl waiting for him upstairs? He stepped out of his car and looked up at the second floor apartment. There were no lights on anywhere.

"Well I'll be damned!" he said into the darkness, and smiled.

He got back into the Corvette and backed out of the alley as quietly as he could, wondering where to go now. He thought of heading back to the motel at the Fox and Ox Camp. Then he remembered that Viola Brown had an extra room.

He turned around in the middle of the street and headed for the Bottoms.

Thirty

He slept late. He got up at nine o'clock to find Viola's note on the kitchen table. She had left early to continue the cleaning chore at Twin Oaks, but he was to help himself to anything he wanted to eat. He made a pot of coffee, but ate nothing.

He waited an hour before going to the hardware store. The space below the outside stairs was empty. He parked the Corvette and went up to the apartment. In the bathroom, he removed the bandage from his face and studied himself in the mirror. The wound was healing, but was still swollen and ugly. He showered and shaved, easing the razor gingerly around the stitches. Then he taped on a fresh bandage, put on clean clothes, and went to the kitchen for something to eat. Famished, he grabbed a quart of milk from the refrigerator and a box of frosted donuts from the cupboard and sat down at the table. He was eating when Aunt Martha came upstairs. "I thought I heard you rummaging around up here."

"Who's minding the store?" he asked.

"Doris Toothman. She helps out sometimes. You need more to eat than that. Let me fix you some ham and eggs."

"I won't argue."

She fixed him a large breakfast of grapefruit juice, country ham, scrambled eggs, buttered whole wheat toast, and orange marmalade. She put it all in front of him, got herself a cup of black coffee, and joined him at the table. He wolfed the breakfast down, the first time she had seen him eat so heartily since he arrived from New Mexico.

At last, he pushed his plate aside. "Damn, that was good. Why can't I convince you to go home with me, Aunt Martha?"

"*This* is home, Josh."

Once that had been an endless contest between them. Time and again he asked her to sell the store and come live with him in Santa Fe, to let him take care of her for a change. He offered to build her an adobe home in the foothills of the Sangre de Cristo Mountains overlooking the city, if that's what she preferred. But she would have no part of it. On the few occasions she had visited him she had been excited with the novel sights and sounds of "The City Different"—for about two days. By the third day she was anxious; by the fourth, miserable. He always had to take her to Albuquerque and put her on a plane for home days earlier than he'd planned. She explained to him that her roots were deep in the verdant West Virginia soil. As the years passed, he came to respect the wisdom of her conviction, sadly reflecting on the sense of detachment that often plagues those who abandon their roots.

"You could move back here, you know," she said.

That, too, had been part of the contest. He smiled and shook his head. "I'm afraid Thomas Wolfe was right about that. But thanks for asking."

After a moment she said, "I'm the one who should be the one thanking you."

"For what?"

"I heard you pull into the driveway last night, then back out. Where did you sleep?"

He started to deny it, but realized that would be childish. "Viola Brown's. How long have you and Carl been seeing each other?"

"Four years. He wants me to marry him."

"Do you love him?"

"I've grown accustomed to him. I like being around him. I miss him when I'm not. If that's any answer."

His face brightened. "It sure as hell is. Carl's a great guy. You should grab him while you can. What's the problem?"

"Oh, I don't know. I'm set in my ways. After Boyd and all . . ."

He grasped her hand. "Aunt Martha, Boyd was years ago. You can't stay shackled to a ghost from the past. That was then; this is now."

"Oh? And just when did you become such an authority on matters of the heart, Mr. Affirmed Bachelor?"

He gave a mirthless laugh. "Yesterday."

"You saw Beth, didn't you?"

"Yes." He released her hand and leaned back in the chair. "I hurt her, I'm afraid."

"How so?"

"I never dreamed that she would have the same feeling for me that I thought I had for her. I can't explain it, but after dreaming of her night and day for fifteen years, suddenly I didn't want her anymore. God knows, she's still as beautiful as ever. But the feeling just wasn't there. I'm ashamed to admit it, but I was relieved. Except for the pain I caused her."

"Don't be too rough on yourself. She'll get over it."

He gave her a telling look. "Precisely what I meant about you and Boyd. It's time to put that dream to rest. Don't let Carl get away, Aunt Martha."

She stood and picked up the dishes and started to the sink. "I'll think about it."

He got up and took the dishes from her. "Let me do that. You sit."

She put the dishes on the sink and returned to the table. "Just the dishes. I'll take care of the skillet."

He smiled, remembering that she never let anyone except herself touch her cast-iron cookware. He ran hot water into the sink, squirted in some dishwashing liquid, and started washing the dishes. "Beth told me something pretty amazing. She said Stewart envied me. Said he told her that once. Envied me because our mother loved me and not him. I just never thought of it that way. I wonder if that might not explain a lot of things."

He turned to face her. "Why did she do that, Aunt Martha?" he asked, his voice heavy with feeling. "How in God's name could a mother desert her own child? How could a woman like that love anyone?"

The implication of the question was as obvious as the pain he revealed in asking it.

Aunt Martha pushed her chair back. "I have something you should see."

She stood up and started toward her bedroom, then paused. "By the way, Carl asked me to have you call him soon as you can. It's going to take me a few minutes, if you want to do it now."

He finished washing the dishes and put them in the rack to dry. Then he picked up the wall phone and called the *Ledger* office. After the first ring, Carl answered brusquely, "*Ledger*. Travis."

Josh smiled at the old editor's gruff tone. Years ago he had learned that Travis answered all calls like that in case it was an irate reader on the phone. He figured it gave him an edge in the argument to come.

"I'm back," Josh said. "I've got a lot to talk over with you. Anything new here?"

"Maybe. I might know for sure by the time you get here. By the way, a Vicki Armijo called for you this morning from Santa Fe. I told her you were out of town."

"I almost forgot. She's supposed to get me some information on Professor Marshe."

"She wants to know when you're coming home, and said she's about ready to toss the steaks out the window, whatever that means."

Josh laughed. "I know what it means. Did she find out anything about Marshe? I asked Annie to have her pass the info to you if I wasn't around."

"She said she'd rather talk to you. Wants you to call."

He pondered it a moment. "Okay, I'll be over there in a little while."

"Do that," Carl said, and hung up.

Aunt Martha entered the kitchen carrying a shoe box. She placed it on the table and sat down. Josh put the phone back on the hook and sat across from her.

"These are letters from your mother," she said. "There weren't many; Jenny was a phone addict." She picked out a time-worn envelope and handed it to him. "I want you to read this one now."

It was postmarked Santa Fe. Feeling an anxiety he couldn't suppress, he took out the enclosed letter, unfolded it, and read:

Dear Martha,

We are so thrilled that you'll be spending Christmas with us. It should have happened long before this. That damned store! Sometimes I wish it would burn to the ground and set you free. But I can't really be mad now, can I? You'll be here soon. And I can't be mad at anyone these days. Life is so worth living—at last!

Estévan is such a dear, loving man. Little Josh (just wait until you see him!) and I are the only family he's ever had, you know. He dotes on us. Now that he's quit that awful marine reserve unit that took so much of his time, we have more of it to spend together.

Oh, Martha, I can't wait to show you around this magnificent country. Remember how I expected to find nothing but sand dunes and cacti and jackrabbits and rattlesnakes? Instead, I'm surrounded by snowcapped mountains and heavenly forests with lush meadows, beautiful flowers, and crystalline streams. Here they call it "The Land of Enchantment," and I do so agree.

There's only one sad note to all this, and sometimes I think it will make my heart break. Little Stewart. I was such a fool to let those damned Dunnings and their blood-sucking lawyers force me to abandon my own dear little boy. They made such vile threats against Estévan. He didn't know about that until recently. He was so angry when I told him, that he took me to see an attorney (there are decent lawyers!). She thinks I have a good case to force the Dunnings to give me visitation rights. Oh, Martha, wouldn't that be wonderful? I could visit Stewart there, and he could come see me here. He would know he has a mother, and get to know his little brother. I'm praying so hard for that to happen. Please pray for it too.

Time to close. Estévan says to assure you that we will all be in Albuquerque to meet your flight. Now I

*must go. It's time for Josh and I to take our daily stroll,
and I have to get him into his snowsuit, always a tussle.
Winter this year is severe.*

Love always,
Jenny

He read the letter through twice, and then looked up at his aunt through watery eyes.

"It's the last letter I ever got from her," she said. "The last letter she ever wrote, I'm sure." She paused. "A few days later, she and your father were killed on the way to Albuquerque . . . to meet me."

"And I lived."

"Thank God for that."

He thought for a moment. "Aunt Martha, did you ever show this letter to Stewart?"

She shook her head. "Stewart felt the same way about me being his aunt as he did about you being his brother. I thought it best to let sleeping dogs lie. If I'd known he was suffering the bitterness Beth told you about, I would have made him read it. But I didn't know."

"I wish you had," Josh said. "I wish you had."

Thirty-one

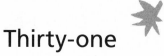

Carl adjusted his trifocals and used his finger to trace Mohawk Creek on the map spread across his desk. "Hess believes the culprit waded from the highway, here, to Dub's cabin and back. Voila! No footprints."

"Not even at the cabin?"

"The cabin door was right on the creek, remember, with a cinder path in front. Tailor-made for no footprints."

"Well I'll be damned!" Josh exclaimed. "The Apaches and Utes avoided trackers that way. Why didn't I think of it?"

"Let's be glad Hess did."

"Yeah," Josh conceded.

Carl said, "The question remains, who did the wading?"

"Does Hess have a theory about that?"

"He thinks it was one of the thugs who tried to rearrange your facial structure."

"I'm not sure I buy that. It might sound crazy, considering what happened up there, but I don't think those two were sent here to kill."

Carl rolled the map and put it in a corner beside the desk. "Well, we can think about that later. Tell me about Washington."

Without mentioning Ramón Torres's name, Josh told what the old FBI agent had found out.

"That means skulduggery between Angus and the mob," Carl said. "I guess I could buy that—father protecting son. How reliable is your source?"

"A-one. But he admits it's speculation. I also went to see Beth." He told about their meeting at her home in Georgetown.

"You buy her story about the ring?"

"Considering everything she told me, yes. She and Stewart were in the process of getting a divorce. Stewart's death put a convenient end to that."

"Convenient? For whom?"

"Think about it." Josh prompted.

Carl did. "I give up."

"Connie Munroe," Josh said. "Beth told me that her mother was obsessed with forming a Munroe-Dunning cartel. Her only hold, however tenuous, on Stewart's estate was through Beth. A divorce between them was the last thing Connie would have wanted."

"Damn. Josh, don't you think we should bring Hess in on this?"

"That's the advice I got in Washington. To bring the sheriff in, and then get out of it."

"Sounds valid to me."

"Maybe. But you know Hess. He's convinced Dub killed Stewart, and once he sets his mind on something, that's it. I'd just as soon keep his stubbornness at bay for a while longer."

He sat back and stared into the middle distance. "I wonder if Connie left that ring there to implicate Beth."

"Unlikely," Carl said. "Constance is nobody's fool. You say Beth has an airtight alibi. If Constance had intended to set her up, she'd have planned better than that."

"I suppose you're right. Anyway, we've got just as much hard proof as we ever had—zilch."

Carl looked at the phone on his desk. "Maybe. Maybe not. I'm waiting for a call from Rachel."

"About what?"

He told about Rachel's visit the day before. "She wonders if her stepfather might have stored something in his safe-deposit box that would shed light on things. I made legal arrangements for the bank to give her access to the box. That's where she is now."

"I wish I'd been here to go with her."

"I'm sure you do. Don't worry. She's one shrewd lady. If there's anything incriminating in that box, she'll find it."

As she had every few minutes since arriving at the Farmers Bank and Trust Company in Morgantown, Rachel glanced at the Seth Thomas clock on the wall above the tellers' cages. It was 12:53. She had been cooling her heels for an hour and fifteen minutes and wondered if she should call Carl Travis to see if anything had gone wrong.

Across the foyer a young woman was breast-feeding a baby. Rachel watched for a moment before purposely averting her eyes. Moments later a chunky, silver-haired woman dressed in a blue pantsuit and carrying a plastic portfolio walked up to the receptionist's desk and asked where she might find a Miss Bond.

Overhearing, Rachel rose from her chair. "I'm Rachel Bond."

The chunky woman scrutinized Rachel through horn-rimmed glasses. Then, offering her hand, she said, "I'm terribly sorry to be so late, Miss Bond. The mayor called an impromptu meeting. That *man*. Can't go to the bathroom without a consensus from his staff. Oh . . . I'm Miss Maples, with the county court clerk's office."

Rachel shook hands. "Miss Maples."

"We were all so sorry to hear about Professor Marshe. He was a frequent visitor to the clerk's office; he came to study the property-owner registers—for his field trips, you know. Do you have the key?"

"Yes. It was in his desk at home."

"I see. Then we may as well get started."

The security teller at the vault required Rachel to sign a registry indicating she was entering Professor and Mrs. Raymond Marshe's safe-deposit box, number 240, at 12:59 p.m. Miss Maples countersigned the registry, signifying that Rachel's access to the box was authorized by the court, that Rachel was acting on behalf of her mother, who was incompetent, and that the bank was not liable for any ramification. Then the teller, a dark-haired woman of Miss Maples's age, but much slimmer, escorted them into the huge vault. She inserted Rachel's key and the bank's key into the dual lock on box 240 and allowed Rachel to remove the steel drawer.

"We will need a secure room," Miss Maples said.

"This way," the teller replied.

She led them to a private room at the end of the hall. "Call me when you're ready to go back to the vault," she said, and left.

Miss Maples locked the door and placed her portfolio on the table beside the drawer. "Did you ever *see* such hair? Straight out of the bottle. She's no spring chicken that one, I tell you."

Rachel said nothing.

Miss Maples pulled back a chair and sat down. "Well, then, down to business. This is a most unusual procedure, you know. It usually takes days for the court to authorize an entry such as this. You must be a *very* good friend of Judge Crockett."

Yes, we screw every day, Rachel was tempted to say.

Instead she said, "No. I'm sure the judge weighed the circumstances quite carefully before he approved." She took the chair next to Miss Maples.

"Oh yes . . . I'm sure that's true. Certainly."

Miss Maples unzipped the portfolio and turned back several pages of a yellow legal-size tablet until she came to a blank one. She took out a pen and wrote "Marshe Estate" at the top of the page. "You understand, I must make a complete inventory of the contents. For tax purposes, you know. And you must sign for anything you wish to remove."

"I understand," Rachel said.

She opened the drawer and removed the items one by one, placing each on the table so Miss Maples could log it. There were deeds to property (all heavily mortgaged), insurance policies (worthless because of the professor's borrowing against medical bills), a woman's engagement ring and wedding band (the other jewelry had been hocked), and various odds and ends. There were no bonds, no stocks, no cash. Miss Maples recorded it all, noting that there was nothing to interest the county tax assessor.

At the very back of the box were nine plastic-encased computer disks trussed together with a heavy rubber band. Rachel recognized the professor's bold printing on the content tabs. Four were labeled for the academic level of the lectures they contained: FRESHMAN

. . . SOPHOMORE . . . JUNIOR . . . SENIOR. The remaining five were labeled: ARCHEOZOIC . . . PROTEROZOIC . . . PALEOZOIC . . . MESOZOIC . . . CENOZOIC.

Rachel shook the box to show Miss Maples it was empty.

Miss Maples nodded. "How in the world do I list these?" she asked, fingering one of the disks.

"Lecture notes. My stepfather kept them here in case he lost the ones in his office."

"He certainly must have given an awful lot of lectures."

"Yes," Rachel said, "all over the country." She reached for the box, knocking the disks onto the floor. "Oh, dammit! How clumsy can you be?"

Miss Maples leaned down to recover the scattered disks. "I must record these too, you know." Thus preoccupied, she didn't notice when Rachel reached into the box and removed a separate disk taped to the top—where she had felt it earlier.

After Rachel slipped the secreted disk into her pocket, she helped recover the disks on the floor. "I am sorry."

Miss Maples finished recording the box contents. "Is there anything you plan to take with you?"

"No," Rachel replied, "there's nothing of interest here."

Miss Maples made a final notation and then closed her portfolio. "We'll just put it all back into the vault then," she said.

"Yes," Rachel agreed. "Thank you, Miss Maples."

"You're very welcome, my dear. I'm sorry you didn't find what you were looking for."

At the moment Rachel was leaving Farmers Bank and Trust in Morgantown with the purloined disk, Joshua Chacón pulled to a stop near an under-road culvert on Mount Canaan. Here, Mohawk Creek passed beneath the highway on its shallow downhill run toward the Potomac River. Just beyond the culvert was the old logging road leading through the deep forest to Dub Oliver's cabin.

Josh surveyed the scene for a moment. Almost hidden by the underbrush, a small spur road led down a sharp incline to the water. He walked down the bank to where the creek entered the culvert. It took only a few seconds to find what he was searching for. Deeply imprinted in the dirt at the edge of the creek were the telltale imprints of inverted-V tread tires with a center split. Where the driver had backed to turn around and drive up the incline, the imprints showed the rear tires to be the same as the front. An all-terrain four-wheel-drive vehicle. Josh studied the scene again. Whoever had parked here to wade Mohawk Creek to the cabin and back was the same person who had tried to run him down that night he went to check out the strange light at Twin Oaks.

Thirty-two

Rachel and Carl watched as Josh inserted into the computer the disk Rachel had purloined from Professor Marshe's safe-deposit box. They were working in the composition room behind Carl's office.

Josh said, "You could probably put everything the professor had stored on those nine disks at the bank onto this one. But it's not unusual to have several put away like that. It's just easier to back up something onto a new disk than it is to go to the bank, retrieve the old one, add to it, and take it back." He pulled the keyboard onto his lap and typed the command for an index reading. In seconds, the monitor screen filled with a catalog of fourteen files stored on the disk. Each was identified by a subject common to university-level geology classes.

Rachel traced her finger down the screen, reading each title aloud. "Dammit! Why'd he take such pains to hide just another stupid lecture disk?"

"Keep your shirt on," Josh said. "All you see here are the file titles. If Marshe was computer savvy he could have buried something inside any of these files."

"He's worked with computers for years," Rachel said.

"Oh, boy," Carl exclaimed. "You mean you're going to read every file listed there?"

"Not word for word, but we've got to scan each page. An unlisted document could be hidden anywhere." He typed in the command to open the first file.

Carl straightened up and rubbed his back. "Well then, it looks like we're in for a very long night. I'll go plug in the coffeepot."

Josh turned to Rachel. "It may take a while. Why don't you keep Carl company. I'll yell if anything comes up."

She waited until the coffee was perked, and then filled three cups, black. She took one to Josh, and carried the others to the table where Carl was using the time to clip and paste ads for the next issue of the *Ledger*.

"Thanks," he said, taking one of the cups.

"He's a glutton for punishment," she commented. She sat down at the table.

"It's in his nature," the editor replied. He pasted an ad for Hugh Greene's Bar-B-Que Pit, centering it carefully between the borders. "He told me once that unless an author's willing to take the risk of doing an awful lot of work and have it come to naught, he'd better take up another line of work. That's the attitude he's taken with this whole mess surrounding Stewart's death."

"I understand he didn't really care that much for his brother."

"Half brother," Carl said, with no additional comment.

"Yeah. Well, anyway, Josh's other work certainly hasn't come to naught."

"No, it hasn't. Justly so. He's quite a guy, really."

She turned and looked back to where Josh was still scanning files on the computer screen. "Yes," she agreed. "He's quite a guy."

"And quite vulnerable," Carl said.

She turned back. "What do you mean?"

"He got burned once. Bad. People like that build walls around their hearts."

"C'est le vie."

"Voice of experience?"

"I've been there," she replied.

"I think his wall may be crumbling a bit. I just hope he doesn't get hurt again."

She smiled, but said nothing.

Josh closed the twelfth file and opened the thirteenth—GYPSUM. It contained a series of lectures about the techniques of gypsum mining in the United States as compared to South America and Asia.

Boring, boring, boring, Josh thought, scanning the pages of the file. And there was only one more to go. If he found nothing there, he mused, it was strike-out time. He started to close the GYPSUM file when a single word at the bottom of the page caught his eye. Four double spaces removed from the last line of text, centered in mid-page, it read "SENDIR."

Strange, Josh thought. He hit Page Down, to scan the text below the entry. The computer hesitated briefly, then highlighted a message at the bottom of the screen: "SUB-DOCUMENT PROTECTED: ENTER PASSWORD."

There was no use in trying again. "Rachel, come here a minute."

She came and looked over his shoulder. "What?"

He pointed to the centered word. "What does that word mean, in the professor's jargon?"

She studied the screen. "*Sendir*? I haven't the slightest idea."

"Find something?" Carl called from across the room.

"Don't know," Josh said. He hit a couple of more keys. Once again the highlighted message appeared: "SUB-DOCUMENT PROTECTED: ENTER PASSWORD."

"A protected document within a document," Josh explained. "Whatever it is, the professor didn't want just anybody to have access to it. Rachel, did Marshe ever say anything to you about a password?"

"Not that I recall. No, I'm sure he didn't."

Carl came to where they were working and looked at the screen. "*Sendir*," he said to himself and shook his head. "Means nothing to me. Now what?"

Josh thought a moment. "Rachel, what was the professor's birth date?"

"I don't remember."

"I think it was in the *Cumberland News* obit," Carl said. "I'll check." He went to his office. Moments later he returned. "February 25, 1945."

Josh typed 022545 and pressed Enter. A different message appeared: INCORRECT PASSWORD: ACCESS DENIED.

Moments later, the first message reappeared: SUB DOCUMENT PROTECTED: ENTER PASSWORD.

He typed in various combinations of the birth date. The messages kept repeating.

He said, "Rachel, get some paper and write down every individual name or date you can think of that may have had meaning in the professor's life. His middle name, his mother's maiden name, his mother-in-law's maiden name, his old girlfriends' names, his wedding date, his nicknames—anything like that you can recall, no matter how trivial."

"I'm afraid I don't remember very much," she said.

"Whatever," Josh replied. "Let me have anything you think of. It's hit and miss, but it's our only chance."

"You'll find a pack of index cards and some pencils on the paste-up table," Carl said.

She went to the table and began to write down names, dates, places, and events she could recall. Each time she finished one, Carl took it to Josh to try against the computer's demand for a password. At the end of an hour, after he had tried everything she had come up with, and variations of them, the computer continued to deny entry to the SENDIR file.

Rachel threw the pencil on the table and cupped her head in her hands. "My brain's exhausted. I can't think anymore." She got up and headed down the hall. "And I've got to get rid of some of this coffee."

Josh looked at his watch: 1:35 a.m. His eyes were blurred from overexposure to the screen. He closed the file directory and turned off the computer. "Let's give it a rest."

They went to Carl's office and slumped into chairs. Moments later Rachel came in and sprawled on her back on the couch.

"Should I make more coffee?" Carl asked, without enthusiasm.

"I couldn't hold another drop," Josh replied. He put his feet up on the coffee table.

Rachel shook her head. "Just wake me for breakfast." She closed her eyes.

Carl tilted back to a position of ease and his chin fell to his chest. Within seconds he began to snore.

Josh wondered if they should all go home and try again tomorrow. There was no guarantee that there was anything important in the protected file. But he was determined to find out, *if* he could break the code. And it was a mighty big *if*.

All at once Rachel swung her feet off the couch and sat upright. "Josh, let's try 'Podge.'"

"What?"

"It's a nickname. Raymond told me that my mother called him that. I have no idea where it came from, but if he intended for her to break that code someday, it's possible he picked one he knew she'd remember sooner or later. I know it sounds silly, but . . ."

Josh was already on his feet.

He switched on the computer, waited until the screen told him it was ready, and brought up the files again. He moved the cursor over SENDIR and pressed Enter. At the command for a password he typed PODGE and pressed Enter again. Within seconds, the screen came alive with the protected document:

SENECA DIRECTORY
    (Dinwiddie/Seneca IX)
FRED KING 2/2
JACOB CORBETT 11/3
CHARLES HENRY 9/4
ALEX QUIGG 22/6
PAUL RAKESTRAW
WILLIAM EASTON 5/7

Carl adjusted his glasses and leaned closer to the screen. "What's this all about?"

"You tell me," Josh said. "What does Dinwiddie/Seneca mean?"

"Beats me," Carl replied.

"Rachel?" Josh prompted.

"Not a clue. But Raymond made that list. He always wrote dates like that, day-slash-month."

Josh studied the names for a while, then looked at his watch. It was a couple of minutes after two. Washington, D.C., was in the same time zone. He made a printout of the names, took the sheet from the printer, and stood. "Carl, I need to call D.C. Which phone?"

Carl gave a puzzled look. "At this time of morning?"

"It could be important."

"You want privacy?"

"Just for a few minutes."

"My office, desk phone." Carl said.

After the second ring, the weary voice of Ramón Torres came through the phone. "What?"

Josh said, "It's me again."

"*Madre de Dios*! You know what time it is? You in jail or something?"

"Not yet. Sorry about this. But it's important. You awake enough to think straight?"

"Straight enough to tell you that I'm not going out to any damned pay phone this time of night. Not in this town."

"I know, I know," Josh tried to assuage the old FBI agent. "We'll have to take our chances. You remember our talk a couple of days ago? And the idea you had about things?"

"What things?" The question was followed by the sound of a weary yawn.

How do I do this? Josh thought. Then he proceeded cautiously, "Garbage chutes."

"Garbage chutes? Oh, yeah. Sure."

"Okay. I'm going to read something to you. Tell me if any of it means anything to you."

Josh placed the printout under the desk light and read aloud, pronouncing each name slowly and distinctly: "Fred King . . . Jacob Corbett . . . Charles Henry . . . Alex Quigg . . . Paul Rakestraw . . . William Easton."

He waited.

"Say again," Torres requested.

Josh repeated the names.

After a moment, Torres said, "Nada . . . absolutely nothing."

"You're sure? There's a date after each name, and all the dates are within the last six months."

"Means nothing to me."

"Could they be code names," Josh persisted, "substituted for real ones?"

"Not likely. They don't operate that way. They might use numbers, or symbols perhaps, but not other names. My experience has been that they don't keep a record at all. Too dangerous."

Josh felt a pang of disappointment. He started to ask Ramón to check with his sources, in and out of the agency, but realized that would be wasted effort. If any of the names on the list were hit victims, Ramón would have recognized them. And he was probably right about no record being kept.

"All right, old friend," Josh said. "Thanks for your help. Go back to sleep."

"Oh, sure. Just like that. I'll be up the rest of the night wondering what the hell this was all about. You will let me know, when you can?"

"That's a promise," Josh said, and hung up.

He had told Torres that each name was followed by a date. That wasn't the fact. He picked up the paper and went back to the composition room where Carl was just finishing the ads. Josh looked around. "Where's Rachel?"

"Had to leave to get some shut-eye. She promised Doc she'd take the day shift at the hospital with Dub. Said she'd catch up with you later today."

"Dub's lucky," Josh said.

Carl smiled. "Yeah, he is. Did your call pan out?"

"Not the way I was hoping," Josh replied. "Carl, when did Doc say Stewart was killed? Exactly."

Carl laid the ad page atop the rest of the paper, now all ready for the printer. "Friday night, late. Let's see"—his brow knitted in thought—"that would have been the seventh."

Josh placed the list of names on the table and ran his finger down the date column. "Every name here is followed by a date except this one—Paul Rakestraw." He moved his finger down one name. "This one—William Easton—is the last dated entry. July fifth."

"What's the significance?" Carl asked.

"That's two days before Stewart was killed," Josh replied. "Think about it. We have a list of names that nobody recognizes;

it was found in a protected file taken from Professor Marshe's computer. There's a dated entry after each name except the last, and all the dates fall within the period when Marshe was working with Stewart. The day after the last dated entry—Easton's name—Marshe had an urgent meeting at Twin Oaks with Stewart. The next day, Stewart was killed. Do you honestly believe all that to be coincidental?"

Carl shook his head. "I don't know. I'm totally confused."

"That makes two of us," Josh said. After a moment he asked, "Carl, has there ever been any talk around town about Stewart and Constance Munroe?"

"Heavens, yes. Those two were always trying to undercut each other. You know that."

"Not that kind of talk. Rumors of a tryst . . . a possible affair?"

Carl guffawed. "Stewart Dunning and Constance Munroe? You can't be serious."

Josh's countenance signaled that he was. "Beth told me that her mother had seduced Stewart. I didn't say anything before because I didn't know what to make of it. But consider this. Hess says that Stewart went to great pains to make everyone believe he was out of town that weekend. Instead, he stayed secreted at Twin Oaks. Why? Hess speculates that he had planned a meeting he wanted to keep secret. I suggested a woman. Hess disagreed—said that Stewart took pride in his satyric reputation and didn't care who knew about his affairs. Well, perhaps there was one affair that even Stewart Dunning didn't want to become common knowledge—one with his mother-in-law."

"You believe Constance was with him the night he was killed."

Josh retrieved the turquoise ring he still carried in his pocket. "If this was in Beth's grandmother's jewelry box, like she said it was, who else would have access to it?"

"All right," Carl said, "you've built a circumstantial case against Constance Munroe. Question is, What do you intend to do about it?"

"Yes," Josh mused. "What to do about it?"

He sat back in thought. After a few moments he said, "I think tomorrow would be a good time to make another visit to Greenleaf."

Thirty-three

David Munroe made a sharp turn off the unpaved road, downshifted the Range Rover, and drove deeply into the darkening forest. He parked at the base of a low hill and switched off the engine. The telltale tremble had already begun in his hands. He took a silver pill case from the glove compartment, flipped it open, licked his index finger, and dipped it into the cocaine. Holding one nostril closed, he rubbed the white powder gently into the membranes of the other and sniffed hard. Then he repeated the process with the opposite nostril. As he tossed the pill case back into the glove compartment, he wondered what Sheriff Hess might do if he knew the cocaine was there. Probably nothing, he concluded. Now that his staunch patron, Stewart Dunning, was dead, the sheriff had nothing to gain from riling the Munroes.

Calmer now, he sat staring at the top of the hill. After a while, he grabbed a pair of binoculars from beneath the seat, got out of the Range Rover, and walked uphill through the thick underbrush toward the crest. Just before reaching the top, he dropped to his hands and knees and crawled the rest of the way. Below the hill was a narrow valley traversed by a rocky stream. Halfway up a hill on the other side of the valley, a grand two-story log cabin with a wraparound porch sat almost hidden by the oaks, maples, black gums, and berry vines that surrounded it. He focused the binoculars on the cabin for a while, and then lowered his head onto his forearms. He had not seen his father's hunting lodge for over ten years and had not expected the rush of nostalgia that hit him at this moment. Nostalgia, and pain.

Once, too many years ago to count, he had found happiness here. Happiness and love. Often when his father was too busy for him, as he always seemed to be, his mother would bring him to this peaceful valley. Here they would fend for themselves, far removed from the pampered confines of Greenleaf. Always, his first chore on such outings was to scout the woods for wild flowers, which his mother would arrange in bouquets to brighten this temporary home away from home. Next, they would break out their fly rods, don waders, and fish the pools and cascades of the icy stream for trout for their dinner. They would frequently detour into the lush hillsides to gather blackberries or persimmons for dessert. Later, watching along the way for the myriad colorful birds, deer, foxes, and other wildlife that flourished in the fertile Appalachian woodlands, they would explore the winding mountain trails. Other times, they would simply sit side by side in the swing on the huge porch until bedtime and enjoy the sights and sounds and smells of the forest.

All too soon, it ended.

When his mother died, the light of his life was extinguished. No one could rekindle it. Not his father, who never tried. Not Constance, whose ambitions lay elsewhere. Not the countless other women, before and after Constance. Not anyone. Except, for one brief shining season, Beth.

He was seized by a sudden chill.

Beth. Sweet, beautiful Beth. The daughter he loved so dearly, and who once loved him—until he turned her love to loathing.

He purged that bitter memory from his mind, raised up on his elbows, and again fixed the glasses to his eyes. In the fading light he concentrated on the two cars parked near the lodge. The black Lincoln Town Car was near the front steps. He focused on the license plate— District of Columbia. He moved the glasses to the man sitting with his eyes closed and his head back against the driver's seat. Chauffeur, David thought, although the man was not in uniform. Perhaps he was a secret service agent assigned to protect the secretary. If so, he wasn't earning his pay at the moment.

David shifted the glasses to the Rolls Royce convertible parked at the side of the lodge. It required no speculation. It was his wife's.

He trained the glasses on the windows of the master bedroom upstairs. The room was dark. Nor were there lights on in any other rooms in the lodge. He lowered the glasses and waited.

A half hour later a light flicked on in the upstairs bedroom. He raised the glasses again. He could make out shadowy figures moving on the other side of drawn curtains, but nothing more.

Ten minutes later, the downstairs lights came on, followed by the bright porch light beside the entrance. David trained the glasses on the doorway. A burly man dressed in a white seersucker suit and a black bow tie stepped out and set a suitcase down on the porch. The man's beefy pockmarked face, a feature that delighted media caricaturists, readily identified him as one of the most powerful, and controversial, members of the president's cabinet—Secretary of the Interior Michael Mulhaney. Standing in the doorway just behind the secretary was Constance Munroe, her sable hair in a tousled fall around her shoulders. The backlighting from the living room revealed that the gossamer nightgown clinging to her body was all she was wearing.

The man in the Town Car stepped out and retrieved the suitcase. He put it in the trunk of the Lincoln, and then held the back door open.

The secretary turned and placed a hand on Constance's bare shoulder. He said something, and leaned forward to kiss her. She turned her head, avoiding contact.

The secretary straightened up and looked at her for a moment, patted her shoulder, and walked down the steps to the car.

David kept the glasses on the doorway. His wife stood watching until the black Lincoln was well down the private road leading to the main highway, then turned, and went back into the lodge.

"Whore!" David uttered aloud, tasting the bitterness in his throat. "Filthy . . . despicable . . . *whore!*"

He scooted backward a couple of yards on his belly, then stood and ran back down the hill toward the Range Rover.

Constance Munroe—impatient to wash away the odious sweat, smell, and touch of the man who had just left her bed—turned the hot water higher and let the scalding shower cascade over her. She thought of Michael Mulhaney's repulsive body and wondered if she would ever feel clean again. Lathering for the third time, she scoured every inch of her skin from head to toe with the coarse loofah, wishing she could wash away the memory, as well as the filth.

"Angus, you *bastard!*" she exclaimed aloud in the steaming stall.

He had done this to her. He had asked her—no, had *ordered* her—to defile herself with the repulsive secretary of the interior.

Defile myself? Well, hardly. Hell, she'd had plenty of men. All shapes, sizes, and, yes . . . colors (she wondered what her dear Virginia-bred mama would have thought about *that*). But they had been men of her own choosing. Never before had she lowered herself to the level of a pimp's whore.

Angus the pimp? She didn't know whether to smile or sneer. Well, it would be a damned cold day in hell before she would spread her thighs for him again.

Wait. Better reconsider. Whatever else Angus was, he remained Lord and Master of Greenleaf, and would be until he died.

She thought of Angus dying. In spite of their in-law relationship, her claim to the Munroe fortune at that time would be tenuous at best. He had made it plain that he would not leave Greenleaf to David. That left only her and Beth in the line of inheritance. No question, Angus loved Beth dearly. She made a wry face. In a much different fashion than he loves me, she thought. No, the only real hold she had on Angus was through the enduring vitality of his loins. And that, she could attest, the old man possessed in full measure. If Greenleaf was to be hers, she must continue to please Angus however she could.

She rinsed, turned off the water, and stepped out onto the deep mat. She ran a towel over her body, went to the vanity, and plugged in the blow-dryer. Surely Angus should be pleased with tonight's work, she thought. Mulhaney had assured her that he would report favorably on Munroe Mining Corporation's compliance with the EPA standards when he returned to Washington. She laughed again. The obnoxious son of a bitch hadn't set foot on one inch of Munroe Corporation property since he had arrived in West Virginia.

She turned the blower on high, picked up her brush, and smoothed the tangles from her dark hair. The rush of warm air drowned out the sounds of the night.

David Munroe let the Range Rover idle on the side road until the black Lincoln Town Car carrying the secretary of the interior pulled out of the dirt lane onto the main highway and sped away toward the Virginia border. Then he turned onto the lane, switched off the headlights, and navigated the way to his father's hunting lodge by moonlight. Moments later he parked beside his wife's Rolls Royce.

He climbed the front steps, key in hand, but found that she had left the front door unlocked. How trusting, he thought. He stepped inside, stopped, and listened. The shower was running in the master bedroom upstairs. Quietly, he climbed the stairway and walked down the hall toward the room. He opened the door slowly, looked inside, and listened again. The shower was no longer running. Then he heard the hair dryer switch on. He stepped into the room, turned off the light, and sat in a deep overstuffed chair facing the bathroom door.

Dried, powdered, and feeling almost human once again, Constance Munroe slipped into the light summer robe she kept at the lodge, and went to the bedroom. She was puzzled to find the room dark; she thought she had left the lights on. She made her way to the wall switch and flipped it up. Turning, she clutched her throat and gasped.

"David! You son of a bitch! What the hell are you doing here?"

"How was the screw, Connie?"

"I don't know what you're talking about."

"Don't lie to me; I'm not in the mood. I was up on the hill. I saw Mulhaney leave. Is he a good lay?"

She gave a sardonic sneer. "Excellent. He knows how to please a woman. It was good to be with a real man again."

"Oh? Isn't Father a real enough man for you anymore?"

She went to the closet. "You bore me, David. Go home and make love to your needle. I've got to get dressed."

She took down her clothes and started laying them out on the bed.

When she looked up again he was holding a gun. "You recognize this, don't you?" he said, cradling the small revolver in the flat of his hand. "You're so damned fond of it."

"Don't be so dramatic, David. It doesn't become you."

"You're a conniving bitch, Connie. A shrewd, conniving bitch. What you can't get by manipulation you get by dealing with a thug like Manny Marconi. None of us are safe while you're still alive."

She dropped the robe. His eyes widened. Her body was magnificent. Still pink and glowing from the scalding shower, it was as erotically voluptuous tonight as it had been that night so long ago in Richmond when he saw her win the Miss Virginia crown, and knew he must have her.

"Are you trying to scare me, David?"

"No, Connie. I intend to kill you."

"Kill me? *You?* What a laugh. It takes passion to kill, David. You don't have the pass—"

The first bullet struck her just above her navel. She dropped to her knees, glanced once at the wound, and fixed her eyes on him in shock.

The second bullet tore through her left breast. Without a sound, she crumpled onto her right side, her eyes still open, but glazed over with death.

He sat unmoving, contemplating her lifeless body. Finally he rose and went to the phone on the nightstand beside the bed. He sat on the bed and thumbed through the book, looking for the home number of Sheriff Russell Hess. Finding it at last, he dialed.

No one answered.

He put the phone back in the cradle and tried to remember the name of the deputy sheriff. It came to him. He looked up the number and dialed. After a couple of rings a voice answered, "Yeah?"

"Deputy Sheriff Mares?"

"Yeah. Who's this?"

"David Munroe."

"Oh . . . Mr. Munroe. Yes sir. What can I do for you, sir?"

"How can I reach Sheriff Hess?"

"He's making rounds over by Mount Hazard tonight. I can get him on the radio. Is it important?"

"Yes. It's important. Tell him to come to my father's hunting lodge at once. He knows where it is. Tell him there's been a shooting."

He hung up and looked at his watch. It was 9:17. It wouldn't take the sheriff long to get here.

He went back to the chair, sat down, and withdrew a minirecorder from his pocket. He pushed the record button and spoke, "Father . . . No, *dear* Father . . ."

Ten minutes later, he turned off the recorder and returned it to his pocket. He went to where his wife lay. He knelt and straightened her body and closed her eyes. There would be other men here soon, he remembered. He took her robe from the bed and draped it over her. Then he lay down beside her and pulled her to him. He lay like that, cuddling her, for several minutes. Then he stuck the muzzle of the gun against his temple.

"Mother," he whispered, and blew away the top of his head.

Thirty-four

There were state police cars parked on both sides of the road in front of the large wrought iron gates. A trooper flagged Josh down. Josh rolled down the window.

"No visitors allowed today," the trooper said. "You'll have to turn around."

Barlow, the gatekeeper, looked out and spotted the red Corvette. "It's okay, Bernie," he called. "That's Mr. Chacón. Mr. Munroe's expecting him." He pushed a button, and the huge gates swung open.

The trooper gave Josh a churlish look and waved him through.

There were more than a dozen cars parked at the house. In the pasture beside the stables was a large helicopter with United States Marine Corps markings. Josh pulled to a stop in the parking area and surveyed the knots of people standing around the large west veranda. He saw Russ Hess standing with others near the wall overlooking Canaan Valley. If the sheriff noticed him, he gave no sign of it. Then he spotted something else. At the far end of the lot, parked well away from the other cars, were a blue Rolls Royce convertible and a white Range Rover. He knew the Rolls belonged to Constance Munroe. Surely the Range Rover belonged to a member of the family also. He made a mental note to inspect the Range Rover more closely before leaving.

Morris, the butler, opened the door. His countenance was grave.

"Good morning, Morris. Mr. Munroe is expecting me."

"This way, sir."

Inside the foyer, somber men and women stood conversing in hushed tones. Josh recognized a few state and county dignitaries, but he couldn't place the others. He followed Morris down a long hallway to where a middle-aged woman with short-cropped gray hair was seated at a desk before a closed door. The ever-present Max was seated nearby. The woman pushed an intercom button. "Sir, Mr. Chacón is here."

"Show him in please, Mary."

Angus Munroe was seated behind a large desk in the richly furnished den adjoining his private library. Josh was taken aback at the sight of him. The old man's patrician face was etched with lines of fatigue. His eyes, so clear and alert during his luncheon meeting with Josh only five days earlier, were now clouded and cheerless. Only his voice, straightforward and sonorous, bore witness to the inner strength that sustained the Lord of Greenleaf.

There were two other men in the room, both seated across the desk from Munroe. Josh recognized the corpulent, balding man as the senior United States senator from West Virginia, but couldn't for the life of him think of the man's name. He didn't recognize the other, younger man seated next to the senator.

"Gentlemen," Munroe said, "this is Joshua Chacón, the young man from New Mexico I was telling you about. Mr. Chacón, you probably recognize Senator Ryan. And this is Robert Lupino, United States Assistant Attorney General."

And that, Josh thought, explains the helicopter.

He shook hands first with the older man, who had not risen. "Senator." He then shook hands with the well-tailored assistant attorney general, who stood. "Mr. Lupino."

The assistant AG eyed Josh's face. "Looks like Martelli's boys did a real job on you, Mr. Chacón."

Reflexively, Josh touched his still-bandaged cheek. "It wasn't one of my finer moments."

The AG smiled and released his vise-like grip. "I was quite impressed with your book *Evil Witness*. Apparently you had a knowledgeable inside source."

Josh acknowledged the lawyer's pointed curiosity with a nod, but didn't comment.

"Ah," Senator Ryan said. "*That* Joshua Chacón."

"Yes, Jacob," Munroe said. "One of the few products of these hills to attain deserved prominence. And now, if you and Bob will be so kind, I would like to speak to Mr. Chacón in private."

The senator clutched his cane. "Surely, Angus. Bob and I will be on the veranda."

The assistant AG helped the senator to his feet. "Mr. Chacón," the AG said, his tone officious now, "I would like to get your version of the incident involving Santino and Bartelli. I'll see you before you leave, I take it?" It was more an injunction than a question.

"I'll make a point of it," Josh replied.

The two men left, the senator leaning laboriously on the younger man's arm.

Munroe motioned for Josh to take the chair Senator Ryan had vacated. "I'm pleased you—"

Just then the intercom sounded. Munroe pushed the button. "Yes?" he snapped.

"Sir, I'm sorry to disturb you, but Mr. Gray just called. Dr. Sites has released the bodies over to him for preparation. He wants to know if he should seal the caskets now, or if you would like—"

"Now," Munroe said, emphatically. "No more interruptions, please, Mary."

"Yes sir."

Josh studied his host during the exchange. Munroe was obviously exhausted from the strain of the past twelve hours. "Mr. Munroe, when I called this morning, I hadn't heard about your son and daughter-in-law. I'm terribly sorry. If you would prefer to postpone . . ."

"No, no," Munroe responded. "I'm interested in what you have to say. First, there's something you deserve to hear. It concerns you."

"Oh?"

Munroe placed a miniature tape recorded on the desk. "This is why I asked Attorney General Lupino to be here today. The voice is that of my son."

He hit the play button. "Father," David Munroe's voice spoke from the tape. A pause. Then "No . . . *dear* Father. Permit me to express affection for you in this, the last time you will ever hear my voice." The tape went on:

Remember the day six years ago when you explained to me why you had passed me over to make Connie your business manager. You made it clear that although you had arranged a generous trust in my name, you would never allow me to gain control of the Munroe fortune. You were right, of course. I would have squandered it—destroyed everything you have built. Now I'll reveal how you nearly destroyed it yourself.

Your trust in Connie was ill placed. From the outset, her singular passion was to gain control of both the Munroe and the Dunning conglomerates and merge them into a single, powerful cartel. She considered me nothing more than her ticket to the Munroe fortune and exploited me to that end. More cruelly, she looked upon our daughter as her ticket to the Dunning fortune and exploited her to that end. I'll not go into particulars about how she used an episode from Beth's past to manipulate her away from the Collier boy—whom Beth truly loved—and into an odious marriage with Stewart Dunning. I'll leave it to Beth to tell you about that, if she desires.

At the time Connie took charge, neither she nor you knew that I was deeply indebted to a mobster in Philadelphia named Marconi. At his insistence, I began selling cocaine to my friends, turning over all proceeds to him. It was barely enough to cover the interest he was charging me. I confessed all to Connie and asked her to finagle funds from corporate assets to pay off the debt. She was furious. She recognized that Marconi had tricked me into becoming vulnerable to criminal charges. She didn't give a damn about me as a person, but she knew that if I fell, her legal claim to the Munroe estate would be weakened at best, and destroyed at worst. She manipulated the books to acquire the necessary funds, and we went to Philadelphia together to buy back my IOUs. But Marconi wouldn't deal. His price to wipe out the debt and keep quiet about my drug transactions was straightforward. The solid-waste contracts between Munroe Corporation and the eastern cities were coming up for renegotiation. He demanded that she renew the contracts, no questions asked. I considered it a simple request. But you know Connie. She confronted him, demanded to know why he was so eager to have access to our pits. He refused to tell her, but at that moment, I believe, Marconi recognized a kindred spirit. They reached agreement; Marconi would have indefinite access to the pits. When the pits were exhausted, he would return all incriminating documents about me.

At first, things went smoothly. Then, a couple of weeks ago, Connie took a call from a man named Raymond Marshe, a state-appointed geologist assigned to take core samples from our pits. He insisted on talking to you. Connie told him that she made all business decisions, and he would have to speak to her or no one. He was reluctant, and told her only that he had found something that Mr. Munroe would consider of immense value. He wouldn't discuss it over the phone. Connie was shaken. Whatever Marshe had discovered of "immense value" in those pits had to be connected with Marconi. She smelled blackmail, pure and simple. She bought time to think by telling him she'd be away for a few days and would contact him later. She told him to never call Greenleaf again.

On the day you and Connie were attending Senator Dunning's funeral, Marshe called for you again. When I told Connie, she became furious. She reported it to Marconi. Two days later, Marshe was blown to bits in his office at the university.

If it had ended there, I'd probably have rationalized it. After all, Marshe had been a threat. But it didn't end there.

When Joshua Collier returned to Seneca Falls, Connie was visibly upset. With Stewart dead, she feared that the spark between Joshua and Beth would re-ignite.

Then, you received him for lunch at Greenleaf, and
Connie was convinced that an old nemesis had
returned to threaten her dream of dominion.

I was in the hallway that night when Connie
returned from your bed."

Here, Josh shot a surprised glance at Munroe. The Lord of Greenleaf, eyes half closed, gave no indication that this revealing segment
of the tape was any more significant than the rest.

She gave me the customary contemptuous look she reserved
for those occasions; then she dressed and drove from the
grounds, as she often did late at night to make an untraceable
phone call. Two days later, two of Marconi's gunmen tried
to kill Joshua. It was clear to me then that Connie would
allow no one to stand between her and her greedy ambition.
Her next victim could just as easily have been you, Father, or
even—God forbid—Beth. Connie had to be stopped.

Tonight I watched from the hillside above the Lodge
while Connie was . . . *entertaining* Secretary Mulhaney.
When the secretary left, I entered and . . . well, the
evidence will be clear.

And so, Father, farewell. I'm sorry I was such a
disappointment to you. You deserved better. But then . . .
so did I.

For a long while after his son's voice grew still, Angus Munroe
continued to stare into space, lost in the visions of his mind.

Josh used the silence to collect his thoughts. David had not
mentioned a collusion between Stewart and Professor Marshe.
Why not? Did he believe it to be irrelevant? Or was he unaware of
it? Nor had he mentioned an affair between Stewart and Connie.
Had Beth been wrong about that? Or was David unaware of that
too? Not a word about Dub or the ransacked cabin . . .

" . . . dreadfully wrong conclusions," Munroe said.

Josh looked up. Angus had extracted the tape and was looking at him. "I'm sorry," Josh apologized. "I'm afraid my thoughts
were elsewhere."

"I said, David and Constance reached wrong conclusions. Dreadfully wrong. Whatever it was that Professor Marshe was trying to peddle to me didn't come from our pits. Marshe never took core samples from them."

This didn't jibe with what Josh had heard before. "I'm not sure I understand."

"I checked with the pit bosses and with the foremen in charge of our reclamation projects. Marshe never once set up his drill apparatus anywhere near a Munroe Mining pit. David might not have known that, but Constance should have."

This was disturbing news to Josh. "Then I took a beating, and two men died up on that mountain, because she made an error in judgment?"

"I'm afraid so. Still, there must be something nefarious going on at those pits. Otherwise, Marconi wouldn't have reacted as he did. Clearly, he agreed with Connie that your meddling—as she put it—was a threat. Why? Lupino intends to follow up on that. I've given him carte blanche to investigate those pits at will, no search warrant required."

Josh wondered if he should mention Ramón Torres's theory about the pits. He decided against it. There was no way to do it without compromising his friend.

He turned the conversation back to the professor. "Then what could Marshe have found that would be of such value to you?"

"Yes," Munroe echoed. "What, indeed?"

He paused a moment. "There's another error in David's mea culpa. He implies that following a call from Constance, Marconi had Marshe killed."

"A logical conclusion, don't you agree?"

"Not according to Lupino. He says Marconi was as puzzled by that incident as the rest of us. And Lupino's in position to know."

It had a ring of déjà vu. Torres, also, had questioned Marconi's involvement in Marshe's death: "A hit like that is not exactly Marconi's style . . ."

Munroe placed the tape aside. "Well, let's hope the professionals can figure it all out. Lupino intends to use David's confession in the case he's building against Marconi."

He sat back. "Now, from what Mary told me about your call

this morning, I'm sure there are other matters on your mind. What did you wish to see me about?"

Josh reached into his pocket. "Mr. Munroe, as inopportune as the timing may be, I believe there's something you should know." He pulled out the turquoise ring and placed it on the desk.

A look of astonishment crossed Munroe's face. "Where did you get this?" He picked up the ring and held it to a better light.

"Dub Oliver found it at Twin Oaks the night Stewart was killed. Most likely beside Stewart's computer, which was still turned on. I believe that the person who left it there discovered the loss, realized it was incriminating, and went back to look for it. Just by chance, I happened to see a light in the house one night and went to investigate. Whoever was there tried to run me down with their car . . . or truck, from the glimpse I got of it. Later—perhaps that same night—I believe that person went to Dub's cabin looking for the ring."

"And shot Mr. Oliver."

"Yes . . . leaving him for dead, not realizing he was merely unconscious from a grazing wound."

"And just whom do you have in mind for these deeds, Mr. Chacón?"

The old man is dissembling, Josh thought. He knows full well what I'm getting at. "I happen to know that ring belonged to your late wife. I saw Beth wearing it one day years ago and asked her about it when I visited her in Washington two days ago. She told me that she hasn't seen it for years, and that it was kept with her grandmother's jewelry. It's obvious who else had access to it."

"I see," Munroe said. "You suspect Constance." There was no hint of surprise in his voice.

"I'm sorry to add additional anguish to this day. But I think there's reason to believe that she was in Stewart's home that night."

"Because of the ring."

Josh paused. He wondered if he should reveal Beth's revelation of an affair between Stewart and Connie. Not yet, he decided. "Among other things, yes," he said. "The ring is pretty strong incriminating evidence."

"I see," Munroe said. He placed the ring on the desk and stood. "Please wait here. I'll be only a few minutes." He left.

Josh looked around the ornately furnished den without really seeing. His mind was fixed on the question of whether he was doing the right thing. Perhaps he should have followed Carl's advice and discussed all this with Russ Hess before confronting Munroe, particularly on this of all days. Maybe that's where Munroe went, to the patio to get Hess. It wasn't a pleasant thought.

Five minutes later Munroe returned and sat again at his desk. He was carrying an intricately scrolled silver case etched on top with the letter *N*.

"This was Nan's . . . my wife's jewelry case," he said, opening the case. He removed the top tray, withdrew a ring, and laid it on the desk beside the one Josh had brought. Dumbfounded, Josh studied the two pieces of jewelry. Only by the closest inspection could he see that the two were not identical.

Munroe said, "I admit I was astonished when I saw the ring you brought, until I examined it further." He took back the ring he had taken from the jewelry chest. "I had this made for Nan in Gallup over forty years ago. The Zuni silversmith etched her initials . . . here." He turned the ring so Josh could see the initials *NM* carved on the underside of the band. "Beth wore it from time to time when she was in high school. She returned it to me before she left for college, and, to my knowledge, she hasn't seen it since. As for Constance, she never wore it."

"Now this ring"—he took the other ring in hand—"is also obviously of fine Zuni craftsmanship. But it does not belong to any member of the Munroe clan. Furthermore, I can assure you that Constance was nowhere near Twin Oaks the night Stewart was killed. She spent that night here at Greenleaf."

"You know that for certain?"

"I'm sure you detected from the tape that I was in a position to know that for certain."

Well, I've really bungled this one, Josh thought. "Mr. Munroe, I don't know what to say. It was presumptuous of me." He started to rise, but then he remembered the list of names in his pocket. It was worth a shot. He sat back down.

"One last thing." He took from his pocket the list he had found on Marshe's computer disk and handed it across the desk. "Do you, by chance, know who any of these people are?"

Munroe studied the list. "Easton," he uttered, thinking aloud. "William Easton," he said again, pronouncing the name slowly. He stood. "Come with me."

They stepped into the library just off the den. Josh looked around the huge impressive room. Shelves heavy with books covered all four walls and extended from floor level to the lofty ceiling. The shelves were categorized for art, geography, the classics, maps, atlases, history, and others, with each section further classified to a lower common denominator such as continent, country, region, and state. Josh had never seen such an extensive private collection. Surely many of the volumes housed here were priceless collector's items.

On a table in a far corner was a computer with a stand-alone central processing unit. Munroe noticed Josh eyeing the setup.

"Miss Mary put everything in here in a database," Munroe said. "I don't allow anyone else to touch the machine. Not even me."

He went to one shelf, pulled down a well-thumbed volume, and flipped through the pages. "Ah, here." He read from the book, "Lieutenant William Easton. War of Independence. Service number s-35508. Buried near Eagle Rocks in the Smoke Hole region."

"The Revolutionary War?" Josh remarked. "Surely that's not the man on my list."

Munroe handed the book to Josh. "Take a look at this."

Josh saw that the book was a nineteenth-century history published by the West Virginia University, just the sort of text a history buff like Munroe would have on hand. He studied the page Munroe indicated. It, and the next page, contained forty-five names arranged alphabetically; all were names of Revolutionary War veterans buried in Seneca County. He confirmed the listing for Easton, then looked under the letter *K*. Sure enough, there was a listing for Fred King, Captain, followed by place of burial—Old Lahmansville Cemetery. All were listed with rank and place of burial; all were officers. He noted that there were other officers in the Seneca County group who were not on Marshe's list.

"Rakestraw's name isn't here," he said.

"So I noticed," Munroe agreed. "Perhaps an oversight. Not uncommon in those old histories."

Josh studied the book again, and then the list he had brought.

"Forty-five in the book, but only six of them on Marshe's list. Is there anything significant about those six? Battle awards or something?"

"Not that I'm aware of," Munroe replied. "Would you care to let me know why you're asking about these men?"

Why not? Josh thought. He couldn't screw up things any more than he had. "I found those names in a protected file from Professor Marshe's computer. He took pains to hide it. I have no idea why."

"Most interesting," Munroe said. "Most interesting, indeed." After a moment he asked, "And what do you plan to do with the information?"

"I haven't the slightest idea," Josh replied.

An intercom on the wall sounded. Munroe frowned, stepped over, and punched a button. "Yes?"

"Sorry, sir," the secretary's voice came through the instrument, "but Senator Ryan says he must be leaving. There are heavy rains forecasted for later today. You know how he is about flying."

"All right, Mary. I'll be right out."

He released the button. "Craven old curmudgeon. Should have abdicated that senate seat to a younger man years ago. Well, Mr. Chacón. I hope the visit hasn't been entirely fruitless."

Josh stood. "Thank you, sir. Once again, my condolences."

Munroe nodded. "May I ask you a personal question, Joshua?"

Josh was pleasantly surprised. It was the first time Munroe had ever addressed him by his first name. "Certainly, sir."

"There's a matter on David's recording that I'm curious about. I've long known that at one time you and my granddaughter were enamored with each other. David was cryptic about how Constance broke up your affair. Are you free to talk about that?"

Anything but that, Josh thought. "I'm sorry. I believe it's best to leave that to Beth's discretion."

"I see. The same opinion her father held. Well, she will be here this afternoon. She's driving. Perhaps she'll stay this time. It's all hers now, you know, or soon will be—Greenleaf, Twin Oaks, and the Munroe and Dunning fortunes. Ironic, don't you agree? She inherits by default what her mother so sorely coveted."

"Yes. Ironic."

Munroe gestured toward the door. "I'll walk you out. Let me know if you decipher that cryptic list?"

"I will, sir. One other thing—who owns the white Range Rover parked out by the Rolls?"

"It is . . . it was David's."

In the foyer, Munroe bade him goodbye and went looking for the senator. Josh remembered that he had promised to speak with the assistant attorney general before leaving. But Lupino was nowhere in sight. It was just as well. He had no intention of discussing his "knowledgeable inside sources" anyway.

In the parking lot, he walked past his car to the white Range Rover at the far end of the lot. He stooped down and studied the tires. They were all-terrain, inverted-V treads. But not center split. This was not the vehicle that tried to run him down that night at Twin Oaks.

Another false lead in an altogether perplexing day.

Thirty-five

Nursing supervisor Charlotte Waller handed the medical chart across the counter to Rachel. "I don't know how to thank you enough, Miss Bond. We're stretched so thin lately, and Mr. Oliver needs constant care. We're all grateful."

"It's the least I could do," Rachel replied. She opened the chart and read through the latest entries.

"His throat wound is healing slowly," Charlotte Waller said. "Dr. Sites says he may be able to talk in a few days."

"That is good news," Rachel said. "Are there other patients in ICU today?"

"No, I'm afraid you'll be the only one on duty there. But don't hesitate to call if you need us."

"Thank you."

Rachel handed the chart back to the supervisor and started the long walk down the north wing. Midway she passed the maternity ward where three newborn babies lay in bassinets just inside the viewing window. She stopped and gazed down at the babies. After a moment, struggling with the heart-wrenching emotion that rose within her, she turned away and continued to the critical care unit at the end of the corridor.

Two of the three private rooms in the ICU were empty. In the third, Dub Oliver lay on the high bed with his upper body elevated.

His throat and chest, where Little Joe Bartelli's bullets had ripped through him, were heavily bandaged. A plastic bag suspended from an IV stand beside the bed fed fluid through a clear plastic tube and into a needle in a vein on the back of his right hand. That arm was strapped to a restraining board.

The attending nurse glanced up when Rachel entered. "Oh . . . hi." She closed the year-old copy of *Reader's Digest* she was reading. "I didn't know you were taking this shift."

"Morning, Harriet. How's the patient?"

At the sound of Rachel's voice, Dub opened his eyes.

"Not out of the woods," Harriet replied, "but his vital signs are stronger today."

"Still on morphine, I see."

"Lowered dose. I just changed the bag."

"Yes, I see," Rachel said. The monitoring screens above the bed were blank. "No monitors today?"

"Doctor says they're no longer needed." She gathered up her personal items. "Julie will relieve you this afternoon. If you need anything in the meantime, you know the routine."

"Yes. Now, you go home and get some sleep."

"Thanks." She gave her patient a parting look and saw that he was staring hard at her. She knew he favored her over the other nurses. "It's all right, Mr. Oliver. Miss Bond is here to take care of you. I'll be back tomorrow." She smiled and left.

Rachel waited until the nurse's footsteps faded down the tiled hallway before she closed the door to the room. She stepped around the bed to make certain that the monitors were, indeed, disconnected. They were. She walked around to where the morphine pouch was suspended and increased the drip rate to quadruple the dosage. Dub's eyes were fixed on her, aware of her every movement. She noticed and patted him on the shoulder, and then sat in the chair Harriet had vacated. She looked at her watch, and waited.

Forty-five minutes later she rose and turned the IV valve back to the previous setting.

A half hour later, Dub Oliver's labored breathing ceased.

Thirty-six

At the bottom of the hill, where the road from the Munroe estate forked toward the highway, the Canaan Valley widened into a lush expanse of bluegrass and red clover bordering both sides of the river. Envision the flora as sage, Josh mused, and the scene would pass for the high-mesa meadows bordering the Rio Grande Gorge just southwest of Taos, New Mexico.

The thought of New Mexico brought Vicki Armijo to mind. He had forgotten to return her call!

There was an isolated general store a few miles down the highway toward Seneca Falls. Five minutes later he parked in the graveled lot beside the store and entered the outside phone booth. He was thankful that a gathering cloud bank was shading what otherwise would have been an unbearable sweatbox. He looked at his watch, interpolated the two-hour time difference, and decided Vicki wouldn't have left for the TV studio yet. He dialed her unlisted number, entered his credit card code at the tone, and waited for the ring. He decided to let it go through the fourth ring, and then hang up. He didn't want to try to explain things to her machine.

After the third ring, she answered. "This is Vicki."

"Hi. Sorry to have taken so long to—"

"Well, it's about time," she interrupted. "When are you coming home?"

"Soon. Did you find out anything about Marshe?"

"Just like that? No 'How are you' or 'I miss you' or 'When are you moving to Wichita'?"

His heart sank. "Are you moving to Wichita?"

"I don't know. You tell me. Should I?"

She hadn't decided yet. "Vicki . . . I wish I were there right now. Hell, I wish I'd never left. I never expected to get so caught up in things here . . . but . . . it's confusing . . . people have been killed . . . it's too much to attempt to explain over the phone. Look, we agreed we'd talk things out when I get back. We will, I promise. But I've got to see things through here before I can give anything else serious thought. Please, please try to understand."

There was a momentary pause before Vicki responded. "I've never heard you talk like this, Josh. Are you all right?"

A twinge of pain shot through his cheek. No need to mention that affliction now. "I'm okay. Tired and frustrated, but okay. It's just that trying to get a grasp on things here is like trying to make sense of Santa Fe politics."

It was an analogy any New Mexico reporter could relate to. She laughed. "That bad, huh? Okay, how can I help?"

"Marshe."

"Oh yes, Marshe. Is he a friend of yours?"

"No."

"Good. I called Mel Simmons, the geologist you went caving with. He said that at one time Marshe enjoyed an excellent reputation in his profession, but then he screwed up."

"Screwed up? How?"

"You ever hear of the Troublesome Creek Mine scam, in Colorado?"

"No."

"Simmons didn't know the details, only that it happened while Marshe was teaching at the University of Colorado. So I did a database search. Troublesome Creek is a deserted gold mine in the high-desert country about fifty miles west of Denver. It played out back in the fifties, or so everyone thought. Then, five years ago, a drunken prospector rode into Kremmling—that's the nearest town—flashing nuggets that he said came from the Troublesome Creek Mine. He claimed he'd discovered a new lode. The mine owners confirmed the find, posted guards on the property, and solicited financial partners to help reopen the shaft. An investment group in Phoenix was the high roller—Henry Broadbent and Associates. They sank four million dollars into the project. Problem was, the whole thing was a setup. The owners took the money and ran—they still haven't been found—and the so-called new lode turned out to be a sophisticated plant. The gold vein was actually melded into the rock strata—something Simmons says only a first-rate geologist could have pulled off."

"Are you telling me that Marshe seeded that mine?"

"Bureau of Mines in Denver was convinced of it—still is. I called one of the investigators on the case. I've got his name and number at the office if you need it. He was able to tie Marshe to two meetings with one of the mine owners that absconded. Both meetings were in public restaurants. Just dinner with a friend, Marshe said. The investigator learned that Marshe had made at least three trips to Kremmling shortly before the new lode was found. Marshe claimed they were fly-fishing trips, and he had receipts from Elkhorn Lodge where he had stayed. Problem was, the Elkhorn is an upscale resort that always assigns a fishing guide to guests, and none of the guides could remember accompanying Marshe. He countered that he had not wanted a guide, and that he preferred to fish alone. Anyway, the bottom line is that it was all too circumstantial. Marshe was never charged. Soon afterward he left CU and moved to West Virginia."

The conversation fell into silence.

"Josh . . . are you there?"

"Yeah. Hold on a minute, Vicki."

He held the phone aside and looked out over the valley. In the distance, dimly visible beyond the rim of the overhanging clouds, a single jet contrail threaded a westward course. He wished he were aboard that plane. He cherished the thought for a moment, but then turned to trying to fit the new pieces into the ever-expanding puzzle. Marshe a crook? In cahoots with Stewart? What sort of scam had they cooked up that required the cooperation of a "first-rate geologist"? There were no gold mines in Seneca County. Certainly a new coal vein was no rarity. Still, according to David Munroe's taped confession, the professor claimed to have found something

Angus Munroe would pay dearly to have. What? David and Connie assumed Marshe had uncovered incriminating evidence about the pit contracts with Manny Marconi. Yet, according to Angus, Marshe never got near Munroe Mining's reclaimed pits.

"Josh."

No answer.

"Josh! Are you still there?"

He put the phone back to his ear. "Sorry, Vicki. I was thinking."

"Josh, you're not tied in with Marshe somehow, are you?"

"No. No one's tied in with him anymore. He was blown to bits by a package bomb last week."

"Madre de Dios! Who? Why?"

"Marshe and my brother were working together on a project when both of them were killed. We've been trying to get to the bottom of things . . ."

"We?"

"Marshe's stepdaughter. Rachel Bond. We've got a common interest in finding out what happened."

"Oh? . . . Is she pretty?"

Josh laughed. "Absolutely ravishing. I can hardly keep my hands off her."

"You're one stinking *bastardo* at times, Joshua Chacón. Do you know that?"

"So I've been told. Don't worry. It's strictly platonic." He started to add *so far*, but didn't.

"Look, I've got to go, Vicki. There are others who need to hear what you've just told me. You've been a real help."

"My pleasure. By the way, Mel Simmons wants to know if you're going to do the book about WIPP."

"Oh, shit." Something else he had forgotten. "Call him for me, will you? Tell him I'll give him a decision just as soon as I get back."

"Will do."

"Thanks again, Vicki. You're a jewel."

"Sure. Hurry home, amigo. It's been a bit too platonic around here lately."

Thirty-seven

Carl Travis's face was a mask of grief.

"When did it happen?" Josh asked, shaken by the news.

Carl was seated at his desk in the *Ledger* office. Ads and stories that should have been pasted by now lay untouched on a side table. "Sometime before noon," he replied. "Rachel was with him. She said his vital signs were looking up. Doc had taken him off the monitors, and hoped he'd be able to talk in a few days. Then . . . he just went . . . all of a sudden." He swallowed hard a couple of times. "We weren't that far apart in age, but Dub was like a son to me, Josh. Like a son . . ."

"How's Viola taking it?"

"Hard. She's at the hospital now. Doc's going to do an autopsy this afternoon. I suspect she'll stay close to him as long as she can."

Visions of the slow-witted giant flashed through Josh's mind: Dub's ransacked cabin splattered with his blood; Dub appearing from nowhere to confront the two murderous goons; the fat man pinned to the cabin wall by Dub's pickaxe; Steelrims firing bullet after bullet into Dub.

"How about Rachel?" he asked.

"Devastated. She left the hospital right after it happened. Said she had to get away."

"She at the Fox and Ox?"

"Most likely," Carl replied.

Josh made a mental note to call her as soon as possible. He wanted to ask her about the Troublesome Creek Mine scam in Colorado. Why hadn't she mentioned that? Did she even know about it? Questions he wanted to put to her as soon as possible. First, though, he owed it to Carl to bring him up to date. Ironic, he mused, that for the second time today he had to infringe on the private thoughts of a grieving man. He wondered if Carl was up to it, and asked.

Carl cleared his throat. "Yes . . . certainly." He shuffled some papers and came up with a track-fed computer sheet. "This is an AP release about David and Connie. Came in about an hour ago. Tragic . . . tragic. How's the old man taking it?"

"Suffering, but he holds his emotions in tight rein. I offered to leave, but he wanted to get on with it."

"And?"

Josh related the details of his meeting at Greenleaf. How the names on Marshe's list were recorded in a history of Seneca County veterans of the Revolutionary War. Except for Rakestraw.

"What in heaven's name has the Revolutionary War got to do with this?" Carl asked.

"Good question," Josh replied. "There's more. I called Vicki Armijo."

He related what Vicki had told him about the mine scam in Colorado. How circumstantial evidence implicated Marshe. How the professor left soon afterward to come to West Virginia.

"Marshe was a crook?" Carl asked.

"It appears so," Josh replied. "I've got to talk to Rachel about that. First, I think it's time we follow your advice and bring Hess up to date."

Carl shook his head. "Your timing is way off. He's in Pittsburgh . . . some sort of law enforcement convention."

"How long?"

"Through Saturday. Maybe longer."

"Would his secretary know?"

"He took Mrs. Thompson with him. He might check in with his deputy. But if you're thinking of briefing Mares, you might as well brief that telephone post out front. Anyway, my guess is that once Hess hears that Dub is dead, he'll consider Stewart's case closed."

Josh emitted an oath of disgust and stepped to the window. Outside, the light was fading fast. The cloud bank he had encountered in Canaan Valley had evolved into an anvil thunderhead, signaling a new summer storm rising west of the Alleghenies. He watched the scene for a moment, and then turned back to Carl. "I can't wait for Hess," he said. "I've got to get to Rachel."

"I understand. If I hear from him I'll—"

The phone jangled. Carl answered, and then covered the mouthpiece with his hand. "It's Mary Henson . . . Angus's secretary. For you."

Josh took the phone. Moments later he said, "Yes, certainly."

He placed the phone back in the cradle. "Angus wants to see me again. Something about our meeting this morning. Says it's important." He paused. "You got the number for the Fox and Ox?"

Carl opened a drawer and took out the thin Seneca County phone directory. He found the number and pointed it out to Josh. Josh dialed. He was greeted by a computerized switchboard. He punched in the number of Rachel's room. After ten rings he slammed the phone down. "Damn!" His mind was approaching overload.

"Calm down, son," Carl admonished. "It's not worth a stroke."

Josh took a deep breath. "Look, if Rachel calls, tell her to stay put. I don't know how long I'll be with Angus, but I'll get back to her just as soon as I can. Maybe she and I can chat over dinner tonight at the Fox and Ox. Tell her I suggested it, okay?"

"Sure. I'm going to be here late anyway. I've got to make arrangements for Dub. Don't keep me in the dark, hear?"

"I'll call you from the Fox and Ox," Josh promised, and left.

A driving rain was sweeping across the estate when Barlow waved Josh through the wrought iron gates. There were fewer cars parked at the mansion now. The Marine helicopter had long since lifted off to ferry Senator Ryan and Attorney General Lupino back to the capital.

Morris, the butler, met him at the car with an umbrella. They ran for the covering porch together. Morris shook out the umbrella and placed it in a stand before opening the front door. "Mr. Munroe is waiting for you, sir. This way."

He led the way to the library, rapped on the door, and pushed it open. "Sir, Mr. Chacón is here."

"Ah, Joshua," Munroe acknowledged. "Come in, come in."

Josh wiped his face and hands with a handkerchief.

Munroe said, "Sorry to call you back through this storm. Would you like a towel?"

"No, sir. It's not that bad."

"Morris, please see to it that we're not disturbed."

"Yes sir," the butler replied, and closed the door as he left.

The master of Greenleaf was seated at one of the large mahogany tables near his extensive historical collection. Books of different sizes lay open before him. He indicated a chair across from him. Josh sat down and looked over the open books. Two of the larger volumes, timeworn and frayed from use, were bound with burlap and leather, a practice abandoned in the mid-nineteenth century. Others, much smaller, were similar to the university-published history he had examined in this room earlier that day.

Munroe said, "I hope you will not consider me coldhearted, Joshua. I'll mourn my loss in my own time. But your visit this morning was so intriguing that I forced all other thoughts aside and returned here, to my books. I've been here ever since. There are things I want you to see."

He pushed a computer printout across the table. "I had Miss Mary do a database search for the names you found on Professor Marshe's computer disk. You have that list with you?"

"Uh . . . yes." Josh pulled the folded paper from his pocket.

"Good. Miss Mary's printout pinpointed certain books in my library—the books now on the table before us—that refer, however briefly, to the six names on your list—"

"Including Rakestraw?" Josh interjected.

"Indeed. First,"—he opened the West Virginia University history pamphlet that Josh had seen that morning—"as you know, this book contains the names of forty-five Revolutionary War veterans who are buried in Seneca County. It contains all the names on Marshe's list, with the exception of Paul Rakestraw."

Josh nodded in agreement.

Munroe pushed the booklet aside, opened one of the burlap- and leather-bound tomes and leafed through it for several seconds. "Ah yes, here we are." He turned the book so Josh could read it. "Do you recognize this name?"

Josh leaned closer and read aloud where Munroe was pointing: "Governor Robert Dinwiddie . . ." He thought a moment before it came to him. He unfolded the list he had made from Marshe's computer and looked at the heading: Dinwiddie/Seneca IX. "Well, I'll be damned." He looked back at the book. "Is that the person on this list?"

"It is," Munroe confirmed, "and it's the clue that sent me back to the library after you left. Does the name mean anything to you?"

"I'm afraid not."

"I doubt that it would to anyone not well-read in pre–Revolutionary War history."

He sat back in his chair. "Robert Dinwiddie," he said, now using a professorial tone. "Lieutenant governor, to be more precise—not governor—of colonial Virginia from 1751 to 1758. 'Seneca IX' on your list refers to the ninth chapter of an exhaustive eighteenth-century history of the Seneca Territories written by Marcus West. West chronicled Dinwiddie's reign in suffocating detail—far more than suits our purpose. Our concern lies with a few months shortly preceding the French and Indian Wars."

It does? Josh thought, wondering why. Nonetheless, he was eager to hear what this history lesson was all about.

Munroe continued, "By 1753, the French were making serious inroads into the Mississippi Valley. Their presence was a thorn in the side of the English, who considered the American continent their private domain. Dinwiddie was determined to thwart the Frenchmen. In 1754, he called on an officer in his service who knew the land perhaps better than any other—a twenty-one-year-old colonel named George Washington—"

"You mean *the* George Washington?"

"The same. During his teens, Washington surveyed much of the territory west of the Alleghenies, including the acreage on which we now sit. Dinwiddie commissioned Washington to carry a communiqué to the French demanding an explanation for their encroachment and warning them to leave the area at once. Suspecting it would be futile, he further commissioned Washington to map all the French bastions along the way, including any wilderness trails over which the French could expect to receive reinforcements from their forces in Canada."

"A spy mission," Josh suggested.

"Exactly," Munroe agreed. "Washington assigned the task of plotting French positions to a man whom he identified as 'my cartographer.' Nowhere, in any of the documents I've searched, is the man listed by any other identity.

"As expected, the French commander scoffed at Dinwiddie's edict and ordered Washington to retreat or face dire consequences. Washington did retreat, but not before he sized up the French forces and had his cartographer record their positions on the charts he had etched each day since leaving Virginia."

Munroe leafed several pages ahead and once again invited attention to the book. "Washington's complement on that mission included six officers. Here are their names."

Josh read the names. The six officers identified in the fading history text were identical with the six names on Marshe's list— including Rakestraw. He glanced up at his host. "This can't be coincidental."

"No, it can't," Munroe agreed.

He pushed the large volume aside, pulled the second one to him, and laid a hand atop it. "This is a collection of Washington's reports made to his superiors when he was billeted at Fort Cumberland. It contains his account of happenings during his retreat from French forces following their rejection of the Dinwiddie edict. It's here for you to read, if you wish. I've researched it thoroughly, and can paraphrase the points that interest us."

"Please do," Josh concurred.

"On the return trek, Washington's small force was attacked by French and Indian marauders on two occasions; first, in what is now Pittsburgh; second, in a lesser-known location, Piawaka Flats."

Something pricked Josh's memory. "Piawaka?"

"An Indian name—a remote tract on the west bank of the Potomac, in what is now Seneca County. In that encounter, the cartographer was killed. Expecting other attacks, Washington feared the documents he'd compiled of French forces would be captured. If so, the French would surely regroup elsewhere, eliminating any element of surprise the English may have gained. So he memorized the data, sealed the documents inside the dead man's saber sheath, and buried them with the body." Munroe paused. "Does this last bit of information tell you anything?"

"I don't . . . no, wait . . . the saber sheath! Only officers carried sabers."

"Indeed."

"Rakestraw!" Josh exclaimed. "It had to be him. The other five officers are listed in the register as veterans of the Revolutionary War. Rakestraw didn't survive to fight in that war."

"Precisely. And if the two of us could unravel that historical riddle, certainly our good professor could have done the same. Which brings us to the odd manner in which he conducted his surveys. Why would Marshe range throughout Seneca county with a drill rig, ostensibly searching for core-sample evidence of mine pollution, yet never set foot on the largest mining operation here—namely, Munroe Mining? Could it be that his quarry was something different? Something of historical, rather than environmental, value?"

"The cartographer's charts," Josh interjected.

"Yes," Munroe said, "the cartographer's charts. Marshe even double-checked his findings along the way. Look at the dates beside the names on his list."

Josh did: February 2 through July 5. A different date beside each man's name, except Rakestraw's. It was clear now. Marshe had visited the graves of the surviving officers of the Dinwiddie expedition and, in true investigative style, had recorded the date for whatever purpose it might serve.

"There's something else," Josh said. "Rachel—Marshe's stepdaughter—was with him when he died. He was trying to talk to her, to tell her something. According to her, his last word sounded like *pyahga*. She had no idea what it meant. But from what you've told me just now, it's almost certain he was trying to say *Piawaka*."

"Most intriguing," Munroe said. A moment later he added, "Marshe made several attempts to contact me. He claimed to have something of great value to offer me. He surely knew that I would have no interest in anything of material value. So it had to be something else."

He sat back in his chair, his countenance pensive. "He was right, you know. If he found those documents, or whatever fragments of them remain, I would have paid—would still pay—dearly for them. Not for my private collection, mind you. That no longer interests me. But as a present to the Smithsonian, where they rightfully belong." He sat forward. "I must know the truth, Joshua. If those documents exist in the professor's holdings, either at the university or at his home, I must have them."

Intuitively, Josh realized what the statement implied. Would he, Joshua Chacón, be willing to help obtain them? He said, "There are things we haven't discussed yet."

"Oh?"

"Stewart Dunning," Josh said.

"Ah, yes . . . they were cohorts, weren't they—Stewart and the professor? Stewart would have been as eager as I to lay hands on those documents."

"And they were both murdered," Josh said pointedly.

The implication reflected in Munroe's countenance. "How obtuse of me." He thought for a moment. "Someone else has solved the riddle, too, haven't they, Joshua? Someone who is so eager to obtain the documents that he is willing to kill for them."

Rachel, Josh thought. She'd mentioned that she was sorting though Marshe's things at his home. Whoever else was stalking the documents would be certain to go to the professor's home. Rachel could be in danger. He looked around the room. "Is there a phone in here?"

"On the desk."

He went to the desk and dialed the Fox and Ox Camp number. This time, when there was no response in Rachel's room, he entered the phone code for the desk clerk. To his question, the clerk replied, "Miss Bond has checked out, sir."

"Checked out? When? Did she leave a forwarding address?"

"Shortly after noon. No sir, no address."

There was only one place she could be. He dialed information and asked for the home number of Professor Marshe in Morgantown.

"I show a Raymond Marshe, 301 Campus Circle," the operator intoned.

"That's the one," Josh confirmed, and took down the number.

He hung up briefly, and then dialed the Morgantown number. After the third ring a recording announced, "The number you have dialed has been disconnected."

Damn! Increasingly apprehensive, he looked toward Munroe, "How long would it take to drive to Morgantown?"

Munroe glanced up from the books. "In this storm, you'd be fortunate to make it in three hours. Are you considering it?"

Josh looked at his watch. He could make it by 9:30. "Yes." He jotted down the address the operator had given him. "First I have to make another call."

Munroe pushed the intercom to his kitchen.

Josh dialed Carl Travis's office number. The editor was still at his office. Josh explained his plan. "There's too much to explain now. If I get a chance, I'll call you from Morgantown. Tell Aunt Martha I may not be back tonight."

Just as he hung up, Morris entered the library with a small picnic bag. Munroe said: "Sandwiches and a thermos of coffee. You'll need them. Call me later, no matter what the time."

"I will." He thanked his host and took the bag. Morris sheltered him with the umbrella as he hurried to his car.

Thirty-eight

Vicki Armijo found a vacant parking space near Scholes Hall. She despised driving on the University of New Mexico campus, but on this occasion she considered herself lucky. Despite the late afternoon traffic, it had taken only twenty minutes of cruising to find a space. Usually she had to park on one of the Albuquerque side streets and hike a mile or more to the school. She locked her Volvo, fed the meter, and walked across the campus toward the quad. Just past the ponderosa-sheltered duck pond, she entered Zimmerman Library.

Inside the mammoth building, she continued past the main desk and descended the petroglyph-adorned stairwell to the microfilm library in the basement. Extending along one wall of the cavernous room, scores of file cabinets contained film copies of major newspapers and magazines, domestic and foreign, dating back to the turn of the century. But it wasn't print media that interested her. Ever since talking to Josh on the phone that morning, she had been obsessed with one of his comments. The only way to satisfy her curiosity was to scan her notes. And to do that, she had to visit the university.

That her notes were on microfilm at Zimmerman Library rather than at the TV station where she worked was the result of an agreement between the station's news manager and the school's department of journalism. Although students could obtain cassettes of actual news broadcasts from the station, the chair of the journalism department wanted students to have easy access to the basic notes taken by reporters in the field—the raw material from which a final story was constructed. Thus, the TV station maintained a library of aired stories, and the school maintained a microfilm library of reporters' field notes. It was a quid pro quo that saved both facilities precious space.

Vicki went to the file cabinet maintained for her TV station, opened a drawer, and fingered through boxes of reels until she found the one marked JAN–JUN. She took it out, glanced around the room, and sighed. Like any major research library on a university campus, Zimmerman was usually crowded. All the reading machines were occupied. She sat in a nearby chair to wait. She noticed others doing the same.

Ten minutes later, a student turned off the microfilm reader nearest where she was sitting. She hurried to it, beating two others who had risen from their chairs. Another black mark on my reputation, she thought. Her face was one of the most recognizable in the state.

She threaded the film into the sprockets, adjusted the brightness and focus, and fast-forwarded through the months until she arrived at April. Then she turned the film forward a few frames at a time until she found the notes headed "Armijo." She continued forwarding slowly until she came to the first note annotated "Women/AIDS." It was the first of sixty-four pages of notes she had taken during that assignment. The original notes had filled two legal-size tablets, but were now reduced to a few inches of microfilm. Beneath the major topic the subheadings read: "Albuquerque," "Tucson," "Flagstaff," "Dallas," "Phoenix" . . . five of the eleven Southwestern cities she had visited to collect data for the report.

She stopped at the first entry for Phoenix, and then read through each succeeding note with painstaking care. Six pages later she stopped abruptly, sat back, and stared at the screen. "Mother of God!" she uttered aloud.

She rewound the film, left the reel on the table, and rushed upstairs to a bank of pay phones. She had to contact Josh as soon as possible.

Carl Travis pasted the final entry onto the makeup boards for the next edition of the *Ledger*. The entire front page was devoted to the heartfelt eulogy, with photos, he had written for Dub Oliver. Now, exhausted from the events of this long day, he returned to his office and slumped down into his chair. He picked up the notes he made about Dub's funeral arrangements, scanned them for a moment, and then shoved them into his satchel. He wanted to stop by the hardware store and see Martha before going home to try to get some sleep. He would review the notes tomorrow when his mind was clearer.

He had just turned off the desk light when the phone rang.

He switched the light back on and picked up the instrument. "*Ledger*. Travis."

"Mr. Travis, is Josh there?"

"Vicki. Good to hear from you aga—"

"Please, Mr. Travis . . . I must talk to Josh."

"I'm sorry, he's not here."

"How can I reach him? It's very important." Her voice was tense with emotion.

"I'm afraid he's out of touch right now. Can I help? Josh is driving to Morgantown to see Rachel Bond."

"Mr. Travis, Rachel Bond is dead."

Carl was silent. There had to be a mix-up. "No, Vicki, I'm talking about Rachel Bond—Professor Raymond Bond's stepdaughter. She's been here for several days helping—"

"*Rachel Bond*," she repeated emphatically. "Professor Raymond Bond's stepdaughter, his wife Gloria's daughter. Rachel Bond is dead, Mr. Travis. She died of AIDS in Phoenix General Hospital last April."

Carl stammered, "I . . . I don't understand."

"I was with her shortly before she died. We'd been talking for two days. I was researching a story." She told him about her TV special, *Women and AIDS*. She had interviewed dozens of afflicted women. In Phoenix General Hospital she met and interviewed Rachel Bond. The dying woman talked in detail about her past: that she had been born and raised in Colorado; that the Bohemian lifestyle she had adopted following her father's death caused an insuperable rift between her and her mother; that her mother had married again—to a geology professor from Denver, who was now at West Virginia University; and that she learned from friends her mother, too, was suffering a terminal illness.

"She told me that neither her mother nor her stepfather knew she was dying of AIDS. I offered to contact them. She was adamant that I not do so. She wanted nothing to do with them, or anyone. She simply wanted to die and be forgotten."

She paused a moment. "Mr. Travis, Josh told me on the phone today that people have been killed there. I don't know who he's going to see, but it is not Rachel Bond. He could be . . ." Her voice cracked. "Oh, dear God . . . I've got to get in contact with him!"

Carl's blood turned to ice water. He had to get control. He took a deep breath. "Vicki?"

Sounds of weeping came through the phone, revealing a deeper emotion than mere concern for the welfare of a friend. "Vicki . . . can you hear me?"

"Yes."

"I'll get your message to Josh. I promise. I've got to hang up now. Understand?"

"Yes." Her soft sobs continued. "Please call me . . . *please*."

"I will." He placed the phone in the cradle.

His mind raced with conflicting thoughts. Could this new information be true? Who was the woman impersonating Rachel Bond? And why? "I'll get your message to Josh. I promise." How in the hell am I going to do that? Think, damn it, think! Call the professor's home? No, Josh said the phone had been disconnected. There had to be a—

Suddenly it hit him. He picked up the phone and dialed Hess's office. No answer. He checked his Rolodex for Deputy Mares's home number and called. Mares answered.

"Bob, Carl Travis. I need Gene Gregory's home phone number in Charleston."

"Colonel Gregory?"

"Yes."

"That's a private number," Mares replied in a practiced bureaucratic tone.

"I know it's a private number. That's why I'm calling you instead of the operator. This is an emergency. Give me the number, Bob."

"I don't wanta get in no trouble."

Carl swore aloud. Then, his voice cold as steel, he said, "Bob, if I don't have that number in ten seconds you don't know what trouble is!"

Mares hesitated. After a silence, he responded, "Well . . . hold on a sec."

A moment later, Mares came back on the line. "Okay, here it is."

Carl copied the number. He hung up, waited a second, and put through a long distance call to the commandant of state police in Charleston.

Thirty-nine

The rain had subsided to a gentle mist by the time Josh reached Morgantown. Still, even with a flashlight, he found it difficult to read the street signs in a night void of moon and stars. He had fought the deluge for four hours, an unnerving experience for one accustomed to driving in New Mexico, where a windshield wiper was more ornament than necessity. Just off I-79 south of town, he stopped at an Exxon station and bought a map. With the map and directions from the station manager, he found his way to the main entrance to the West Virginia University campus, where he turned east in search of Campus Circle. From the address given him by the phone operator, he figured that the professor's house was on a corner lot. He soon found the street, and a sign indicating he was at the one hundred block. He turned north. Two blocks later his headlights illuminated a curbside number—301—outlined in reflective paint. He pulled into the down-sloping driveway and checked the car chronometer. It was 10:27 p.m.

He shut down the car and sat for a moment observing the scene. The house was a modest one-story brick cracker box built above a full basement, a typical east of the Mississippi middle-class home. There were no lights on inside or out. There were no other vehicles in the driveway. He had a sinking feeling that something was amiss.

Grabbing the flashlight, he walked down the yard to the front porch. There was no response to the bell. He tried the door; it was locked. Both front windows were blocked by venetian blinds. If Rachel was in there, she could be in trouble—or worse. He left the porch to circle around to the back door. He found a side door and tried it. It opened. He stepped inside, focused the flashlight, and saw that he was in the utility room. The next door led into the living room. He hunted for a wall switch, found it near the front door, and turned it on. Sparsely furnished, the room contained a single overstuffed couch, frayed from long use; two matching chairs in similar condition; and a Formica table in the offset dining nook. All the furniture was sitting on a hardwood floor covered with a couple of shoddy throw rugs. The professor and his wife had led a frugal life; most likely, considering Rachel's summary of their medical bills, of necessity.

"Rachel!" he called. There was no response.

He made his way down the hallway and checked the bedrooms. No one was there. Nor in the bathroom. At the end of the hall, another door led to a small book-lined den. He flipped on the lights. A desk near the window held a laptop computer. Opposite the desk, a full-size drafting table sat against one wall. On the floor beside the table were several sheets of parchment paper seemingly yellowed from age. Another sheet, held to the table by a T-bar, contained the outline of a crudely sketched map, easily recognizable as the Ohio River Valley along what was now the West Virginia-Ohio-Kentucky borders. Entries on the map identified the location of rustic fortifications or trails leading to them. Most of the original pencil sketches had been etched over with black ink; some had not yet been inked.

A book stand near the table held a voluminous, burlap-bound book similar to the ones Josh had seen that afternoon in Angus Munroe's library. He read the title: *A History of the Seneca Territories*. The author was Marcus West.

He knew exactly what he was looking at. There had been no momentous unearthing of historical documents at Piawaka Flats. Marshe had been creating his own history, right here in this room. Like the seeded Troublesome Creek Mine in Colorado, this was another scam in the making.

Another thought hit him: the den was not locked. Anyone in the house would have had easy access to it. Surely Rachel had seen this book. Did she know what it meant? Where was she now?

Josh left the den and went to the kitchen where a staircase led down to the basement. He descended a few steps and shined the flashlight around to reveal a work table, tools, a furnace, and gardening equipment. The beam also illuminated a vehicle parked just inside the garage door. He went to examine it. It was a four-wheel-drive Isuzu Trooper, chalk white. He knelt and ran his fingers over the back tire. Inverted-V tread, center split, precisely the type tire that left the telltale tread marks in the garden barn behind Twin Oaks and at the side road pulloff at Mohawk Creek just below Dub's cabin. He stepped forward and shined the light on the right front fender. Wedged beneath the forward edge of the chrome tire-well guard was a tiny fragment of gray cloth. A twinge of recalled pain shot through his left leg. There was no question where the tattered remnant came from. It had been ripped from his trousers the night a vehicle—*this* vehicle—attempted to run him down in the front driveway at Twin Oaks.

Pulse racing, he stood and shined the light inside the Isuzu. There were two suitcases, closed and strapped, on the rear seat. An ice chest, easily accessible to the driver, rested on a towel in the passenger seat. Behind the backseat, the floor of the cargo area was caked with dried mud. Lying on the dirty carpet was a pair of rubber boots. They were only knee high. Nonetheless adequate, Josh thought, for wading the shallow stream of Mohawk Creek. He noted the diminutive boot size and wondered if Marshe had been a small man. A decal pasted in a corner of the rear window caught his eye. He shined the light on it. It was a permit for the staff parking lot at Phoenix General Hospital. Instinctively, he shined the light on the license plate—Arizona.

Arizona plates . . . Phoenix General Hospital . . . small boots.

"Ah, shit! NO . . . NO!" He struck the top of the vehicle with his fist.

He was suddenly blinded by a burst of light from overhead.

He wheeled about. Rachel was standing at the top of the stairs, near the light switch. "I wasn't trying to run you down that night at Stewart's home," she said. "I didn't even know it was you. I was trying to get away."

"Is that a gun you're holding?"

"Yes. I'm sorry you came here, Josh."

"So am I," he replied.

She gestured him forward and watched closely as he mounted the stairway. "Slowly. No sudden moves. I'm a good shot."

She led him to the living room and ordered him to sit in one of the overstuffed chairs. She sat on the end of the couch, facing him. She was wearing the same outfit as the first time he had seen her: western snap blouse, jeans, and rawhide boots. Her auburn ponytail was held in place by the same leather barrette. She rested her hand, still gripping the gun, on the arm of the couch.

"Why the gun, Rachel?"

"Don't be cute, Josh. I saw your reaction to the Isuzu. You know."

He was sitting rigidly upright, studying the distance between them. Six, seven feet. He might be able to do it, if he could push himself out of the damned low-slung chair quick enough.

She raised the gun slightly. "Don't try it, Josh."

He shrugged and slumped back into the seat. "May I ask what you were doing at Twin Oaks that night you ran me off the road?"

"Looking for my ring."

"*Your* ring?"

"I thought you'd have pieced that part of the puzzle together by now—Zuni jewelry, reservation pawn, a woman from Arizona. It was all there, right in front of you."

Her tone was not chiding; still, it was a bitter point to concede. The connection had never crossed his mind. Now, he carried it further. "If you went back for the ring, you must have left it there that weekend. Are you telling me that you shot Stewart?"

"With more enthusiasm than you can imagine."

He gave an involuntary shiver. This was a different Rachel from than the one he thought he knew. Deadly serious, firmly in control, she was a far cry from the perplexed young woman who was seeking the answer to her stepfather's death. He sensed that his best chance to survive was to keep her talking until an opportunity to overtake her presented itself.

He thought of the rubber boots in the back of the Isuzu and

decided to let her know he hadn't overlooked that link. "Is that why you went to Dub's cabin, to look for the ring?"

"No. I didn't know he had found it. I went there to silence him because he saw me with Stewart Dunning that night—at least I think he did. I shot him through the window. I was certain he was dead." She gave a disheartened laugh. "Doesn't say much for my professional acumen, does it? I didn't even check his pulse. I was too busy tearing up the place so it would look like something other than a planned murder."

Another point for Hess, Josh reflected. The sheriff had guessed that the ransacked cabin was a ruse, and that the real purpose of the shooting was to keep Dub from talking.

He said, "If you weren't looking for anything in the cabin, why'd you try to burn it?"

"To destroy any clues I may have left. Look, I'm not proud of what I did up there. But it was necessary. I had to finish what I came here to do, and I didn't want Dub turning me in before I could get Raymond."

"Raymond! Your own stepfather!" It was becoming more bizarre with every word she spoke.

"He wasn't my stepfather. My name is Rachel, but not Bond. I'm Rachel Broadbent—Mrs. Henry Broadbent. That name doesn't mean anything to you, but—"

It certainly did. He had heard it that morning from Vicki Armijo. "Broadbent and Associates," he blurted. "The Troublesome Creek Mine fraud."

It startled her. "How did you know that?"

He told her how he checked up on Professor Marshe's background and how a friend in New Mexico had uncovered the information about the gold-mine scam and Marshe's involvement. "At least they think he was involved. He was never indicted."

"No," she said, bitterly. "He was never indicted. But he was guilty, Josh. Guilty of murder."

"Murder? I know nothing about that."

"My husband Henry made a small fortune in Arizona real estate. When he learned about the gold find at Troublesome Creek, he was convinced it was authentic. He persuaded several of his friends to invest in a company to operate the mine. They lost millions. Henry did everything he could to repay them; he sold everything we had and borrowed against his insurance. It wasn't enough. He couldn't handle the guilt. One day he drove into the desert, walked down into an arroyo, and . . . shot himself. The coroner ruled it a suicide. But it was murder. Raymond Marshe and the scum who hired him to seed that mine pulled that trigger just as surely as"—her voice was breaking up—"just as surely as if they'd been there in the desert with him."

Her eyes watered, and she took a deep breath. "Henry had been one of my patients. He was older . . . May-December, that sort of relationship. But he meant everything to me. Do you have anyone like that, Josh . . . someone who loves you so much they will do anything for you, even sacrifice their dreams for you?"

He didn't respond.

"I was pregnant," she said. "Two months. Henry wanted a child so much. He didn't know; I was saving the news for his birthday. When they came to me that day and told me how they'd found him in that arroyo, I went into hysterics. That night I miscarried.

"With Henry and my baby dead, there was nothing left for me. Except revenge. I was obsessed with it. I vowed that someday, somehow, I'd avenge them. I had no idea how. Then one day, Rachel Bond became a patient at Phoenix General.

"At first I didn't make the connection. One evening I walked into her room while a television reporter was interviewing her. She was terminal then, with AIDS. The minute she mentioned that Professor Raymond Marshe was her stepfather, I knew who she was. She told the reporter how her mother was so ill she no longer recognized anyone. She said she'd never met her stepfather. She insisted that no one tell her parents where she was or what had happened to her. She just wanted to die and be forgotten. That gave me the idea. We were approximately the same age and size. We had the same color hair, and the same general features. Marshe had never seen her, except perhaps in youthful photos. I couldn't get to the crooks who had fled to God knows where, but I could get to Marshe. So I became Rachel Bond and headed for West Virginia."

Why is she telling me all this? Josh wondered. It was as if she felt a compulsion to justify herself to him before . . . before what? He didn't want to think about that.

"Excuse me, Rachel, but this isn't making a lot of sense. If Marshe was your target, why didn't you just go to Morgantown, shoot him, and leave? Why the charade? Why the phony dramatics to Carl and me about being the aggrieved stepdaughter? Why steal the disk from Marshe's safe-deposit box? Why erase Stewart's computer and take his backup disks? In fact, how did Stewart fit into this thing at all? He certainly wasn't in on the Troublesome Creek scam."

"He was a crook, Josh. He and Marshe were vultures in common. It didn't take long for me to determine that."

She had to be talking about Piawaka Flats. He wondered if he should mention that he knew about that too. He decided to let it go for the moment.

"I took Rachel Bond's identity because I wanted to study Marshe for a day or so, to learn his routine so I would know where to put the bomb."

"You made that bomb? Come on, Rachel. That's pretty intricate work."

"I've worked with surgical tools for years, Josh. As for a bomb, anyone can pull down the blueprints from the Internet. Besides, as your skepticism just implied, it's not the sort of thing a woman would do, is it?"

Touché. "No, I guess not. But that still doesn't answer my questions."

"Remember our talk at the Fox and Ox the first day we met? I told you that Marshe had confided in me. There was more to it than I let you know. He was in agony over 'my mother,' and feared that she'd be kicked out of the private hospital and moved to a state institution. He said he had a plan that would make enough money to keep her in good care for the rest of her years. He knew that I, or the person he thought I was, had been no angel. So he had no qualms about showing me the fake documents he was creating in the den. I'm sure you saw them when you were in there."

"Not very convincing work, from what I saw."

"That's the prototype. The final was to be etched on flax paper with ink made from coal soot, and then tattered, like the Dead Sea Scrolls. It was all part of a scheme to swindle money from Angus Munroe. Your brother came up with the idea."

"Marshe told you that?"

"Yes. Dunning drew the first maps. Marshe said he was an amateur artist. Dunning offered him $25,000 for his part in the plot. That was okay, until a curator at the university told Marshe that the value of the authentic documents—if they existed—was a million dollars, minimum. He confronted Dunning, demanding a fifty-fifty split. Dunning was enraged, and even threatened Marshe.

"The story infuriated me. It was Troublesome Creek all over, perpetrated by a couple of loathsome bastards like those who drove my husband to his death. At that moment I began hating Dunning as much as I hated Marshe. I decided to get him too, and everyone else involved, if I could find out who they were.

"I called Dunning, identified myself as Marshe's stepdaughter, and said I knew how to patch things over. I asked to meet him in secret to discuss it. He asked me to meet him late Friday night at Twin Oaks, and said he'd fix it so no one would know he was there. I parked a couple of blocks away and walked down the back alley to the house. He met me at the kitchen door and led me to his office."

"How was he dressed?" Josh asked.

"Short-sleeve shirt, slacks. Why?"

It didn't jibe. Was she making this up? "That's not how he was found, Rachel."

She gave a wry smile. "I knew his reputation. I wore a thin halter dress cut low in front, and no bra."

"Seduction? I thought you hated him."

"He was a big man. Big men tend to be strong. I had to distract him, get his mind on things that would cloud his judgment. It worked. My dress, a couple of admiring glances—I hadn't been there fifteen minutes before he ran his hand up my thigh. I told him to get into something more comfortable. While he was upstairs I looked through his wall safe—"

"It was open?"

"He had opened it to show me the contract he had with Marshe. I pretended interest. While he was gone, I looked through the safe for names of anyone else who might be involved in the fraud. It was to be my hit list. But there was nothing like that in the safe. Then Stewart came back downstairs wearing a Chinese kimono—"

"Japanese," Josh said.

"What?"

"It was a Japanese kimono. I saw the photographs."

"Okay, Japanese. He sat on the couch and gestured me to him. There was a bathroom just off the office. I took my purse—with my gun inside it—and told him to wait a minute. I stripped, then held the gun behind my back and went back to the office. He was lying on the couch, nude now, and quite obviously ready. He reached out and drew me to him. I shoved the gun in his face and fired."

Josh winced.

"I went back to the bathroom and took a shower to wash off the blood. I dressed and wrapped a towel around my head to dry my hair. Then I searched through all the files on his computer looking for any cohorts in the scheme. That's when I removed my ring to make typing easier. I printed a couple of documents, but it was taking too long. So I took the backup disks and stuck them in my purse to check later at home."

"Weren't you worried about fingerprints?"

"Latex surgical gloves. I have a big stock of them."

"Why did you erase the hard drive?"

"I didn't want anyone else getting the information from the disk before I did."

"Why'd you leave the computer on?"

"There was a storm that night. Lightning, thunder. Then I heard a different noise, like a truck starting up. I opened the window blind and saw a light in the barn behind the house. A man was sitting just inside the door trying to start a riding mower. He looked right at the window—right at me. I grabbed the gun and ran out the back door. But he had disappeared. I looked around for a while, then went back for my things, ran to my car, and got out of there."

"Forgetting the ring," Josh said.

"Yes."

"And leaving the back door open?"

"I guess . . . yes."

And that, Josh thought, explains how Dub Oliver got into the house without using the key.

She said, "It didn't take a lot of research to learn who I'd seen—

Dunning's handyman, Dub Oliver. I didn't know if he'd be able to identify me or not. Afterward, when I discovered that I'd left my ring and went back to search for it, I saw that things inside the house were not as I'd left them. I suspected that Dub came into the house after I had left. That night, I drove directly from Twin Oaks to Dub's cabin."

"And almost ran me down in the process."

"I waited in the barn until I thought you'd left. If I'd really wanted to run you down, I would have."

He wasn't convinced. He'd had to make a pretty hard leap that night to escape the truck. Even then, it clipped him on the leg.

He said, "Then you went after Marshe."

"Yes. He was ecstatic when he read about Dunning's death. He would have all the money to himself now. The following Saturday he went to the hospital to see his wife before teaching a class that afternoon. His office building is always deserted on weekends, so I was able to put the package on his desk while he was at the hospital."

"What about the disk you later took from his safe-deposit box? Another search for anyone else involved?"

"Right. When you broke the code and found those names, I knew who they were; Marshe kept a list of them with him. After that, I decided Dunning and Marshe were the only ones involved, and I'd already gotten them. It was time for Rachel Bond to disappear from West Virginia and for Mrs. Henry Broadbent to reappear in Phoenix. But there was one last thing to do."

"Dub," Josh said.

"Dub," she agreed. "When I walked into his hospital room that first day on volunteer duty, he took one look at me, and the monitors went crazy. Pulse, blood pressure, respiration—all off the charts. The staff was puzzled, but I wasn't. I knew what it meant. He recognized me all right, and all indications were that soon he'd be able to talk again. So this morning I increased his morphine drip to a lethal dose. It was an easy death. But it was my biggest mistake."

"In what way?"

"He was in a small-town hospital with overworked staff, so I assumed they'd call it respiratory failure, and let it go at that.

When I learned they planned to do an autopsy, I knew the real cause of death would point right at me. I hurried back here to grab my stuff and get away. I was packed and ready to go. Then, once again, you showed up in the wrong place at the wrong time."

She stood and took a step back.

His body stiffened. "What are you going to do, Rachel?"

"What I have to do, Josh," she said, and leveled the gun at his chest.

Forty

State trooper Bobby Crites awoke with a start. He sat bolt upright in his patrol car and glanced around furtively. "Geez!" he moaned aloud. "Not again!"

This was the second time this week he had fallen asleep on duty. If that ever got back to Captain Brimley, his ass would be mud. He couldn't afford to lose this job, what with another baby on the way and Sue on extended leave-without-pay from the paper mill. He grabbed the thermos of black coffee she had prepared for him, poured a cup, and tasted it. "Shit." It was cold. I've got to get another thermos, he thought. Oh well, caffeine is caffeine. He downed the coffee in three gulps and glanced at the brick house sitting on the corner lot. The hard rain that had fallen earlier had turned into a slow drizzle, and now he could see more clearly. Everything looked in order.

Trooper Crites was parked curbside on Campus Circle in Morgantown, three houses down from number 301. He had been there since 9:05 that night. His orders were to intercept a red Corvette and keep the driver from entering the house at 301 Campus Circle. Brimley had been emphatic. "These orders are from Colonel Gregory himself."

Strange way to do things, Crites thought, and he said so to Brimley. Why a one-man stakeout to stop someone from entering a house? If there was danger, why not storm the damned house, and be done with it?

"Because," Brimley had replied in that arrogant CO-to-private tone that Crites despised, "that's not how the colonel wants it done. He's expecting more info from Phoenix. When it comes in—*if* it comes in—then maybe we'll take the house. But for now, do what you're told, and don't screw up, Crites!"

Asshole! Crites thought, recalling the conversation.

His body was stiff from confinement. He opened the car door, eased out, and stretched long and hard, raising on tiptoe to stretch his leg muscles. As he did, he glanced toward the house again, and his heart skipped a beat. A car was parked in the driveway where none had been earlier. "Oh, God!"

Crouching low, he raced toward the house. At the driveway his worst fears were confirmed. The car was a Corvette—a *red* Corvette. ". . . don't screw up, Crites," Brimley had told him.

Lights were on inside the house. He eased down the sloping yard toward the porch. A short way down the hill he stopped short and stared at the window. The venetian blinds had been closed with the slats pointing downward inside. Looking through the tiny slits, he could see a person holding a gun leveled at someone or something that wasn't visible. He unstrapped his holster, thought better of it, and ran back to his patrol car. This called for the SWAT team.

He grabbed his radio mike from its mount and promptly dropped it on the floor. While fumbling for the mike, his hand brushed against the butt of his .12-gauge riot gun. He stared at the mike. Could they get here in time? He stared at the shotgun. Which? Which, dammit . . . which?

Rachel kept the gun pointed at Josh as she crossed the room to a desk near the dining area. She opened a drawer and took out a small plastic container. She came back to the couch, remained standing, and tossed the container to Josh. "Shake out two capsules and swallow them."

Josh looked at the pill case warily. There was no label. "Ah, come on Rachel—"

"It's not poison, Josh. If it were, I'd make you swallow all of them. I don't want to harm you unless I have to. Two capsules, and you get a nice sleep. By the time you wake up, I'll be out of your life forever. Phoenix is out for me now, but I have friends. I think I can pull it off."

"Why don't you just trust me to give you a head start?"

"Oh sure. Maybe, if it weren't for Dub. But I don't think you'll cut me any slack for that. Two capsules, Josh."

He shook out two capsules, tossed them into his mouth, and slipped them under his tongue. He made a swallowing motion and opened his mouth for her to see.

"You're being cute again, Josh. I've been giving pills for years. Now, out from under the tongue and down the throat. Either that"—she made a gesture with the gun—"or this."

Not much choice, he thought. Anyway, where could she get by morning? Kentucky? Ohio? They'd have her in custody before the day was out. He rolled the pills to the top of his tongue and prepared to swallow.

Just then there was an ear-splitting crash, and the front door splintered inward off its hinges. Rachel whirled. A uniformed patrolman was standing in the doorway, shotgun in hand.

The officer swung the gun toward Rachel. Josh spit the pills so hard they flew to the opposite side of the room. "NO-O-O!" he yelled.

Too late. Confronted with a pistol aimed point-blank at his belly, Trooper Bobby Crites did what every police officer in the country is trained to do. The shotgun roared. The blast struck Rachel in the chest and head, propelling her backward over the couch and onto the floor beyond.

Glued to the chair, Josh stared in horror at the mangled form that had once been Rachel Bond–Rachel Broadbent. The auburn hair that once shone like burnished copper in the sunlight, now matted with blood and splayed to all sides, formed a macabre frame for what had once been a beautiful face.

Forty-one

Russell Hess read the single-page report for the second time. He glanced at Carl Travis, seated at his roll-top desk, and then across the room to Josh. "You faxed this to Carl from Morgantown?"

"Yes," Josh replied. He was slumped on the couch in Carl's office, head resting against the wall, legs stretched out in front of him. The strain of the past twelve hours had taken its toll. "The DA let me use his machine," he added, wearily.

"Why didn't you send it to me?" the sheriff demanded.

"Because I didn't know you were back in town. I knew Carl would provide you with a copy."

Hess looked back at the paper. "Most of this is just your word about what happened—not very reliable evidence."

"Oh, Russ, come off it," Carl protested.

"It's okay, Carl," Josh said. He looked at Hess. "My word—plus the gun the state police took from Rachel's hand, plus the bullets you retrieved from Stewart's couch and Dub's cabin, plus the autopsy report on Dub, plus Rachel's fingerprints all over Dub's hospital room, plus the report Colonel Gregory got this morning from Phoenix. I think even Mares could make a case out of all that."

Carl laughed.

Hess let it pass. He tossed the report onto Carl's desk and stood. "Send me a copy of that." Then to Josh, "You sticking around?"

"Not on your life. I'm taking the first flight available this afternoon from Dulles to New Mexico."

"There'll be a lot more questions for you before this is put to bed."

"They can depose me in Santa Fe. If they subpoena me, I'll come back. Either way, I'm outta here today."

"Suit yourself," Hess said, and turned to leave.

"Russ," Josh said.

Hess stopped. "Yeah?"

"A friend of mine who's in position to know asked me to warn you that Manny Marconi's not going to be happy about what you did to Little Joe Bartelli. Manny's got a lot of button men working for him."

Hess gave a disdainful snort. "There's enough room in these hills to bury them all."

He left.

Carl watched the sheriff stride out the door. "He'll never change."

"Nope, never," Josh agreed.

Carl studied his one-time protégé. "Are you sure you're up to driving to D.C. today? You need sleep, son."

Josh detected the paternalistic concern and was touched. When he got back from Morgantown earlier, Carl had jumped from his chair and embraced him in a prolonged bear hug that belied the old editor's frail appearance.

"The DA let me use a couch in his office," Josh said. "I got a couple of hours. Anyway, I can sleep on the plane today."

Carl leaned back in his chair. "I reckon we were driving down blind alleys all along on this thing. It had nothing to do with the environment, or with Dunning's anti-strip-mining bill, or with a mob connection." He shook his head. "That lovely young woman a killer. It's just too mind-boggling to grasp."

"Revenge," Josh said. "Obsessive. It drove her over the edge.

I want her buried in Phoenix, Carl, next to her husband. I'll pay all costs."

"I'll arrange it. Are you stopping by to see Angus on the way out?"

"No. I called him late last night. He was both furious and amused that Dunning and Marshe thought they could trick him with a fake map."

"I still can't grasp why Stewart would do such a thing," Carl said. "He certainly didn't need the money."

"He despised Angus," Josh said. "He knew his reputation as a historian. My guess is that he wanted to see him humiliated. He would never have brought it off, though. Angus would have spotted those fake maps in a second."

"Sounds like you've got a lot of respect for the old man."

"That, I do," Josh agreed. He pulled himself up on the couch. "I've got to make a phone call."

"Vicki?"

"Yes."

"I called her last night when I learned you were all right," Carl said. "She's waiting to hear from you."

He grabbed the report off his desk and stood. "Use my desk. Meanwhile, I'll go fax this to Hess." He left for the makeup room.

Josh moved to the desk. He picked up the phone and punched in the number in New Mexico. After a couple of rings, he heard her voice. "This is Vicki."

"Take those steaks out of the freezer."

"Oh, Josh. Really? When?"

"Tonight. I'm leaving for Dulles in a few minutes. Don't know what flight but I'll call you from the air."

"Should I meet you?"

"My car's at the airport. I'll come right to your place."

"Oh, Josh. I'm so happy. I've missed you."

"Same here. Look, do me a favor? Call Mel Simmons. Tell him I'll have to pass on the WIPP book. I've got another project that takes priority."

"Really? Anything you care to talk about?"

"Greed, wrath, revenge . . . ruined lives."

"Sounds exciting. I'll call Mel. I'll be waiting, Josh."

"One last thing, Vicki . . . do you think you can teach me Spanish?"

She laughed. "About time. *Sí, amante, sí.*"

"Well, I know the 'sí' . . . but 'amahntay'?"

"Amante," she repeated, giving it the proper tone and inflection. "Your first lesson, Josh. It means *lover.*"